Benghazi-Bergen-Belsen

By **Yossi Sucary**

Translated by Yardenne Greenspan

Translated from Hebrew by Yardenne Greenspan

Contact: yossi.sucary@gmail.com

ISBN-13: 978-1533529817
ISBN-10: 1533529817

Benghazi

At the end of April 1941 (she) saw the desert defeat
itself. The steady, confident ground of the Sahara
could no longer withstand its own winds. The moment
when the wind usually abated, no longer tampering
with the sand, never came. It appeared to her that
this phase had been entirely lost. It appeared to her
heart that the desert itself was lost, too. The wind
feverishly peeled away the earth's top layers and
created more and more sand whirlwinds, thickening
by the minute. The air grew murky. The sun blazed
and disappeared in turn. For one long moment, a
great shadow darkened it all. *what happened before*

Ever since her fourth birthday, the desert had been
a warm blanket that covered her being. From the day
her father first took her there on an excursion, being in
the desert made her feel cozy. Now that she could no
longer recognize the desert, she felt entirely exposed
to the world. From beyond the cloud of smoke that
swirled throughthe air, she stared at the five camels
that walked only a few feet away, expecting the
desert to become reflected in their demeanor once
more. But their naturally calm, languid walk became

quick, nervous stomping, until they appeared to be attempting to rid themselves of their own humps. She looked up at the sky, wishing to hold onto the sight of the eagles' familiar wings, to fly with them over this foreign image. But it was all for naught. From beyond grains of sand, she saw birds flapping in a panic—predators shaking off their reputations as kings of the sky. She wanted to go home. The strong winds of the desert had blown away not only the cloak of her being, but also the clear memory of home. She wanted home to be hers once more.

She got on the truck that had taken her to the desert and waited for the other travelers to get on as well. Whenever she could, she'd feed her constant yearning for the desert and join the truck leaving central Benghazi for a few days' trip. The majority of passengers were Jews and Arabs wishing to forget the burden of existence and be forgotten by it. The owner of the truck, a man named Zoheir, wanted to associate with her father, who was famously wealthy, so she was never charged for the trip. Moreover, she always received special treatment on the ride: Zoheir made sure to provide her with quality food and warm blankets.

Now she sat in the truck, her eyes closed. She wanted to see her desert, the one she knew. She didn't want to watch it drying up quickly inside another, foreign desert. She stayed seated, her eyes closed, even as the truck made its way back into town.

Until they reached Al-Jabal Al-Akhdar. Then she let her eyes open slightly. She knew this mountain range, which separated the desert from Benghazi, by heart. There lay the building blocks of her desires. There, on the range between her city and her desert, is where she dreamed of building a modern high school for the Jews of Benghazi. She thought the good earth of Al-Jabal Al-Akhdar could help this dream bloom.

Now she heard the sound of planes, and from the cracks of her eyes she saw people shifting in their seats inside the truck, their faces irritated, their bodies searching for a comfortable position, attesting to a gnawing fear that something awful had happened in Benghazi. She noticed some of them pointing accusing fingers at the driver for going too slowly, urging him to speed up, as if reaching their destination would remedy their long-lasting illness.

As the truck approached Benghazi, her eyes opened completely, until they threatened to eat up the houses that began emerging beyond the sand. When the truck reached Piazza del Municipio, she watched the white roofs, the narrow alleys where children played soccer, the mothers washing diapers in square yards, and the round fortune fountain, always sparkling clean. To her surprise, there was no sign of the British soldiers who had occupied the Cyrenaica region four months earlier from the Italians that had ruled it for almost thirty years. She breathed in the Benghazi air, which was saturated with the fragrance of the sea. She could rest. Just as the desert was a warm blanket that had covered her since childhood, the sea was the bed on which she lay. Its smell always healed her exhaustion. The sight of its waves washed away all hardships, distress and aches.

She got off the truck and walked down Via del Municipio. Her eyes were now able to see what she hadn't been able to spot from the truck: the faces of residents of the city from which she'd been gone for four whole days were not the same. They implied something completely new; especially the faces of the Jewish residents. Their expression gave away the terror of entrapment felt by those entirely submitted to the graces of fate. Some glanced surreptitiously at the blue sky, as if wishing to be seen, and others curled up and lowered their faces to the ground. She hastened her steps and told herself, *Aadi* Silvana, *Aadi*, relax, but her attempts failed, and as she neared Via Generale Briccola, her heart beat faster and faster; as she approached the street where she lived with her family—her father, mother and sister—she felt her pulse defeating her heart.

When she arrived at the door, she could no longer feel her heart. She opened the green iron gate slowly. Its screeching was more grating to her ears than ever before. She walked on the tiled path, glancing at the sand to the sides of the path so as to avoid looking at the concrete steps toward which she was advancing. She put the key in the lock and opened the door, and then sensed something seemingly impossible: the house wasn't her home. The large record player her father had brought back from one of his many trips to Naples, the four Caucasian rugs her mother had worked so hard to place just right, so that they covered the entire floor of the living room, the *orologio* that only rarely showed the right time, the *lampadario*—the chandelier her father liked to move so that he could properly read the documents he'd received from Fratelli Capone, the Neapolitan construction company owned by the Capone brothers, whose products he imported to Libya—the two red armchairs her younger sister Toni liked to point at, announcing to her friends, "*Un appartamento arredato*," a furnished apartment, though they lived in a house, rather than an apartment—these were all in place, and yet, the house wasn't her home. The safe, pleasant atmosphere that had defined it had been ripped away.

She quickly left and made her way to her father's shop. On her way, she walked through Souk Delam—the Dark Market—and saw the vendors saluting sunset and submissively folding away their stalls. Imad, the owner of the jewelry stall, an emaciated man with a vulture's nose and fairly light skin who often gave her a free necklace or ring, approached her and asked, "*Sha Halec*, Silvana?"[1] She told

---

[1] From Jewish-Libyan Arabic: How are you, Silvana?

herself this question was asked just as it always had been, but once again she had trouble believing her own thoughts. She couldn't help but notice the slight tremor that had made its way to the tail end of Imad's question just as he'd spoken her name.

She searched for Rabah's eyes as she walked past the peanut and seed stall. Rather than welcoming her warmly as he always did, he only muttered a quick hello, and then bent his long, slender neck and fixed his gaze upon one of the large sacks that were stacked below him, as if wishing to bury his eyes among the seeds.

When she arrived at Via Calanzzo, the light begged the dark for just a few more moments of life. She was afraid to keep walking. She stood at the southern end of the street and stared in the direction of her father's shop, about a hundred meters from where she stood. After lingering about half a minute, she gathered her courage and began walking toward it. The heavy heat and humidity didn't make things any easier. Each step she took drew her thoughts backward and reminded her of a previous moment in that day's chain of events. When she was about ten meters away from the store, her mind lingered on the foreign, lost desert she'd seen that morning.

The store was locked. The metal shutter sealed it off completely. She knew it shouldn't be so; her father, or Ziad, the shop manager, whose wisdom and gentle manner always impressed her, usually only locked the door and lowered the shutter later in the evening. Helplessly, she began running down Via Calanzzo without considering exactly where she was headed. All she wanted was to escape the thought that something bad had happened to her family, but this thought chased her like a predator. She wanted to go to a place where she could drown the thought and think something different, more rational.

The Jeliana Beach was that kind of haven for her. Of all the beaches of Benghazi, and even of all of Libya, it was her favorite. She never stopped missing the Jeliana Beach, even when she sailed with her family on the Carrera, a ship that traveled from Benghazi to Tripoli, to visit the Zaruk family in their home above Lido Beach, who many Libyans considered as the most gorgeous beach in Northern Africa. To her, the Jeliana bay was a living, loving thing. She didn't see it as an object dropped into the world against its will. In the soft, white sand of Jeliana Beach she could truly sink into herself. Among its rocks, she could escape the invasive eyes of men—Jews, Arabs, and Italians—sunning themselves on the sand. If the sea served as her bed, Jeliana Beach was her pillow. Now she began running to the beach, widening her stride as she approached. When she arrived at Via Roma it was already pitch dark. She told herself it would be sufficient to reach the Lungomare, the boardwalk, where she could stop under the friendly lights and watch the beach.

When she arrived, breathless, at the boardwalk, she didn't see any need to descend unto the beach. She only stood behind the concrete railing and watched the sea in the light of the moon and the lamps. The water roared, the waves crashed against the mighty rocks. She relaxed a bit. She remembered her mother mentioning the wedding of the daughter of one of her friends taking place tonight, and guessed her parents and sister had gone to the wedding, assuming she wouldn't be returning from the desert until the next day. She put her hand in the pocket of the pants her father had brought her from Rome, probably against her mother's wishes, pulled out a hairband and tied it around her long, smooth black hair, bleached white by the desert dust, leaving only a trace of the black beneath. The first thing she always yearned for upon returning from the desert was a shower. She liked to stand below the water for a long time, soaping herself slowly, seeing her tan skin revealed, washing her hair with Trozzi, a luxurious soap she only used on special occasions. And now, instead of the beloved shower, she was busy rinsing the remains of terrorizing thoughts from her head.

Silvana leaned against the concrete railing and continued to watch the sea. The terror that had plagued her was swept away with the waves, almost drowning in the water, but suddenly the rustle of waves was interrupted by a strange sound, something between a screech and a dry slap. She looked left and right, trying to locate its source, but saw nothing but the row of lamps illuminating the boardwalk. She looked back, but saw nothing but the line of trees that served as the rear border of the boardwalk. She turned to watch the sea again. A few moments later she heard that sound again, much sharper this time. She had no doubt it wasthe sound of footsteps, though she'd never heard footsteps like these before. They sounded nothing like the footsteps of Benghazi natives, nor like the footsteps of the Camicie Nere, the Italian Fascists, whose fast, compressed marching was familiar to her ears. The footsteps echoing in her ears now were slow and very loud. A mysterious thought suddenly pierced her mind: these footsteps existed independently, not necessarily obeying the person producing them.

She looked to her right again. The water sprayed the wall that stood against the concrete railing. The fresh moistness exacerbated her anxiety. For a moment, it looked different to her; it wasn't the same wall she liked to hide behind in her childhood, playing hide-and-seek with her Arab friend, Nassarin. Nor was it the wall that, in her early childhood, she and her friend Lizzy Saban called *Heit Lehlamat*— Wall of Dreams—because they liked sitting beneath it and dreaming aloud. Now the weeds, which had always only covered the cracks between the bricks, had invaded the bricks themselves. Now there were cracks in the wall she'd never seen before.

She looked back and suddenly identified the source of the sound. Her heart thumped. Just a few meters away was a man the likes of which she'd never seen before. He looked nothing like the Italian and English soldiers she'd seen in Benghazi. He was wearing tall, black boots in spite of the heavy heat and stifling humidity. His carefully pressed pants were tucked into the boots, and the long sleeves of his shirts were tight against his arms. The buttons of his shirt were done almost halfway up his neck. Its pockets were decorated with ornaments, and his head was covered with a cap adorned with a shiny metal vulture. Her anxious eyes moved between each detail of his outfit, trying to decipher their meaning.

She pushed up against the railing. The soldier approached her, removed his cap and addressed her in a language she'd never heard. The patience and kindness of his eyes were in complete contrast to his appearance and the sound of his language. Alarmed, she shook her head to indicate she couldn't understand, but he repeated his words again and again, until a coherent stream of sound bubbled between her ears: "*Guten abend*."[2]

She stuttered, "Tayeb, tayeb," and began retreating against the railing, hastening her steps, praying for a *carrozza*, a horse-drawn carriage serving as taxi for the wealthy residents of Benghazi, to appear.

---

[2] From German: Good evening.

Normally, she was deterred of riding the *carrozza*. She didn't like the black wheels, which always reminded her of enormous ears glued to a small head; she didn't like the rough combination of wood and metal in the center of its body, and more than anything, she was revolted by the frequent beating the coachmen gave the horses, supposedly to please customers, and in fact out of an unbridled desire to bring a new customer onto the wagon as quickly as possible. But in those moments, as the soldier repeated his greetings and uncertainty gaped before her, the *carrozza* seemed to her like a protective baby carriage. She yearned to hear the rattling of wheels, the bothersome bell announcing its arrival, the groans of the tortured horse.

She heard nothing of all these. Instead, the streets of Benghazi appeared before her, one by one, submitting without the slightest protest to the authority of darkness. She saw the moonlight briefly dipping into the sea and the weak light of the lamps of the Lungomare. She crossed the street quickly and began running along Via Corsa Italia. Searching for an illuminated route, she went against her habit and turned onto Piazza Penne. It was out of the way, but the area of the old mosque was almost always well-lit, thought in recent months it sometimes went dark as British planes bombed the city.

And indeed, she felt some relief the moment she arrived at el-Masjad, the biggest, most central mosque in the city. This building was the antithesis of the soldier she'd just seen at the Lungomare. There was nothing threatening about it, and it appeared before her as the familiar home of her city's legal residents. Its surroundings were illuminated with heavenly light. Two men wearing white *galabiya* and wide, white skullcaps, passed her by without paying her any notice.

It wasn't obvious that she would feel relief at the mosque. In the eleven years that preceded this moment, since she was ten years old and began wandering the city without her mother's supervision, el-Masjad was like a minefield within her city, a place she always preferred to bypass. Her mother never gave her any other option. As a child, whenever she expressed a wish to watch what happened behind the iron gate leading onto the tiled yard, her mother pulled her the other way and treated her as if she were possessed. When she was older and left the house without announcing her exact destination, her mother told her, "*Ya Silvana, ya azizti*, baby, *ma tamshis min hanaya*, don't take that route." Normally, she ignored her mother's prohibitions. They were swallowed like tiny grains of sand in the wide berth of liberty her father granted her. "*Binti, a-dinya camla kedamc, wada'a*. My daughter, the whole world is your playground, your space, and your comfort," he sometimes old her, but for some reason, this one instruction of her mother's, to stay away from el-Masjad, always glowed like a beacon before her. But now all her mother's warnings collapsed and the fuzzy feeling that being close to the mosque gave her grew stronger. Even a distant buzzing, likely the engine of a fighting jet, did not take away from this feeling. Silvana opened the iron gate.

Though she'd lived around Muslims her entire life, she never opened up to their faith. When she saw their Arab neighbor, Samira, covering her face with a *hijab*, she didn't ask her what it meant. When she saw Ziad, her father's trusty shop owner, kneeling on the floor of the office in the afternoon to pray, she had no reaction. Not that she wasn't curious about these customs, and not that she didn't feel close enough to these people to ask. Her reason was entirely different: Rita, her father's younger sister, had converted to Islam before Silvana was even four years old. The event had shaken the family up, a true disaster, and was forbidden to speak of. It hovered like a bird around the family tree that could not linger on any of its branches. No one in her extensive family could bring themselves to say out loud that the younger sister of Eliyahu Hajaj, one of the most important people in the Benghazi Jewish community, had converted to Islam and married an Arab. No one could bring themselves to say out loud that Eliyahu Hajaj—Lilo, as he was nicknamed—the tall, broad-shouldered man with the piercing black eyes and the commanding voice had been so bluntly betrayed by his younger sister.

Now this forced silence was behind her. She reached the door to the mosque itself, which was open to the public, and walked in silently. Inside, she gazed with wonder at the golden dome and the walls covered in arabesques. She stepped forward, trying to find the best viewpoint, but stopped cold three steps in: the shouts of Italian soldiers echoed from the nearby streets, mixed with the sharp, hard words in the language of the foreign soldier she'd just met. The image of Rabah, the peanut vendor, who avoided looking in her eyes as she walked past him in the market, flickered in her mind. <u>Now she vaguely remembered he'd mumbled something:</u> *Ahrab minhem*, <u>run away.</u> She froze for a few seconds, then ran toward an especially wide pillar tiled with emerald and hid behind it. The shouting outside grew louder, resembling the beating of a hammer: "*Achtung!Achtung!*" She couldn't stop shivering. She yearned to blend into the mosque completely, becoming one of its pillars. But the mosque resisted. In fact, it was as if her presence there purposefully stood out. Whenever she tried to find a better hiding place she became even more exposed in its empty space, and whenever she tried to step on its floor, it sounded an echoing screech.

Outside, people were banging loudly on the walls of the mosque. She was afraid the soldiers would invade and began devising an escape plan. After rejecting the idea of going out onto the backyard, she finally walked through the back gate, taking the quickest route, her face downcast. Unlike the inside of the mosque, the backyard seemed to cooperate, providing her with a hiding place. Now darkness was her guiding light. She left the yard and walked as quickly as possible down the darkest streets. When she crossed Via Corsa Italia, she noticed an *azuza carrozza*, an old wagon, in the distance. She chased it, crying toward the coachman, the moonlight reflecting in his blue velvet cap, "*Stena, stena!* Wait, wait!" The man heard her and pulled over. She'd never seen a more crowded wagon. She immediately recognized the kind face of Said, Nassarin's older brother. They said nothing to each other during the ride, but their silence spoke volumes: the love they had for each other ever since childhood, a love never realized, their hatred for their country's foreign conquerors, the vague feeling that now they were being introduced to a conqueror of a new breed.

As they neared her home, she squeezed his hand. Said didn't let go. For the first time in their lives, he fixed his big brown eyes on her big black eyes, straight on. Suddenly, she didn't think of him as Nassarin's older brother, but as a man with a strong face, a long, muscular body, and a good mind. The lilting voice of the *muezzin* sliced the hot night air at once. Said continued to hold her hand, and only let go after the voice of the *muezzin* fell silent. Silvana kissed his cheek lightly and disembarked the *azuza carrozza* without looking back. She walked down the path, trying as hard as she could to keep her fear for her parents and sister at bay. It clung to her, rising and falling. When she saw no sign of their return, she tried to calm herself by thinking that the wedding must be dragging on, and that they were still out. She was unsuccessful. To push aside her sense of failure, she held on to the thought of kissing Said.

The kiss did her good, liberating her for a moment from the restraints of time and place. She realized that her actions were out of character; she was a different person. True, ever since her bat mitzvah she hadn't always obeyed the norms of Benghazi Jews; true, from time to time she acted against what was expected of a Jewish girl. For instance, she freely conversed with the Italian soldiers, or wandered Souk Delam till the late hours of the evening. But kissing an Arab boy on the cheek—this was highly unusual.   ↵ isn't she two arub. what makes a jew not arub

In her mind, she was now floating within the body of this other woman, who was opening the door to the house. But even the other woman could not make the world behind her disappear. She barely even turned on the lights, the door still open, when she heard a loud shout behind her: "*Halt!*"[3] She turned back. Three soldiers—two of them dressed exactly like the one she'd seen at the Lungomare, and the

---

[3] From German: Stop!

third in the familiar Italian uniform—stood in a row behind the green iron gate. They'd returned her to herself only to once more spit her out of the world. Their threatening looks made Silvana feel that she and the world had not been meant for each other, that the world was about to go their separate way. She was planted in place for a few seconds, and then began walking toward them. She wanted to cling to the possibility that appeared at their side in the form of a fourth soldier: that they might take her to her parents and sister. "Where are they? I know that you know where they are!" she called in English. They didn't answer, instead shouting and pushing her onto a truck covered with green tarp.

As they rode, the two foreign soldiers spoke amongst themselves, from time to time delivering what sounded like a scolding to the Italian soldier. The sound of their words contoured the limits of her anxiety again and again. She watched her city from beyond the hatch of the truck, which was uncovered, and thought bitterly of Benghazi and its residents, her city that did not stand by her side when she needed it the most, which abandoned her to the soldiers, accepting this loathing that was directed toward her rather than serving as her safe haven. Could Benghazi have truly betrayed her?

When they passed by Teatro Berenice, Benghazi's pride and joy, she recalled walking arm and arm with her parents on Saturday nights, going to watch a play. She wanted to cry, but couldn't. The cold gaze Benghazi directed at her as it was moving farther and farther away forced her to do the same. The younger of the two foreign soldiers watched Silvana with hungry eyes, ran his hand over his cheek and whispered, *"Du bist ein schöneFräulein."*[4] She turned her cold gaze to him as well. His comrade also fixed him with an angry look, and the young soldier didn't say another word till the end of their journey, instead lowering his head with forced restraint.

The truck stopped. They'd arrived, but she didn't know where. The soldiers ordered her to get off the truck. The hope that she'd soon reunite with her family enveloped her anxiety like a protective shield, but only for a moment before the silence and dark pushed all positive thoughts away at once. One of the soldiers turned on a floodlight that revealed a large, white structure, which Silvana immediately recognized as the Italian school at Bab a-Jedid, twenty-five minutes south of Benghazi. The soldiers pulled her along the path marked by the light, illuminating the suffering on her face. Within a few steps she began sobbing, *"Ya ma, wenec? Ya buya, wenec?* Mama, Papa, where are you?" The soldiers tried to hush her, but in vain. They covered her mouth forcefully and hit her back, but she managed

---

[4]From German: You're a pretty girl.

to scream between their fingers: "*Ya ma! Baba!*" She didn't make do with screaming, but also punched the chest of the soldier closest to her, kicking another who stood farther away. The soldiers kicked her all over and dragged her into the Italian school.

She never imagined entering the school this way. As a child, she often imagined walking into the Italian school, the best school in Libya and, some said, the best in all of Africa. She often imagined being accepted among the sons and daughters of Italian government officials and walking proudly to school with them every day. It wasn't enough for her to have completed her schooling at the Jewish school Talmud Torah. It wasn't enough that every day until she turned eighteen she studied a plethora of subjects with private tutors and fervently read history, poetry, and philosophy books—philosophy books were her favorite, though she didn't always understand everything that was written in them—brought back from Italy especially by her father. Her entire being yearned for an official, Italian education. Something inside her always told her that was the only way she would be considered a natural daughter of culture.

But now she didn't want to go in. She didn't want to see the two rows of trees in the front yard, the white walls, the long hallways, the ceiling fans, the façade decorated with the portrait of *Il Duce*, and she certainly did not want to see the large gymnasium, which she was pushed into, not once allowed to stretch her hunched body. The soldiers pushed her to the edge of the hallway and gestured for her to lie on a mattress. In spite of the partial darkness, she could easily see the holes and spots that adorned the mattress. She preferred to lie on the cold floor than feel the hard press of exposed springs. The soldiers didn't seem to mind. Two of them left the gym together, and the younger one sat in a gray chair that stood ten meters away from her, close to the doorway leading to the lit hallway. She couldn't see a thing. Her eyes were so red and puffy that she thought they would pour down her face along with her tears. She was restless. Her past and her future were no more. Her presence was still alive, but as dark as the Valley of Death. For hours she thought only of her parents and sister. At first she hoped they hadn't met this new breed of soldiers, but as time went by she only hoped they were still alive. To survive the rest of the night, she turned to math, which often gave her comfort in difficult situations. She calculated all sorts of math problems to distract herself from thinking of all she'd been through since she left the desert that day. She only managed to ignore her aching body and soul and fall asleep as the dawn light of the desert filtered into the gym through its long, narrow windows. She'd never felt as awake as she had during this sleep. Her dream seemed much more realistic than her reality. In her dream, she could clearly see her parents, her sister Toni, and herself, on a family vacation at

Positano, which she'd never been to, but which she'd heard plenty about from her father. They were sitting at a table laden with giant fruit, laughing to the point of tears, when an Italian police officer approached their table and roughly demanded that they follow him. He pointed at her and said, "*Tu no*. Not you."

She couldn't remember how the dream ended: her sleep was disturbed by screaming in a mélange of Arabic, Italian, and the language of the foreign soldiers. She opened her eyes, feeling herself thrown at once from a bright reality into a vague dream. The feeling lingered for weeks after. That sharp turn was like a bridge that collapsed beneath her whenever she tried to shift from thinking that reality and dream were indistinguishable to thinking that they she could tell them apart. Now—attempting to perceive her specific whereabouts, pushing away the terrorizing reality behind the bothersome dream and holding onto it with all her might—dozens of people suddenly strode into the gym, and the soldier who watched her through the night directed them toward the farthest wall while screaming, "*Schneller, Juden! Schneller, Juden! Schneller, Juden!*"[5]

She sat up on the floor, her back against the wall. The image gradually became clearer: along the wall in front of her, dozens of people swayed, hunched and helpless. She recognized most of their faces

---

[5]From German: Faster, Jews! Faster, Jews! Faster, Jews!

from random encounters at Harat al-Yahud, the Jewish neighborhood, or from the walk to the large synagogue of Tzala Lekbira.

She tried to spot someone she knew among them, so she could ask if they'd seen her family the first chance she got. On first and second glance she didn't recognize anyone she knew, but then suddenly, at the edge of the wall, she spotted a friend of her sister Toni. She couldn't recall the girl's name, nor catch her eyes. Toni's friend's face trembled, her eyes were puffy, her hair unkempt. She seemed to have grown old overnight.

As the soldier slowly counted the newly entered, as if to stretch the pleasure their terrified expressions gave him, Silvana dragged her body along the wall. When she reached the point exactly across the way from Toni's friend, she looked straight at her. The girl continued to tremble, but Silvana imagined that, in her shaking, the friend was trying to articulate that she'd seen Toni. She wanted very badly to make sure she'd understood correctly. A few minutes later, when the soldier called her over, she faltered toward him, intentionally taking her time so she could get closer to Toni's friend. As she passed by her, she asked if she'd seen her family. The friend mumbled a few words from which Silvana gleaned, with some difficulty, that the answer was yes. Carrying this interpretation with her, she stood before the soldier. He said nothing and the silence seemed to stretch forever. Silvana was terrified of the possibility that constantly flickered in her mind: the possibility that her life was about to end. She told herself that if she was fated to die, her last request would be to see her parents and Toni.

Then something happened that made her feel she was about to return to reality: instead of punishing her for speaking to another detainee, the soldier gestured to her to walk past him and leave the gym. "*Frei*," he said. "*Du bist frei.*"[6] He turned to a tall Italian soldier with sunken cheeks who stood nearby and gestured for him to let her go.

She did not return to reality. The horrified faces of the people who were left behind in the gym and the missing faces of her parents and sister accompanied her on her way out. She didn't just watch them; they served as the eyes through which she saw the world. The desert sun hit her with such intensity that of all the fateful things that could come to mind, she happened to think about how part of the reputation of the Italian School might have to do with the caressing chill between its walls. But the thought of the pleasant cool breeze blowing through the school evaporated with the speed of the desert light, and in its place, her consciousness was invaded by the most terrible scream she'd ever heard: *Silvanaaaaa!*

---

[6]From German: Free […] you're free.

Silvana saw her mother striding over in a frenzy, all the while mumbling, "*Henan nigliz, henan nigliz,* we're British, we're British." Now she truly returned to reality. Her mind made a quick, cold calculation: perhaps, as British citizens, they were a burden on the Italians' allies. If they were detained, they would have to be treated as prisoners of war. Her mother's hug almost crushed her to death. She pushed her away, meanwhile feeling her father and sister hugging her as hard as they could from behind. After filling her lungs with air, she joined her family's sobs.

She'd never seen her father cry before. She never even imagined he was capable of it. As far as she was concerned, crying was an action everyone but her father was capable of. Even when she once overheard her mother telling one of her friends that Eliyahu had cried at night because of some trouble or another, she blocked out the words like the irritating chirping of a cricket. And now, though the unusual circumstances justified his crying, she imagined that his tears poured away all the times he'd protected her—even the time he slapped an Italian soldier who bothered her on her way home from school, and even the time he told the teacher Roberto Kachlon, a tall, skinny, and bitter man, in front of all the girls in her classroom, because he'd abused her. "*Tzid mara ma telkash sha tackel,*" he told the man. "You do that one more time, and you won't have food on your table." All the times he'd defended her slipped out of her mind, one by one. <u>She began fearing that her father would no longer act</u> as a buffer between her and the world.

The family members raised their heads one by one, weeping and attempting to share their experiences without much success. The dust of the desert sprayed at them from the wheels of a military jeep that rode nearby. One of the soldiers in the jeep said something to the other, signaling to him not to pay any attention to Silvana's family. They began walking in a row, her father first and Toni last, holding each other's hands, toward a large Arab tent about a hundred meters away, where, her father assumed, they could receive some help.

Silvana yearned for the sun that was beating down on them to invade her soul and burn down the flame that was raging within her. She yearned for it to consume the reality around her. They walked into the giant tent that was divided into four separate areas, each one with a different colored mat covering the floor. They were welcomed by a young man with especially large hands and curly hair. He introduced himself as Jalal. Eliyahu Hajaj told him, trying hard to conceal the tremble in his voice, that he knew his father, Muhammad e-Razni, very well, and added with respect that he knew Muhammad wasn't only the head of the largest Arab clan in Cyrenaica, but also the head of one of the two largest Arab tribes in all of Libya. Jalal led them to the most pleasant spot in the tent and told them his father wasn't in Bab a-Jedid, and therefore he would take care of their every need.

Silvana hoped they could stay inside the tent. Its walls became the walls of her world, and its pegs anchored the heavens. All at once she realized she was hungry, that she hadn't eaten in a long time. A girl wearing a white dress and golden bracelets served her some pita bread, which expanded before Silvana's eyes, as if threatening to swallow her up. With each bite of pita her yearnings subsided and with each taste her thoughts evaporated. She ate, feeling as if she herself were being eaten, until finally she perceived herself as a tiny creature devoid of any soul, a crumb of a satiated person. But within a few moments the image of her mother threw her back into reality.

Her mother didn't seem like herself. She looked nothing like the Julia Hajaj she'd known for years. Even on regular days she was unable to reduce her mother's image to clear, permanent descriptions, but nevertheless she now thought that her mother was unlike herself. There was no trace of the wise expression that normally adorned her face. Her eyes, which were always sharp, both in sadness and in joy, seemed to have been pulled out of her face, and in their place were only two dull sockets that revealed nothing of what was going on in her soul. After seeing her father losing his confidence for the first time in her life Silvana had trouble accepting that her mother was helpless too, and that no movement was happening inside of her in an attempt to release them from their wretched situation and transfer them to safety. This thought would have forced her to feel that she was truly alone in the world, and so her heart forbade it. Sometimes she enjoyed imagining she was alone in the world, but only when she was certain there was nothing to it, knowing that reality afforded her with a strong grasp on the world and that these were moot thoughts.

Now things were entirely different. The knowledge that she wasn't alone in the world was necessary for her to piece together her own reality. She yearned for her mother to take her hand, and so she gave her mother her hand and caressed her, so that her mother would return her caress. "*Tuwel balec, ma ikon can l'hir*. Patience, it'll be all right," she told her mother, hoping she would repay her with a similar statement.

Her mother ran her hand slowly through Silvana's hair and mumbled that she'd always known their British citizenship would come in handy one day. With broken words, she praised her husband for having insisted on living in Egypt for a short period a few years earlier, so that they could use the British people's readiness to grant easy citizenship to some of their colonies' residents. Silvana moved her head in an indulging movement, demanding that her mother run her hand all the way to the ends of her hair, combing it with her hand as she used to when Silvana was little.

The girl in white placed four glasses of tea and a plate of cookies on the red mat. Eliyahu Hajaj spoke to Jalal, who made sure to emphasize that he would take care of them, both through words and body language. They trusted him as if he were Muhammad a-Razni, the head of the clan, himself. After they finished drinking, Silvana's father and Jalal stepped outside of the tent for a few minutes. When they returned, her father wore his usual expression again. Her mother's caressing and combing hand and her father's familiar face planted Silvana's feet back on Earth. She felt herself moving safely through the world again, and no longer needed the tent in order to feel sheltered.

Her father told them that Jalal was arranging for a truck to return them to Benghazi. Silvana allowed herself to feel some joy; the thought that she would sleep in her room that very night swept aside some of her fear. The same thought occurred to her mother, who began mumbling in a mixture of Jewish-Libyan Arabic and Italian characteristic of Benghazi Jews, "*El-hushi. A-casa! Voglio andare a casa.* Home! I want to go home." Some time later, when her mother heard from one of Jalal's people that the truck taking them back to Benghazi would be there any minute, she raised her left eyebrow, as happened whenever her heart was filled with sudden joy. But when

Silvana heard the engine thundering, her happiness was shaken; she wanted to be in her room, but she also realized that she didn't want that room to be in Benghazi. At least, not the same Benghazi she was forced to leave the day before. She wanted a room outside of this world, one that would have nothing to do with countries. She loathed countries. She couldn't bear to think about them. She felt all those countries coveting her city now chasing after her, not only her land.

One of Jalal's men helped them onto the truck. Silvana's father and sister sat on the left bench and she and her mother sat on the right. The truck began to move and Silvana lost herself in the desert landscape. It regained its old appearance. It was everything it always had been for her; it was a blanket, but now also a bandage to soothe her wounded being. The serenity it exuded shielded her from the rough impression of recent events. During the ride, she watched the cars driven by the *Tedeschi*, the German soldiers; they sliced through the desert with the confidence of masters of the universe, as if a red carpet had been spread out in their honor. Her gaze was interrupted by Toni's stuttering comment regarding Jalal's kindness. Silvana let her eyes linger on her sister. She'd never looked at her sister as carefully in the seventeen years they'd known each other. Following the recent events, her sister seemed interesting, fresh, as if they'd just met. Silvana couldn't explain to herself how her sister—who always demanded that everyone around her remove all obstacles out of her way, using indulgence as a machete with which to clear the forest of life—was able, in these moments, to withstand the difficulty which was her share in the past day without complaining even once. Toni's face revealed nothing, only emphasizing its own riddle. Toni's eyes were soothing and understanding as a pair of coins with which to buy some relief.

Silvana lowered her eyes. She didn't want anyone to think she was the younger sister. Even in these circumstances she was loathe to give her sister any precedence in their relationship, even for a moment. She knew that if she leaned on her now, she'd pay for it in the future; she knew Toni would never miss a chance to use a favor performed for a friend or relative to condescend later. Silvana recalled the time Toni gave her a silver bracelet as a gift before their cousin's wedding, showering her with compliments, saying how the bracelet suited her, and then two days later remarking in the presence of her friend Lizzy Saban that all the pretty things Silvana owned she'd gotten from her.

Silvana shook the thought off and focused her eyes at the sound of her mother's sobs. It wasn't a wild sob, nor a quiet one, and it wasn't stifled either. Silvana rubbed the back of her mother's neck, this time not with the intention of being repaid. She knew that her touch could not comfort her mother. She knew that, along with her mother's intense desire to be home as soon as possible, she was also afraid; she knew her mother was anxious of the vision she would be faced with at home: the sight of the shattered dishes on the floor would shatter her, the torn pictures on the wall would tear her apart. The house was like a womb to her mother, from which she emerged into the world each day. The stability of the house is what allowed her to be fully comfortable in the world. "*Ya ma, nehabek bezaid*, I love you so much, Mama," she whispered in Arabic, wishing for her words to create an alternative home for them.

"*Anch'ioio ti voglio bene*," her mother answered her in Italian, fixing scared eyes on the entrance to Benghazi, which was gradually revealed. "I love you too." Silvana also watched the long, white row of houses that appeared to her like a fortified wall, but a moment later the facades no longer turned their backs on her; Silvana actually felt them opening to her, telling her not to fear the city hidden behind them.

And indeed, the closer they got, the more Silvana's attitude toward her city softened. Her usual yearning awoke once more. She imagined the city turning to her like a mother to her daughter, pleading with her to come to the rescue, fighting against the strangers trying to claim it. Her entire will was devoted to removing the Italians, the British and the Germans from Benghazi once and for all, to clean it forever from all its ill-wishers, to live only among its deserving residents, to play *Hatota*—hopscotch—with her Arab and Jewish friends, without seeing any foreign soldiers walking by; to play *Giran*—jacks—with Lizzy Saban on the boardwalk, beneath the Wall of Dreams—*Heit Lehlamat*—without hearing the thunder of fighter jets.

The truck entered the city. The city returned to itself, demonstrating its old ability to quickly adapt to a new conqueror. The tense silence that had enveloped her only the day before now evaporated almost entirely. The Arab vendors offered their goods with roaring cries, students trudged on their way home from a school day, exchanging light punches; in the dock, ships anchored, waiting patiently to unload their merchandise. But the comforting image of the city was tainted by the behavior of its Jewish residents. As the truck entered Hara Lekbira, the large Jewish neighborhood, Silvana noticed that even the thick beards didn't conceal the odd pallor of men's faces, and that they were wandering in circles, lost. She saw enraged, alarmed women dragging rebellious neighborhood boys into hiding places. She saw a short woman, her black hair flowing below her waist, chasing a limping ten-year-old boy, ordering him to put down his ball and come into the adjacent yard immediately. Silvana followed the woman's frantic eyes as they shot all over again and again, like the eyes of a terrified animal surrounded by hunters.

The women seemed to seek a hiding place from the uncertainty.

The truck's passengers quickly fit in. They disembarked in the center of the neighborhood, near the covered market, and began walking home. The rumors that were filling the air around them were like the wobbly floor tiles; they felt an enormous hole opening up beneath their feet. A passerby told them the *Tedeschi* were planning on banishing all Jews from Libya, and his friend who was arguing with him said that the soldiers were going to send them to a work camp in the desert, in the heart of Cyrenaica Province; a neighbor said that the foreigners would allow them to continue their lives as usual. This third rumor continued to echo in their hearts as they entered their home, which had been defiled by the feet of foreign soldiers. They nurtured this notion, keeping it safe, as they rearranged the house, throwing out shattered dishes and scrubbing the floors.

In the next few days the rumor seemed to have been verified. The *nuovi soldati*—the new soldiers, as Benghazi residents called them—allowed them to continue their lives as usual, and the old order was more or less restored. The Italians seemed to have convinced the Germans that the Jews were essential to Benghazi commerce. The detainees of the Italian School were therefore also released, all but the Boaron Family. Silvana and her family resumed a slightly dimmed version of their lives: her father walked to his shop every day, using the same route he always took, but the presence of Germans turned his stride more demure, less confident. Her mother, after having resurrected their home, returned to her old habit of assisting her neighbors, Arab and Jewish alike, providing food and clothes or coins and bills she slipped into the hands of the less fortunate with her husband's knowledge and acquiescence. But the frequency with which she offered help had diminished. Silvana quit her old habit of joking around with the Italian soldiers, the allies of the *nuovi soldati*, and no longer hung out at Café Italia, below the Teatro Berenice, where they liked to convene. Instead, she spent longer periods of time in her father's office and shop, assisting Ziad in filing orders, preparing import files for their customs broker, and sometimes, when Ziad wasn't looking—she was forbidden of performing any physical labor in his presence—piling the large cans of paint and sacks of cement in the large storage basement.

Keeping order in the shop was an anchor that helped her sense that her inner world was in order and push away the chaos that lurked on the threshold of her soul. Among rows of cement sacks and paint cans, she thought long and hard about the "*Henan nigliz, henan nigliz*" slogan that her mother had repeated again and again at Bab a-Jedid. She always knew of her mother's distaste for the British, in spite of the fact that they'd granted her citizenship. She

knew her mother viewed herself as Italian, though
the Italian government had never viewed her as such.
She knew she also thought of herself as a bit of an
Arab, because of her mother tongue. Most of all, she
knew her mother saw herself first and foremost as a
Jew. → engrossed w/ nationalities.   language

And so, often, as she sat to rest on a sack of cement,
she pondered the fact that her mother was grasping
at the citizenship of her enemies in order to protect
her Judaism against the allies of the country of which
she saw herself as a legitimate citizen, doing it all in
a language representing an entirely different side of
her personality. She often wondered if she too were
as split and divided as her mother.

She had no clear answer to this question. She
knew that, just like her mother, she also felt first
and foremost Jewish. The fact that she was fluent
in Arabic and Italian and that the Hebrew she'd
learned at Talmud Torah sounded in her mouth like
an exhausted sigh didn't matter. Unlike her mother,
she thought that what defined her more than anything
else was being a woman. The condescension she
suffered because of her gender and the expectation
that she accept her inferior position in the community
always awakened a strong resistance within her.
Thus, she developed an independent consciousness;
for example, when she wanted to join the Maccabi
Benghazi youths who plays ball on the beach and
they refused with ridicule just because she was a

girl, or when she wanted to sit in one of the market taverns and the Jewish male patrons rejected her with disrespectful gestures.

She remembered one instance well, because it was a milestone in her rejection of the social structures that prevailed in the Jewish community. One afternoon in early 1940, a heavy rain poured ceaselessly on the city, washing away the dust that had been collecting in Benghazi for months. The unusual brightness that followed fleshed out the murky sides of residential life: collapsing buildings, dilapidated sheds, filthy water wells, broken windows and broken wagons deserted on the sides of the roads. Even old-time customs, and mostly the superiority of men over women, seemed to have become more prominent than ever before. Images of aggressive men ordering women to perform a variety of physical labors could be seen more than usual in yards and on streets. This made Silvana more upset than normal as she listened to Esther, her mother's tall, pockmarked sister, recounting with submissive dryness how she'd aced the exams taken by all Libyan teachers, and would nevertheless not be appointed principal of Talmud Torah, since, according to tradition, only men were permitted to fill this position.

"*Questo e impossibile!*" Silvana shouted at the principal of Talmud Torah the next morning. "No! It's impossible!" The man had no answers for the twenty-year-old girl who had burst into his office, never hesitating to criticize one of the harshest rules of the institution he ran. Silvana kept his embarrassed silence in the back of her mind, and it imbued her with confidence whenever she decided to protest women's status in the community or voice her opinion on a matter that was considered masculine.

The same happened now, as she listened beyond the living room door to her father and his friends forming a plan of action for the Jews in light of the growing knowledge that the *Tedeschi* were preparing to leave Benghazi and leave them under the control of Italian soldiers. She heard the contractor Hlafo Barbi saying they needed to use this opportunity to return the Boaron family, who were still trapped in the Italian School, to their home, and then she walked into the room with a tray of tea cups and said they were able to do it. She didn't give her father and his friends a chance to overcome their shock, and instead repeated her statement three times, "*Tikder Ta'mel li thav!*" In order to strengthen her argument, she added that a different Arab family detained for spying, just like the Boarons, had been released two days earlier. "*El-bint ma tigdibsh*," said Hlafo Barbi. "The girl isn't lying." Her father looked at her softly.

In the next few weeks, Silvana did her best to enter her father's world. When he drank his beloved black coffee in his office, she conversed with him about his love of the Bible, his friends in Rome, Naples and Sicily, about his dream of seeing her and sister married one day to boys who would become involved in the family business, about his relationship with her mother, which was never simple, in spite of their great love, and even, only insinuatingly, about Claudia, the Neapolitan secretary of Fratelli Capone, who, rumor had it, was having an affair with him for the past two years. The memory of her father's tears outside of the Italian School stayed with her in their conversations, never relenting. Just as it had bitten into his authority, affording his words with a somewhat vulnerable quality, it also softened him in her eyes, allowing her to speak to him with more openness than in the past.

She accompanied him on many of his errands: at meetings of the Maccabi Benghazi Athletic Committee, for which he raised funds; in conversations with commanders of the Italian Army in Cyrenaica, which ended with warm hugs, reflecting his special relationship with the Italian government, which survived alongside German presence; and even to Via Veneto, the barbershop where he was shaved with a golden handled razor, then sprayed with a blue cologne, the fragrance of which she found addictive.

She took great care of her appearance whenever she joined him on his errands. She never used to join her mother with her friends and their daughters at their hairdressers, their *barbieri*, or when they waxed each other's facial hair, a custom that she viewed as frivolous torture. But now she wanted to make her father proud, yearning to improve her appearance, and so before accompanying him she plucked her eyebrows with her mother's turquoise tweezers, painted her eyes with gentle coal and covered her head with a silk green headdress that brought out her eyes. She didn't know this was not customary. The community women didn't walk around town all dolled up, but since she was already used to the community making invasive remarks about her being over twenty and not yet married, she easily ignored all the chastising looks that were sent her way. And on top of that, she had her supporting father at her side.

The deeper she invaded her father's world, the more she felt he trusted her. She wasn't surprised, then, when one morning he announced his wish for her to replace Ziad in managing the shop and office. He'd initially destined this position for a man and dreamed that, in the future, after she and Toni married, their husbands would run the business, but he was always realistic about his dreams, and acted out of the assumption that his hopes wouldn't necessarily come true. This might have been one of the main reasons for his financial success. After he announced his wishes to Silvana, and she answered with the words, "*Come vuoi*, as you wish," she had to ask herself if she truly wanted to take Ziad's place. She couldn't come up with an immediate answer, neither clear nor vague. She dreamed of running the shop and the office, but simultaneously didn't want to. She wanted to prove to herself and to those around her that a woman could succeed in doing this job, but also yearned to stretch out her youth in a way that no one else in the community ever dared do before; it excited her to think that, as soon as the coming spring, she would be allowed to do financial planning or consult with customers, but she also longed to lie on the sand of her beloved desert or the traitorous beach. Her father was aware of her dilemma and didn't push her.

Eventually, he was left with no other choice: in mid-August Ziad once again came to him to discuss his plan to quit his job in favor of architecture studies in Italy, and asked for his help. Silvana's father did what he'd always planned to do: he promised Ziad to help pay his way through La Sapienza in Rome, and told him he would help find him work at the Roman branch of Fratelli Capone. Then he told Silvana, without much to-do, that on September 1st she would have to take over management of the shop and office.

The next day she spent several hours wandering around their house, whispering to herself again and again, allowing herself to be a girl for a day: "*Il mio primo lavoro importante*. My first important job." Excitement and fear mixed together in her heart. Her enthusiasm seemed to contain all other occasions when she got carried away by first time occurrences: the first time she stood on one of the peaks of Al-Jabal

Al-Akhdar, watching the Sahara Desert spreading below; the pounding of her heart as she walked into the sea on a winter day, and her body, initially taken aback, quickly began enjoying the caressing chill that sunk into her; the elation she'd experienced at the quick, lustful look one of the handsome Benghazi boys shot her outside of Talmud Torah. At the same time, she was worried about letting her father down or failing the test, the same way she always feared the unknown: the fear of failing the final Bible exam at Talmud Torah, the fear of having her first period, the fear of not loving the boy her family would choose for her, the anxiety about being mocked for wearing a *reggiseno*—a brassier—at an early age, and the vague choking feeling she had at the thought of British bombs reaching her before she managed to reach the *riparo*, the bomb shelter.

She didn't stop pacing even as night descended, but rather than circling the family home, she was now circling her own mind. She asked herself again and again, as she lay in bed, if she would be able to fill the role her father had destined for her, and answered herself again and again that she'd be able to do it as long as she believed in herself. Finally, she fell asleep.

Doubts returned to plague her after dawn, and the same question and answer circled each other with endless repetition. She sipped the black coffee her mother served her with jingling bracelets, and with each sip she hoped for the end of this vicious circle. But the more she drank the tenser she grew, and the questions bounced around in her head faster and faster. Only around noon, as she hurried among the stalls of Souk Delam to buy fruits and vegetables for her mother, did the doubts finally let go. The intense heat, which paralyzed all movement on the street and caused the Italian soldiers walking by to remove their shirts, seemed to burn her thoughts to ashes.

Her body remained calm through the cooler hours of the evening. And so, when her mother said with seeming innocence that David, the son of Sarah and Abraham Lagziel, had been chosen to sing in the next community meeting at Teatro Berenice, Silvana didn't react as she normally did whenever her mother talked up the boy, urging her to meet him for marriage purposes. Moreover, rather than getting upset, she just said calmly, *"Bravo. Bravissimo."* She was still pleased with her response the next day, feeling a quiet confidence bubbling within her. By the time she went into her work meeting with Ziad, excitement had taken the place of anxiety.

Ziad thought her exaggerated excitement would hurt her focus and took action in order to cool her off immediately: he showed her the rough skin of his palms, the result of years of contact with construction materials. Her father had already clarified that, when she ran the office, laborers would perform the physical labor, but still, she suddenly worried for her tender hands. Ever since she was seven people always spoke of the beauty of her hands. Many times they told her, "*Rabi Yahfadlec yadic*, God save your hands." With the years she fell in such deep love with her hands that people often thought she was serving them rather than letting them serve her. And indeed, she often disobeyed her mother, sneaking into her parents' bathroom in the middle of the night in order to moisturize them with Nivea cream, which was her mother's favorite not only for its softening abilities, but also because of the colorful tin can in which it came. During her trips to the desert she kept her hands in the pockets of her skirts to protect them. In spite of her great love for the desert, she was sometimes worried that its winds would dry out her palms and its sand would roughen her skin.

Now Ziad led her to the corner of the shop that contained mostly foundation materials such as bricks, cement, metal poles and wood used for cement molds. He explained in detail the role of each and every material in the building process. She focused on his words, fishing the most important term from each statement, and memorizing it. Ziad was so impressed by her that he cut his explanations short and asked for her opinion on his nearing studies in Italy. At first she wanted to lie and tell him she thought he was making a mistake, but her intense jealousy of him didn't stop her from telling him the truth: "*Inta ta'amel el-haja il-malzuma*, Ziad, you're doing the right thing." Ziad smiled with satisfaction, led her to the finishing products, such as spackle, copper pipes, lead pipes, paint, bathroom fixtures, tiles and wood for roofs, and explained their uses.

Even as a small child, Silvana loved watching the products that covered the shelves of the shop. Her heart had foretold her what her mind later realized: with these products, she would be able to affect people's choices. With time, she saw from up close how most customers asked for her father or with Ziad's opinion on their choice of finishing materials. Ziad, who was now reading her mind, smiled as he pointed to the paints and the fixtures.

The thoroughness with which Ziad explained the products persisted through his descriptions of Fratelli Capone's most important customers. He characterized each and every one in such detail that Silvana felt she'd known them for years before ever meeting them. This was of utmost important to her; it enabled her to prepare in advance and restrain her explosive opinionated manner, which might have made it harder to serve her customers.

Ziad's explanations came in handy as early as September 1st, when she took over management of the shop and office. Had Ziad not explained to her how to treat Aziz, the youngest son of the Hamduns, a family which was involved in every profitable endeavor in the city, she would have surely lost his business at once, having become infuriated with his little snarky remarks about her people. Ziad knew to elegantly change the subject whenever Aziz mocked him for working for Jews.

As the days went by, she felt that not only Ziad's explanations were aiding her in her task, but also his spirit, which seemed to continue to roam between the office, the shop, and the large storage basement long after he was no longer there in body. Whenever she was met with a problem, she talked it over with Ziad in her mind, avoiding bothering her father or the three employees he'd assigned to her. Ziad's spirit only rarely let her down, and when it did, it was only because she hadn't imagined him in full. In those cases, she had to wait until she could consult with her father. If he was in Benghazi at the time, it was simple, but if he was on a business trip, she had to go all the way to the Italian Governor's Building at the edge of the Lungomare and send him a telegram.

One problem that kept recurring, and which she couldn't discuss neither with Ziad's spirit nor with her father, was the wonder mixed with contempt that customers demonstrated at the sight of a woman running a construction material business by herself. This was a problem she solved on her own: sometimes she answered customers with the same logic by tossing their change at them with ridicule; other times, she reacted more harshly, telling them explicitly that their money was too dirty for her to accept it. This kind of reaction usually erased the contempt off their faces, and they left the shop, shocked and shamed.

On one occasion, her response to a customer's mocking did not go over well. The man's behavior was so extreme that no reaction on her part could send him away, and certainly not one of her rote responses. The customer was a stocky man with rather light skin for a dweller of the desert, dressed with foreign elegance. He had gestures and an accent that made it difficult to ascertain his exact identity. He reacted to everything she said or did with a belittling laugh that sparked rage in her, and the more he laughed, the angrier she became.

As he stood on the doorstep, a moment before stepping out onto the street which was teeming with an Italian Fascist Youth Movement parade, he turned back, looked her right in the eyes, and released a surge of laughter, louder and meaner than his previous ones. This offensive laughter didn't let go of her for the rest of the day. It echoed in the back of her mind whenever doubts pierced her faith in her ability to successfully run the business. On the one hand, it shook her confidence, but on the other hand it encouraged her to outdo herself in performing the mission her father had given her. She floundered between feelings of inferiority and elation. Nevertheless, her doubts subsided as the days went by, and by the middle of October 1941 they'd become vague memories that evaporated with each compliment she received from the customers, the workers, and her father. Once, her father was overcome with joy, having returned from Italy and been stunned by the perfect order he found in the storage basement and the thick accounting books. His cheers echoed between the walls of the office for a long time: "*Hadi binti—ya Tza'adi!* This is my daughter—this is my blessing!" family name sun

The following weeks were wonderful. Silvana felt better than ever before. Her trips to the desert warmed her soul, swimming at the Jeliana Beach soaked every bad feeling with water, and the look Said had given her also struck a secret chord within her heart, but these were nothing compared to the joy she felt during those weeks. It was nothing like floating. On the contrary, it was a joy that pulled her down to earth, into a very positive reality: for the first time in her life, she felt she'd earned her father's respect, and that it accumulated within her rather than passing right through her. More than anything else, she felt her femininity blossoming for the first time. It wasn't because of the realization that she could manipulate the men who walked into the shop with her looks, nor was it because of the affection and respect she received from the men who worked under her supervision. It was for one and only reason: her refusal to accept the role society had chosen for her ever since childhood now received its tangible expression in the business that earned her family's living.

She was overjoyed and completely distracted from the state her country was in. At nights she no longer pondered those soldiers whose presence in a desert not their own had turned the whole world foreign. She ignored the shockwaves of explosive conversations in her community on the second week of German presence: for example, the ongoing shock over the fact that five *Tedeschi* soldiers had shot, one by one, for no good reason, the head of a young girl, daughter of David Halfon, the collector of Tzala Lekbira. It seemed that the German occupation of Benghazi really had stopped at the doorstep to her soul.

But this bubble of safety popped in mid-November. Silvana was enjoying a lunch in the back of the office when she heard a mighty explosion followed by a series of other explosions, the time between each one seeming to be divided into equal units again and again. It seemed that silence would never be restored. After shaking off the initial shock, but with a great anxiety still brewing in her belly, she stepped out of the store. An upset city was revealed to her: fires burning in all directions, roofless buildings, wooden shutters scattered on the ground, trees hunched toward the earth rather than standing erect. Crying and screams shook the streets. Benghazi was begging for God to remove the stifling smoke, but to no avail. People seemed to think that standing in place was a sin. They scampered aimlessly this way and that, their screams forming a tyrannical verbal fog in which even one clear sentence could hardly be spotted. Silvana ran with them. In fact, her body was running, because in those moments she was nothing but a body, a non-person rushing toward nowhere. She only paused when she was very close to the crater. She heard screams, the wailing of the wounded, and the ear-grating honking of ambulances. Standing breathless in front of the crater that spread before her, her mind grasped what her heart had foretold her: an inconceivable number of bombs dropped from the air had completely erased the Italian Headquarters, a walking distance away from Piazza del Municipio. She trembled. She knew the faces of many soldiers who served at Headquarters. Her father knew the commander of the camp well, an officer named Massimo who held a high position in the command center and received a plate of *mafrum* from Silvana's mother every Friday afternoon.

Silvana turned her back on the crater, the nowhere, and walked away, thinking she'd best find shelter from any further aerial attacks. She started running again, this time with a specific destination in mind. The sea was not only a shelter from bombs, but also from the feeling that building up within her, that she was about to collapse. The sea, she hoped, would bring solace to her soul, a measure of stability. Her anxiety would dive to safety on its waves, to a place where she could control it, rather than tremble like a leaf in a gust of wind.

She walked past Café Italia, which, even deserted, had a noble air about it. Beyond the curtain of smoke, almost as think as a concrete wall, she heard the call of the *muezzin*. Suddenly she yearned for it to never stop, hanging on to it as an emotional crutch. In the chaos that had taken over Benghazi, the *muezzin* was a sign of life from the old world, a tangible sign that the natural order of things had not been buried beneath the ruins of the Italian Headquarters.

A few minutes later, the Jeliana Beach was revealed from beyond the smoke and dust, and the old world returned to its new status: a horrid siren shook the entire city. Broken, interrupted, truncated sobs were heard. Dogs and cats crashed into each other, mad horses strode aimlessly down the streets, abandoned *carrozzas* rolled into the small potholes that were a regular feature of the city landscape and became lodged in them. Though she was already exhausted, Silvana sped up, encouraging herself, reminding herself that, even while tucking her dainty palms in her shirt, she always finished first in every school race. "Silvana *numero uno*," she thought, conjuring the words of Abraham, the Talmud Torah gym teacher, from the back of her mind.

Suddenly, a mighty squadron of jets appeared from the direction of the sea. The call "*Ingliz zhao!* The English are coming!" were heard from everywhere. Beyond the terror that plagued everyone at the vision of British planes about to bomb the city again, Silvana sensed something else, a tender sound that attested to the yearning of all residents, Arab and Jewish alike, for the Brits to conquer the country once more, liberating them of the burden of Fascist Italian rule and its allies; especially its allies. "*Nehabo izhio bash itlaohom min ardna*," she heard people whispering. "Let them come and kick them out of our country."

When she reached a stone house standing robust on a cliff across from the sea, she pressed her back against it and waited. She'd seen heroes do this in war films at the Bendosa Theatre, which she liked to visit with her father on Thursdays. She liked the gunshots and blood splattering all over in those movies, but was also deterred by her love for those images. She liked being the only girl watching those movies, but didn't like her pride. But now, pressing her back against the stone house, watching the British jets fly overhead, she didn't even ponder her actions. Any twinkle of a thought was beyond her, as if the ability to conceive thoughts had been plucked from her being. Wait did the British ac attack.

She was all action. Action and nothing more. When she heard the bombs going off, one after the other, she sunk her head into her hands and pushed harder against the wall. She waited this way for an immeasurable time, all the while seeing the waves of the sea crashing before her. She'd never experienced such quiet before; she never even knew it existed. It was nothing like the quiet that was often broken by natural interruptions, such as bird song; nor was it the quiet after a storm, or before a storm. It was not quiet as in the opposite of noise. It was a kind of final, ultimate quiet that all the noise in the world wished to disappear into rather than fight for its prominence over it.

Only one thing was able to interrupt the global quiet that enveloped her: the cry of a mother. About twenty meters from where she stood, a woman in a long dress ran around as if possessed, tearing her hijab off her face and crying, "Samir, Samir, *ya ibni*… Samir…."

The vision horrified Silvana more than all the bombs that had been dropped, and shot an anxiety for the fate of her family into her heart. She didn't know where they were. She knew her mother and sister were supposed to visit her aunt and uncle in the southwest corner of Benghazi, far away from the Italian headquarters, but had no idea if they'd actually gone. She knew her father was meant to return to the office in the afternoon, but she didn't know where he was returning from.

Rather than continuing to run toward the sea, she hurried toward home. She could make the way back with her eyes closed, quite literally; and the smoke billowing over the city and the dust taking the place of the air was no hindrance. The closer she got to home, the less she wanted to reach it, not because she thought something had happened to it, not because she was afraid she'd find testimony to the ill fate of its dwellers, but because she wanted that all-encompassing quiet she'd just lost. She wanted neither to see nor to hear the crowd that must have been hiding in the shelter outside of her house, as happened whenever bombs were dropped on the city. She had no patience to listen to the conflicted mélange of Italian and Arabic, which was surely escaping the throats of panicked people.

She stood planted in place, debating which way to run, until a siren sounded throughout the city, one she unthinkingly construed as an "all clear" siren. She stopped debating and walked back to the shop, which she'd left only an hour or two earlier, though it seemed more like a year or two. The walk back felt longer than ever, and Silvana now realized that the friendly greetings of passersby, as well as the calls of market vendors—"Good morning," "A glorious morning, Silvana," or "A morning of roses"—usually made her walk to the office seem short and sweet. She now noted the neglected streets, the neglect that had always been hidden in the light of people's warm smiles. When she reached Via Calanzzoshe received confirmation that it had indeed been an "all clear" siren. People slowly emerged from homes, shops and the central public shelter. She looked over the street, wanting to stop her gaze at the shop, but her eyes rejected her wishes and stretched her gaze all the way to the edge of the street, where a man who resembled her father stood, repeatedly beating a young man who covered his head with his hands. She walked, hesitant, to the edge of the street, and the closer she got, the crueler the blows became, and her heart yearned not to find that her father was the beater.

Since childhood, Silvana had always suppressed the cruel side of her father's personality, though more than once she'd seen him abusing his workers or manipulating business people until finally taking over their assets. She didn't realize then that this behavior was an expression of part of his personality, and unknowingly treated Eliyahu Lilo Hajaj the way everyone else did: she fused all the problematic parts of his personality together, buried them beneath his protective authority, and coated it all with pure gold. Even now, as she saw the strong, determined punches her father continued to throw at the young man, who was bleeding and about to pass out, or possibly die, she didn't even realize it had anything to do with his cruelty. Shop owners who huddled around told her that some of their workers had taken advantage of the commotion to loot the shops, and from the moment this news reached her ears, she began silently cheering for her father. In his ceaseless punches she saw the long arm of the law. She remained steady in her opinion even after the young man died and her father's friends swiftly carried his body off to an unknown location. Her opinion didn't change even after she heard Saida— whose hair reached all the way down to her behind, and whom everyone called the Witch of Benghazi, because she was an old beggar who pounced on any passerby—saying that Lilo had mistaken the identity of the young man, that it wasn't him who had looted the shop. "*Mush hua*, it wasn't him." The old witch's words circled in her mind, never landing.

When she came closer her father put his arms around her, comforting himself by saying that they'd replace everything that had been stolen that very same week. Silvana walked into the shop and her eyes grew dark, not because of the chaos, not because she felt that all her hard work had been lost, but because the broken mirror on the wall reflected her image as she'd never seen it before: instead of Silvana, the glowing young woman whose face was filled with a natural joie de vivre even in the worst of situations, she saw a woman whose face left no room for doubt. It was a face that had given up on life in this world.

This reflection of her image made Silvana uncomfortable for the next two months. She tried to wipe it off whenever she recalled it because she couldn't bear its ramifications. This reflection ripped the buds of her growing world view: that we ourselves design the world in which we live. It marred the image she had of herself as an optimistic person. Even the war that had been raging for quite a while hadn't hurt her self-perception so deeply, except for one event that had imbued her with incurable doubt.

It was more than two years earlier, in the beginning of 1939, when Silvana visited the Sarusi family with her mother and sister on a rainy afternoon that filled all the ditches of Benghazi with water. As they stepped into the living room, which overflowed with furniture in spite of its considerable size, they saw four people other than the Sarusis. They looked like nobody Silvana has ever seen. They looked neither Arab, nor Jewish or Italian. The skin of the two children and two adults was almost see-through. The four souls seemed scared, shaken-up.

"*Hadi familit Rosenzweig,*" Salvatore, the head of the Sarusi family, said, pointing at them. Salvatore was a man of the world, fluent in many languages.

One by one, Silvana, her mother, and her sister, offered their hands in greeting to the Rosenzweigs, who answered with a weak shake. Their faces showed gratitude, and the mother, a tall woman wearing a long black dress, its top part adorned by an elegant silver pin, mumbled, "*Grazie… danke… grazie.*"[7]

Silvana, her mother, and her sister, all looked at Salvatore, imploring him for an explanation.

---

[7]From Italian and German: Thank you.

The man spoke succinctly, only saying that the Rosenzweigs had fled Berlin to Czechoslovakia after the Kristallnacht, had come from there to Benghazi with three other families, and were now on their way to Palestine. To Silvana's question about the meaning of "Kristallnacht," Salvatore answered dryly that it was the name of the night when the Germans had destroyed all Jewish businesses in their country. A hint of emotion could be identified in his words only at the end, when he said, "*Harko hata Tzlat'hem*, they destroyed their synagogue, too."

Silvana, her mother, and her sister were all stunned, unable to say anything but, "*Elash*? Why?"

What shook up Silvana's regular optimism was the story of four-year-old Rachel Rosenzweig, which was told an hour and a half later by Salvatore in the presence of Rachel's mother. Silvana knew she'd never forget her sharp body movements and her terrified look as Salvatore removed his glasses, describing how German soldiers slammed the heads of little Jewish girls against the sidewalks outside of the synagogue. Silvana thought the world could not contain such an act. She thought an act like that could not even knock on the doors of the world. At that moment, a rift was formed between her and God. Silvana never accepted religion's stature as a given like the rest of her community. Naturally, she participated in the religious ceremonies held in her home, but was never part of the zealousness and excitement that ignited her sister. Still, <u>never before</u> <u>had she given any thought to the possibility that</u> <u>God didn't exist</u>. Until she met the Rosenzweigs, who'd come from afar, it was never an option. But from that point on, her attitude toward God was a mixture of contrasting elements, whose dosage changed according to circumstance: confirmation and negation, yearning and revulsion.

Her father kept the promise he'd made to himself, and within a day and a half returned everything that had been looted. Just as she didn't ask him what his friends did with the body of the young man he'd killed, so did she refrain from asking how he'd gotten the stolen goods and the black safety deposit box back so quickly. The knowledge that her father was expecting her to turn a blind eye blocked out her curiosity completely.

But the return of the goods and the safe was meaningless, since in November of 1941 the British conquered Benghazi once more, and the order that had been kept in the days of the Italian-German government, sometimes thanks to the remaining authority of the heads of Arab and Jewish communities, collapsed completely. The residents of Benghazi preferred British rule to Fascist rule, but they were so exhausted with their war over the city that they no longer had the power to establish normal life in the shadow of a new government. The fear of the return of Germans and Italian Fascists to conquer

their city once again, punishing anyone who joined
the British, also took its toll on them. Many Benghazi
residents dragged themselves, worried and haggard,
through the city streets, listening for any crumb of
news, as doubtful as it may be, as if alert for a higher
power that would decide the fate of their city.

Even her father, who'd always maneuvered among
the city's rulers, managing to create bonds with the
most important ones, was showing signs of weakness.
Silvana sometimes thought he was speaking to the
young sergeants only to practice his rusty English,
and not in order to promote his personal agenda or
the community's interests.

Even winter, which had been waiting in the desert
until the English arrived before it attacked Benghazi
with almost unprecedented force, did not manage to
rejuvenate the city, instead driving it years backward.
Via Calanzzo became a small pond, and people
began calling it *La Piccola Venezia*, Little Venice.
Everyone said—some jokingly, others enslaved to
the new genre of bitterness—that the Italians had
left just when the weather felt like home to them.
The Lungomare, the pride of the town, no longer
looked like a beloved boardwalk inviting residents
to parade around in their finest outfits and watch the
Mediterranean in peace, but rather like a temporary
blockade erected in haste in order to protect the city
from the invasive waters of the sea; dirty rags blown
by the wind clung to its walls and piles of broken

branches and leaves stacked on top of it. The dome of the el-Masjad was covered with mud, making the Muslim house of prayer resemble an incomplete, enormous, ugly municipal statue.

Silvana stopped caring about the small bedlam that took over the city and the alert waiting for things to come in December of 1941. She stopped seeing them and focused on something completely different: The encounter with Hebrewsoldiers from the Land of Israel who were serving in the British army. She'd heard word of previous meetings between Benghazi Jews and Hebrew soldiers, but had never attended one before. Now she was as excited as a little girl before her bat mitzvah. When she went to the meeting at the synagogue, organized by the heads of the community, she wore a blue dress adorned with two long golden stripes beneath her old, gray woolen jacket. She wore the turquoise headdress she'd inherited from her grandmother for the first time, grabbed a blue purse and went to Tzala Lekbira with her sister and mother.

The synagogue was crowded that Saturday night. About ten Hebrew soldiers stood at the center of the temple. The yarmulkes on their heads and the pressed British army uniform made them seem flawless. To the Jews of Benghazi, they appeared as demi-gods. Men wanted to touch them, and a few fingered the Stars of David attached to their lapels in disbelief. The women looked at them longingly from the elevated women's section, regretting the fact that they weren't allowed to go downstairs and take a closer look. Silvana stood at her mother's side throughout the prayer. At some point, when the soldiers joined the community in singing *Lecha Dodi*, the singing so loud that the synagogue seemed too small to contain it, Silvana saw a large tear running down her mother's left cheek. She watched the tear, mesmerized, and realized that it must contain a profound pain: her mother's long lived yearning for a place that would provide an independent home for her Judaism, the memory of her son, Judah, who was supposed to be the same age as these soldiers had he not died of illness at three months old, and the sight of the warm hug her father had given one of the soldiers, as if he were the son he never had.

[handwritten margin note: She had a brother]

She looked away from her mother, wishing to look over the entire synagogue, allowing her eyes to roam free among the brown benches, almost swallowed in the giant crowd, and up to the ceiling, which used to be white, but had grayed with the years.

Her eyes fixed on one of the soldiers—average height, skinny, muscular in spite of the long uniform that hung on his body, his arms slightly long, his face bright and his smooth, black hair longer than the other soldiers'. She followed his eyes. He seemed to be looking around him with a combination of power, tenderness, wonder and bashfulness. She felt herself pulled into his gaze, which contained the image of the man she'd yearned for. Ever since recognizing her feelings toward men, she pictured her knight in shining armor as a self-assured, gentle, and curious man who wouldn't be deterred by her power and would sweep her off her feet without demanding that she adopt the traditional role enforced upon the women of their community. A man that wouldn't be threatened by the desert, but rather open to learn from it that he was no more than a grain of sand in this universe.

As the prayer continued, so did her excitement over the Hebrew soldier of Palestine. His soft, careful body movements as he gulped down the words from the prayer book in his hand made her want to hug him. The speed and determination with which he went to help a congregant who'd slipped on the synagogue floor made her want him to hug her. Toward the end of the prayer she found it hard to breathe and stepped outside. She stood at the edge of the yard, breathing in the Benghazi winter air, focusing her eyes on the doors to the synagogue, lest she miss the soldier as he left after the prayer. He went out after all the other soldiers, surrounded by many people who cleared the way for him with reverence, as if he was the chosen ruler of the Hebrew people, not just one soldier out of many in the British army. Children clung to him with endless love and pride. Women, who now got a closer look, walked over and mumbled blessings in Arabic and broken Hebrew, some of them even taking his hand and kissing it. She didn't want to be one of them. She didn't want to be one of those women. She wanted him to look only at her, but she didn't have a chance to make that happen. He walked past her quickly on his way to Saturday night dinner in the home of one of the large families, as she'd gathered from the excited talk around her. A moment later, she shook herself off and decided to create the opportunity herself. She returned to the synagogue and asked the assistant to the beadle where the soldiers dined. "Ah… *il bel soldato*, the handsome soldier," the man answered without looking up from the chairs he was arranging. She didn't answer, waiting impatiently for him to continue. She thought he was taking pleasure in his own words, teasing her. After a long moment, he finally muttered, "Hachmon, *famiglia* Hachmon."

Luigi Hachmon, the father of the household, was one of her father's old enemies. For the past two decades, the two of them had competed over the supply of building materials for the governments controlling the city, their animosity on occasion reaching the point of insults and threats. Only the mention of Luigi Hachmon's name was enough to deter her. But the image of the soldier quickly took over again, and her desire to see him took precedence over all other thoughts. She also recalled that in spite of their bitter rivalry, whenever any member of the Hachmon family met her they always greeted her warmly.

Emboldened by this thought, she said goodbye to her mother, but not before she made her swear not to tell her father where she was headed. She then made her way to the Hachmon house on Via Generale Briccola, about a hundred meters away from her own home, on a hill that, on normal days, overlooked the ships sailing far away from the beach. She thought of the soldier the whole way there, other than the moments when she wondered, somewhat worriedly, how she'd be accepted at the Hachmon house. She no longer focused on his powerful, awkward, and confused eyes, as she had in the synagogue; now her thoughts were taken with his head. She had a strong desire to run her fingers through his smooth black hair, to stroke it. Halfway to the Hachmon house, she was already yearning to hold his head and softly kiss his lips. Her desire shifted according to the light of the moon, which poured over Benghazi: in places unreached by moonlight, her desire to kiss the soldier abated; in areas flooded with moonlight, her desire exacerbated. For days later she couldn't find a good reason for the game the light and shadows had played on her heart. She guessed it might have been related to the light depression she suffered ever since childhood when the sun disappeared behind clouds, or when the light of the lamps in their house suddenly dimmed. On her desert trips she always made sure to go to bed early; while the other travelers were still chatting enthusiastically, she was cuddling in her blanket, looking forward through shut eyes to the rising of the sun.

Now that the moonlight glowed over the Hachmon house, and two street lamps added golden light like two muscular bodyguards protecting it against the invasion of darkness, her desire to kiss the soldier reached its peak. She walked to the door of the house that she hadn't set foot in for almost three years, and just like the ceremony of *Tashlich* on the first day of Rosh Hashanah, she tried to throw away the lump in her throat, an expression of both excitement and fear. The moment she crossed the threshold, she was relieved: the entire Hachmon family welcomed her with visible joy. "Silvana, Silvana," Yolanda, Luigi's daughter screamed, at once hushing the tumult of the house.

"Silvana, *ya buya*, my baby, *bella*, so beautiful, *capara*," called Yona, the dolled-up lady of the house, and kissed her.

Luigi Hachmon walked over, hugged her just as her father would, and said, "*La mia casa è la tua casa.*" Yona took her gray woolen coat, and Silvana removed her turquoise headdress, ran her fingers through her hair, and smoothed the blue and gold dress. She glanced at the long dinner table, around which twenty people were convened, wishing to catch the soldier's eyes for a moment. She didn't have the courage for more than that.

But before she was able to do so, the lady of the house sat her right across from him. Silvana had to look straight into his eyes and introduced herself with visible excitement. The soldier shook her hand warmly and said shyly, "I'm Amos Rosman." Silvana saw that his eyes were blue. Their color was so deep that she thought they'd been forged in a sea before a storm.

She gently picked up a plate from the stack on the tableand ladled two *mafrum* patties, three spoonfulls of couscous and two ladles of *chersi*, her favorite spicy carrot salad. Yona Hachmon told her off, "*Medi yidic latzinia, shawa int tzaima, ula mereida? Kenti Tzoroy na nehar kippur, khir?* Eat, eat, what are you, sick? Or is today Yom Kippur?" Yolanda added some mesayer, salted vegetable crudité, to Silvana's plate. On a different night, Silvana might have pushed her away, because she hated to be force fed, but now she only mumbled, "*Tayeb.*"

The table was in a tizzy, energetic conversations all around, but Silvana only cared about the dialogue between her plate and the plate of the Hebrew soldier. Whenever his spoon touched his plate, her spoon followed suit and touched hers. Silvana was certain the soldier had noticed their musical rhythm, though she had no proof. She'd never believed in female intuition before, and the notion of it had always seemed ridiculous to her, a notion that only served men's perception of superiority, as if rationale was

(handwritten margin note: "huha Jewish women")

their sole domain, while women were compensated with gut feelings. But tonight she let go of her decisive position and accepted that it was female intuition that was telling her to communicate with the soldier through the improvised, humorous music of dishes.

Finally, she gathered her courage and addressed the soldier. Disguising the light tremble in her voice, she told him that her father had said that Jews in the Land of Israel had Hebrew names. "Is it true?" she asked in English.

The soldier stuttered, saying he'd indeed considered Hebraizing his name. "Maybe I'll change it to Amos Vered, the Hebrew word for rose," he answered.

His embarrassment gave her confidence, and she asked about his family.

The soldier sat up, looked into her eyes and told her that his family had come from Germany. "They ran away from the Nazis."

She told him about the Rosenzweigs. "They are like you," she said. He mumbled something she couldn't understand and glanced briefly at her breasts, which were fastened into their brassier. That moment, Yona Hachmon walked by, pointing to a small glass table on which some silver teapots were placed alongside plates of large almonds. "*Chai beluz*," she said, nodding her head with satisfaction. "Tea with almonds. Hmmm."

Silvana asked the soldier if he liked chai. He laughed and said he had no choice because the British Army had daily five o'clock tea. "Every day," he emphasized with laughter.

A new excitement took over her in the face of his sudden lightness, and she smiled freely and generously. In her heart she wished to kiss him before he returned to the battlefields. In her mind an idea emerged, to ask him to step outside with her for a moment. She would offer him, she thought, to share a Toscana cigar she had in her purse ever since her father had given it to her as a gift on her last birthday. Until that moment, she had no intention of smoking it. On this matter she refused to cooperate with her father's need to sporadically treat her as the son he'd never had. She pointed to the blue purse hanging at the edge of the living room and suggested they step outside for a cigar. Before she could even blush over her offer the soldier walked over to the hangar, pulled a silver cigar cutter from his pocket with childish glee and said, "What a coincidence." Then he told her he saved the apparatus in order to cut Sergeant Moore's cigars. "So you see, I've become an expert."

They took advantage of the commotion and the fact that most guests were already tipsy, put on their jackets and stepped outside. Silvana muttered "*Un momento*" at Yolanda Hachmon, who responded with a wink.

They were greeted with intense cold. The wind knocked the words out of their throats. The soldier invited Silvana to lean against him as he cut off the end of the cigar with his silver knife. She leaned in, shy, a little dizzy from the alcohol. The soldier pulled a worn silver lighter from his coat pocket, lit the cigar, inhaled calmly, and exhaled expertly.

"*Sahtein*," she said, forgetting for a moment that he didn't speak Arabic.

With one hand, the soldier put the cigar in her mouth, and with the other he held her against him. She inhaled, trying unsuccessfully to copy the slow, assured way her father smoked his cigars on their balcony at night. She was tormented. Gripped with excitement, she wondered again and again whether to ask the soldier to kiss her.

"You also know how to smoke a cigar," he told her in a voice that disclosed his excitement. *smooth af*

"But I don't know how to give a kiss," she answered. As if unaware of her actions, she dropped the cigar to the ground and brought her face close to his, surprised by how naturally she did this.

The kiss sent tremors through her body. She felt a physical pleasure the likes of which she'd never known, and an emotional joy she never imagined was possible. Her heart pounded. She was so moved she imagined the entire world had melted like an iceberg heated by an eternal sun, leaving intact nothing but their kiss. While their tongues became friendly,

Silvana and the soldier held the backs of each other's necks, as if trying to stop the moment from passing, delaying the necessary sobering.

A few moments later, they returned inside wordlessly. They imagined that other than Yolanda, who opened the door for them, no one had noticed they were gone. As dinner went on, Silvana and the soldier heard none of the conversations bustling around them, and if they listened, it was only for show. They were constantly busy sneaking each other breathless looks.

To her surprise, in the following days she hadn't let her heart linger over her encounter with the Hebrew soldier. She didn't want to wear it off, wishing to preserve it for a time of need, like a sacred object. Once more, Silvana was absorbed in the crawling chaos of the city, waiting with everyone else to see what would happen to them under renewed British rule. Waiting was difficult. Passivity, alertness, hope, and despair all mixed together. Whenever it seemed that the British were about to win the war over Libya, and that the Italians and their German allies, whose horrific actions began bubbling up in whispered rumors, would be forever defeated, a wave of enthusiasm rose among the Jewish community, and the quiet patience was replaced withthe buds of activity.

Thus, in the afternoon of a day in late December, a man on a bicycle with huge wheels rode beneath the dark clouds from one neighborhood to the next, cruising the streets, and announcing with excited shouts that the *Corriere della Sera* had reported that the Italians and the Germans had given up the African fight, and that they were concentrating their efforts on the European front. The rumor quickly circulated among Jewish residents, who all walked out onto the streets and roared as one, "*Viva il inglese!*"

A few days later, a senior British officer arrived at Silvana's house, wishing to speak to her father about the establishment of a British school that would replace the Italian School. "They will never come back," he said, sipping the martini Silvana's mother had served him. "Cyrenaica will stay British." The next day, the streets were filled with talk of the Jews' duty to help the British destroy Italian establishments and erect British ones in their place.

It now seemed the entire city had come back to life. A mysterious festive cheer bubbled in the streets, and a strange whisper fermented among its residents—a subtle sigh of relief for the instant disappearance of a great darkness that had come out of nowhere and taken over.

But one night in January 1942, all rumors of a final victory for the Brits were crushed under the chains of German tanks. The Germans entered the city in a convoy that only stopped when the first tank reached Piazza del Municipio. "*Un carro armato!* A tank!" people shouted on every corner, frantically

*included
the kiss +
the holiday
b/c its
a sense
of normal*

74 | Benghazi-Bergen-Belsen

describing its enormous size. Not only tanks invaded Benghazi territory against its will that night. A myriad soldiers entered the city from different directions, equipped with heavy artillery and a deluge of aimless aerial attacks.

Silvana heard the news from her father as he walked into the public shelter, drenched to his bone. He did all he could to soothe the people in the shelter, but the turmoil apparent in him put a damper on his attempts. The air in the shelter grew thin and was replaced with fear. It seemed that everyone was inhaling and exhaling only terror.

One of Eliyahu Lilo Hajaj's legs trembled, and all his efforts to hide it were fruitless. His entire body spoke of horror. Silvana was appalled. She was thrown back into memories of her first encounter with the Germans, a few months earlier, with the strange soldier at the Lungomare. For the first time in her life she knew complete fear. She only now realized how much that man had scared her.

As the minutes ticked by the sounds of gunshots and explosions grew nearer. Grown men sobbed inside the shelter. Babies' ear grating screams competed with the thunder of bombs. Migla, a close friend of Silvana's mother's who'd come to visit from Tripoli and spend a few nights in their house, cried, "*Halas!* Enough!" and plugged her ears. Another woman alternated between vomiting and crying. Silvana tried to calm down the dwellers of the shelter, but fear and anxiety were battling for her soul. At moments, she felt scared of the Germans, and at other moments her anxiety seemed aimless and undefined. Nobody listened to her. In fact, the panic in the shelter only exacerbated. It reached its peak when the contractor Halfo Barbi, that same venerable man whose opinion on any and all matters her father valued so much, soiled his pants, and the stench of his feces made the air unbreathable.

Occasionally the horror seemed to be over, or at least to have been abated, but it was merely a mirage. The babies stopped screaming only out of exhaustion, and the men and women stopped their sobs because of the paralysis forced by their desperate thoughts.

As morning rose and the noise of war subsided, Silvana could no longer take the exhaustion, and fell asleep. Years since the first time she'd done so, she rested her head on her mother's feet, the way she liked to do as a child, when her mother told her adventure stories about Hercules and King David.

She woke up at noon. The many sounds in the shelter were joined by a thunder of violent banging on the iron door. On the other side she heard a concoction of shouts that slowly separated into identifiable syllables: "*Machen siedie Tür öffnen!*"[8]

Silvana got to her feet. She felt she could not lean on her parents, who stood, slumped, on both her

---

[8] From German: Open the door!

sides, like a pair of useless, crooked crutches. None of the shelter's dwellers went to open the door. It seemed that beyond it waited an abyss, and whoever fell into it would continue to fall forever. The banging grew louder and louder, and everyone looked to Lilo Hajaj, including his bitter enemy, Luigi Hachmon. Lilo Hajaj was released at once from his terror, and walked ahead confidently, gesturing to everyone else to stay quiet and stand against the walls, hushing the screaming babies. About thirty seconds later, there was silence behind the door. The voices of the foreign soldiers seemed to have been wiped out in the fire that was raging outside. Silvana watched her father. She watched herself in his eyes. She saw her old, familiar image, the strong, confident Silvana. She was moved and filled with pride for her father. She was proud of herself, too, for having spent her entire life absorbing his determination, initiative, leadership skills and values of friendship, which were his signature marks. Pride averted fear from the center of her attention.

Then a German bullet pierced fear right into her heart: shortly after silence fell outside, a gunshot broke the lock on the door. Three Italian soldiers and three German soldiers hurried inside, accompanied by an enormous dog, and began screaming and pushing people outside. Silvana felt even more humiliated than in her previous encounter with German soldiers, when they'd locked her in the

Italian School. In spite of this, and against common sense, humiliation benefited her by somewhat dulling her fear. The German soldiers' vulgar attitude toward her, as if she was a soulless creature, enraged her so much that she harnessed the remainder of her strength toward resistance. She pushed away the butt of a gun directed at her by a tall German soldier with dark hair and eyes, and shouted, hoping he would understand English: "Don't touch me!" To her amazement, he let her go.

Encouraged by his reaction, she went to help the women and children, who didn't stop weeping as they left the shelter in a row. "*Tzbar*, patience, God is with you," she said, trying to calm them. From the corner of her eye, she noticed her father cheering his friends up in a similar fashion. Her mother took all the blankets and bedding they had on her way out, and helped other women do the same. From the moment they walked out onto the street she was overcome with the smell of gunfire. It was so strong that she thought it had taken over her soul. She felt herself surrounded by a huge heatwave, walking within an inextinguishable flame. It was the strangest sensation she'd ever felt, much stranger than the experience she'd had when she was fourteen, when one night she thought she saw a foreign object outside her window, something that was in no way a plane or a bird, flying through the moonlit Benghazi sky.

The German soldiers pushed the children, women, and men with the butts of their guns, urging them on. No one had any idea where they were being led. In spite of their flawless order, it seemed that even the Germans didn't know where they were headed. They walked by a scorched British jeep, and Silvana saw before her the image of the Hebrew soldier. She pondered the fact that they hadn't said goodbye, leaving their initial contact intentionally broken. And suddenly she was worried she'd never see him again. All at once she began longing for him. She hoped he'd been captured, and that they would soon meet at some detainee camp. "Do you have a prisoner by the name of Amos Rosman?" she practiced the question she would ask one of the German soldiers the moment she had a chance.

After the scorched jeep disappeared from her line of vision she turned to look at her parents and sister. The horror that had spread over their face in the shelter was gone, replaced with a different expression for each of them: her father clung to his traditional role and forced himself to keep his cool, but his mask of calm evaporated whenever a German soldier looked his way. Her mother seemed to be hallucinating, and only her sister continued to ridicule her old perception as a spoiled child. Rather than the alarm she'd expressed at the shelter, she had the expression of a confident girl who knew how to withstand bitter battles. Toni encouraged the anxious people around her with all her energy, and called upon them to walk proudly and not to fear the *Tedeschi*, the Germans. Most of them could not absorb the encouragement. It was enough for them to look at the soldiers, whose language seemed to slice through the soft desert air of Benghazi, to feel that breathing was suddenly difficult. They swayed, walking unassured, as if no longer knowing their place in the world. An odd sensation filtered into Silvana's soul: she didn't like the idea of Toni demonstrating leadership skills.

People continued to march. The visions she saw paralyzed her once and again. The most important sites of her life were ruined, becoming building blocks in the defeat of the British and victory of the Germans: the roof of Talmud Torah had become a pile of ruins in its large yard; the large synagogue of Tzala Lekbira was sliced in two, as if its elevated women's section and its men's section had been separated; all that was left of the Giardino, the public garden, whose rosy paths she'd often strolled, was a giant hole; and Souk a-Tzazara, the meat market, had been ploughed open, the large turquoise dome that used to cover it was shattered.

"*Afrikaner!*" the mocking voice of the German soldier walking beside her pulled her out of her shock. She'd never before given much thought to the concept of her Africanness, but now she was given to the authority of a stranger who knew nothing about her, and his voice expressed a ridicule that crossed borders, a hearty portion of degrading condescension and directed insult, fed with self-pleasure. At that moment, the soldier wasn't only her enemy, but the enemy of all of Africa. Their mutual enemy turned them into soulmates, mother and daughter: Africa had adopted her. It was the first time in her life that Silvana thought of herself as African. Black Africans sometimes came to Benghazi by ship, and her father often spoke of them as inferior. "*Hadon suadin Africani,*" he said, "they are African Sudanese," writing them off, as if he and his entire family were not children of Africa. Now Silvana began to view the Africans as her brothers, blood of her blood. With great difficulty, she stopped herself from spitting at the German soldier. She wanted to scream at her father, but held back. The soldier continued to urge her and others: "*Juden. Afrikaner. Schneller.*" She kept going, pondering Africa, the great desert and its sands, her father's negative attitude, the German soldier's milky white skin. Twenty minutes later, they arrived at a wide tent that looked ornate on the backdrop of ruins.

The Germans arranged them in rows without separating women from men and children from adults. They stood in fifteen rows of tens. Silvana's mother held onto her daughters' hands. Her grip weakened Silvana. Her heart told her that other than fear, her mother's grip contained the foreknowledge that this time their fate would be entirely different than on the occasion of the previous German occupation.

Indeed, there was no reason to believe they'd be released soon, and as the hours ticked by it seemed the Germans were intent on keeping them away from their homes forever. The captured people were sent into a rather large tent. Beyond its rectangular windows they saw the German soldiers in the midst of activity: filling water tanks, bringing in jerry cans filled with fuel, packing cases, cleaning weapons, polishing boots, brushing uniforms, shaving, and combing their hair.

The captives were concerned with one question only: where were the Germans planning on taking them? Many guesses were voiced into the space of the tent, including the most unrealistic ones. The need for a sure thing, and the necessity to imagine something defined, were stronger than any cold logic. From time to time, her father tried to calm some of the adults, saying that they would be released either that night or the next morning, at the latest, as they had a few months earlier. But the tension in his forehead attested to his lack of faith in his own words.

Around six o'clock, as the sun was about to set and the winds whistles loudly, a tall soldier, his nose protruding father than the rest of him, walked into the tent and announced in a broken Italian and a heavy German accent that in about an hour they would receive something to eat. One woman, no taller than a meter and a half, whose long hair fell down to her waist, walked over, took hold of his hand, kissed it and said, "*Comandante, voglio tornare a casa!* Officer, I want to go home!" The soldier shook her off, rubbed his hands as if to remove some dirt, and turned to leave.

Silvana's father went to the woman and put his arms around her. Silvana remembered that the woman was called Judith; she was one of the women her mother gave money to before the holidays, but who was never invited into their home.

The long hug her father gave the strange woman pulled her mother out of the shock she was in. "*Halas!*" she shouted at her husband. Her shout seemed out of time and place, as if meant to fly out through the windows of the tent, floating over all the places where her mother heard about her father spending time with other women, toward all the moments when she never stood her ground about it. Her father let go of the woman, returned to her mother's side and lowered his eyes, as if he'd just heard all of her mute screams of the past.

An hour later a young soldier entered the tent. He placed a box of loaves of black bread on the ground beside a military helmet filled with green olives. None of the members of the Hajaj family approached the food. For years they'd only eaten what they thought of as refined food. Even among members of the community stories were told about the delicacies served at the Hajaj home. Silvana and her father took pleasure in those stories and protected thesacred illusion. Toni liked to say any chance she had, "*In casa nostra mangiamo solo il migliore cibo*," waving the Baci chocolates her father brought from Italy.

But it was Toni who now deviated from the family way. When her father's watch showed the time to be a quarter to midnight she walked slowly to the center of the tent, picked up four dry pieces of bread and gave one to each of her family members. Silvana was once again astonished by the change that had taken place in Toni since they'd entered the shelter. She couldn't explain to herself how in the toughest moments her sister was able to remove her spoiled girl façade, revealing instead the personality of a responsible, practical adult. This time she didn't mind her sister overshadowing her. She was so cold and exhausted, and all she wanted to do was cover up and go to sleep. A few moments later she lay down on the cold floor, allowed her father to roll her into his Zegna coat, and fell asleep.

"*Achtung!*" A shout woke her. "*Achtung!*" A harsh ray of light penetrated the tent and fell on a tall, fat German officer with a bulbous nose and bulging eyes, and on a short Italian soldier with a thin mustache and black briliantined hair. The Italian soldier translated the German officer's orders, instructing the captives to collect all the valuables on their person, other than their clothes, and pile them in the center of the tent.

"*Avanti! Più veloce!*Let's go! Faster!" he yelled, trying to please the German officer. Silvana removed the golden necklace that had been passed down from grandmother to granddaughter. The slowness with which she did this was nothing compared to the slowness with which her father removed the Panerai watch he'd gotten as a gift from Maurizio Albertosi, Benghazi's young deputy governor. It was a large watch of the kind used by Italian military divers. He removed it with long motions, as if wishing to stretch out time and give himself a chance to take it back; as if the moment he gave over the watch, its hands would begin to show a different time.

After placing the necklace she'd gotten from her grandmother in the center of the tent, Silvana felt what she wanted to repress the previous day when she found a small brownish red stain in her underwear: a thick stream of blood. She was alarmed because she didn't know where she could find a cotton ball to wrap with a clean piece of fabric and insert inside her, the way she did whenever she got her period. At the same time she was glad, because she realized that the stomach aches, the tension in her head, and the general fatigue she'd been feeling all day were not merely a result of stress. It was only natural for her to feel stressed in the situation they were in, and still she didn't want to appear nervous in light of Toni's calm.

This double sensation was broken at once by the rattling of engines. Beyond the windows of the tent, Silvana saw three trucks, their tires spinning through the mud. She assumed the trucks were unloading more people, but the German officer shouted, "*Schneller, schneller!Sie sind zu langsam!*" The short Italian soldier translated the order—"Faster! You're too slow!"—and instructed them to leave the tent.

Silvana hid behind her father and ripped a tiny piece of the sleeve of her white undershirt. The moment she crossed the threshold of the tent, she saw the scared faces of dozens of helpless people, many of them familiar to her. Their helplessness gave her thought new power. She realized what she and her family looked like to a bystander. Only people she wasn't spending time with could serve as her mirror. Spending time in the shelter seemed to have concealed the faces of other people from her. Now she could see the men's eyes were tired, dark rings sketched around them for lack of sleep; the women's hair was unkempt, other than Yona's, Luigi Hachmon's wife. Shock and confusion appeared on the faces of children. Some of them had developed a strange rash.

Silvana, wishing to calculate her steps, could not figure out if her brisk walk toward the fence that surrounded the tent was a result of her fear of disobeying the orders of the Italian soldier, or whether it was a symptom of her wish to push off the image of her family's faces. Her mother let go of Toni's hand and hurried to grab Silvana's. This was no small thing: since they were little girls, her mother always helped Toni before she helped Silvana. Her mother always tried to find the way to Toni's heart, even when it meant losing the way to hers. Now Toni avoided joining them, but the call of the Italian soldier, "*Avanti!Più veloce!*" this time accompanied by the raising of his shotgun into the air, did not allow Toni to dawdle anymore, and she walked over and clung to Silvana and her mother, who were surprised and delighted to get a last whiff of her Cerruti 1881 perfume.

Silvana's father approached the Italian soldier, urging or begging him to take a look at some documents he pulled out of his coat pocket. The soldier ignored his pleas, but took advantage of the German officer's distraction and avoided being rude toward Eliyahu Hajaj. Instead, he only told him to go back to his wife and daughters.

Her father came over, waving his documents and shouting, "*Siamo Inglese!* We're British!" At the sound of his shouts, the German officer approached him, took his documents and flipped through them. When he finished, she was afraid he was about to put an end to his efforts. She almost collapsed with weakness, but then she heard him say, "*Engländer, Engländer*," and saw that he was motioning to them to step away from the others and stand by his side.

They were cloaked with unbelievable relief, so great that it seemed nonexistent, as if it were nothing but their desire for the idea of relief, for its superior, perfect being. A few moments later the German officer also looked at the documents served to him by Luigi Hachmon, and determined again, "Engländer," motioning for the Hachmons to join them.

Eliyahu Lilo Hajaj and Luigi Hachmon shook hands for the first time since their bitter rivalry began fifteen years earlier, when they publicly accused each other of stealing customers. Silvana noticed that warm expressions also spread over the faces of her mother and Yona Hachmon, having been trapped inside their souls for years. They looked at each other with love, appreciation and compassion. Silvana was moved to see this. She felt their gazes woven into one shared expression that served as her safety net. She sensed that this expression would last forever, and would no longer depend on the men's unstable relationship. She saw it as the forming of a new, unbreakable female solidarity. Silvana felt that whenever she fell, her mother and Yona's eyes would be there to spread beneath her, catching her before she crashed.

The German officer mumbled something that even a native speaker would have had trouble deciphering. The statements escaped his mouth in sharp, choppy syllables, as if they'd been dissected between his teeth. The Italian soldier asked him to repeat himself, listened carefully and put his hand around his ear, touching his brilliantined hair. Once the German officer repeated himself more clearly, the Italian soldier instructed everyone but the Hajaj family and the Hachmon family to go outside the fence and board the Mercedes trucks, which had giant wheels decorated with German letters. Two young soldiers threatened to sic four big black dogs pounce on anyone who showed even the slightest hesitation. None of the captives knew where the trucks were headed. They only knew they didn't want to be in them.

Silvana's eyes focused on skinny Liza Genish, only a few years younger than her, a fellow Talmud Torah student with short black hair and enormous brown eyes. Silvana remembered that her mother used to tell her that if she truly wanted to understand people in distress, she had to choose one person to focus on, because watching a large group, no matter how miserable its members, inevitably became an abstract endeavor paralyzing any true powers of empathy. Beneath the layer of Silvana's protest against her mother and her ongoing anger for having played the traditional role of a woman in their society, she respected her mother's wisdom and experience. In those moments, her rebellion peeled off completely.

Liza Genish watched Silvana from inside the truck. Her eyes seemed to be growing larger as the truck drew away. Her eyes took over until Silvana felt they were no longer fixing upon her from the outside but were within the depth of her soul; that Liza's eyes were looking at the world through her. But the world was blind to her piercing look. The more desperate Liza's eyes grew, the more indifferent the world became to the guilt her eyes tried to instill in it: the German soldiers argued vehemently over a pack of Ariston cigarettes; three smiling Italian soldiers kicked a soccer ball, calling to each other loudly; one of the dogs walked over to his master, an arrogant Italian soldier whose long hair flowed beneath his beret, and licked some food off his hand with slow pleasure.

The sky brightened. Luigi Hachmon rubbed his chest and said, "*Meno male che non siamo su quei camion.* Thank God we're not on those trucks." Silvana's mother mumbled something as she looked up to the sky. Their words and gestures were broken when Yona Hachmon commented, "Poor things, who knows where they'll take them?"

The Hajaj and Hachmon families clung together, closing all distances between them, as if wishing to expand the distance between them and their town's people who'd been taken away. They waited for a sign. None of the German or Italian officers and soldiers broke their apathy in order to hint at what was to come. Silvana's father and Luigi consulted and appealed to the Italian officer, but to no avail.

Only one simple German soldier muttered in Arabic, "*Bila'kl, bishveya*, slowly." A smile of emotionless satisfaction spread across his face in light of their surprised expressions. He added in German, "*Alles klar.*"[9]

Silvana's mother and Yona Hachmon were the first to acknowledge the possibility that their families wouldn't be moved from this location any time soon. They spread two sweaters on the muddy ground and stretched them out carefully, as if making a fancy bed. In spite of their exhaustion, none of the family members sat down. Only time seemed to take a breather, moving backwards: as Silvana watched the handsome Italian soldiers playing soccer through tired eyes, noticing the nervous looks her father was giving them, her thoughts wandered to the soccer tournament her father once held at the Maccabi Benghazi field, in which a few Italian military units participated. In her mind's eye, she saw the soldiers' begging eyes and could even hear their repeating requests to be assigned a spot in the tournament. She recollected the body language of the officers who approached him then, all awe, devoid of any condescension. Even the ball that now accidently hit her head didn't shift her thoughts from the past. Neither did the distracted stroke the Italian soldier who came over to retrieve his ball gave to her hair. In

---

[9]From German: Everything is fine.

those moments, she was not comparing the past and the present. In those moments, she was so invested in the images of her recollection that she wasn't able to rid herself of the past. She was absorbed in it, so immersed, until suddenly she heard the words coming from the German soldier who'd just appeared: "*Guten abend.*" His soft voice didn't completely pull her out of the past, but it did launch her from the distant past to the near past. She recalled the first time she heard the words "*guten abend*" who knows how long ago. She wanted to forget the paralyzing anxiety that had plagued her then, but the eyes of the German soldier in front of her reminded her so much of the eyes of the soldier she'd met at the Lungomare back then, that for a moment she even thought they were one and the same. His eyes projected tenderness and patience, but seemed prepared to change entirely at any given moment. She noticed her mother also looking at the soldier with express doubtfulness. She remembered her mother once told her there was nothing wrong with trusting your eyes, that reality is cunning and lives beyond the realm of our eyesight, even using it to hide. Silvana played around with that statement. She thought that everything she saw before her was nothing but an illusion, and that in another moment the trucks carrying their community members would return, rejoicing people stepping out of them, praising their desert voyage, and that the German soldier would soon announce that the Germans' lovely visit to Libya was over and they were about to return to their homeland; she even thought her father and Luigi would quickly put an end to their truce, becoming bitter enemies once more.

In the midst of her fantasies reality gave her another wake-up call. Evening began to descend, gunshots were heard from up close, as was the barking of faraway dogs, conversing with the dogs of the young soldiers. The two families began to accept the possibility that they'd been deceived, that they would have been better off joining the others on the truck. Silvana, her mother, and her sister, looked at each other with newfound anxiety. Silvana began missing the fear she'd felt in the shelter. She struggled under the weight of an anxiety that was not directed at any tangible object. Her father, who noticed her mood, wished to calm her nerves. "*Rabi ma ya'mel can el-hir*, God will do what is best," he told her, looking for approval to Luigi, who looked at his wife, who looked at Silvana's mother with endless awe and supplication, as if she were God Himself.

Tripoli

They were finally saved of their uncertainty when the German officer ordered the Italian soldier to put the two families on the Mercedes truck that had just arrived. This time, the soldier didn't translate the order, but only said, "*Avete sentito o no?* Did you hear him or not?" He meant the word Tripoli, which the officer had repeated twice.

On normal days, the name of that city had a double meaning: as many Benghazi Jews, the Hajaj and Hachmon families saw themselves as slightly culturally superior to the Jews of Tripoli, but also simultaneously inferior to them, because Tripoli Jews lived in the big city. Some Tripoli Jews even considered the literal meaning of the city's name, seeing it for what it actually was—*tri polis*, three cities, entirely different from one another, and arbitrarily glued together to form one city lacking in any unique character. Now the mention of Tripoli was a source of solace and hope to the families.

Silvana quickly pictured an image of her family getting off the truck at Lido beach and heading toward the Zaruk family home without looking back.

The Zaruk would welcome them with hugs and kisses, providing them several rooms in the house (the room she imagined herself staying in faced the sea), but not before Rebecca, the mother, prepared a meal for them, made of their favorite dishes, such as *mechuma*—a beef stew in garlic sauce, *bazin*—a doughy pastry eaten on Shavuot and Rosh Hashanah, and *atzeyda*—crispy dough.

A moment later, she imagined the German and Italian soldiers leading her to a wide single story structure, a kind of small-scale Pisa Tower on its roof, where the governor of Libya, Rudolfo Graziani, would appear before them in all his glory, with his long face, wearing a jacket adorned with military insignia, immediately recognizing her father, hugging him and rebuking the soldier for daring to remove him from his city so aggressively.

The next moment, she pictured Omar al-Khayyam, one of her father's influential Muslim friends, bribing their captors at one of the dusty checkpoints in the entrance to the city, promising the Hajaj family he would take them under his wing.

She went on and on until her grand imaginings evaporated like the dust that rose from the tires of the truck as it rode through the desert. There was no clear clue that the soldiers were about to transfer them to any of Tripoli's infamous jails, and none of the Italian and German soldiers sitting across from them looked at them in a new way, and nevertheless, the truck's bumpy ride, its lights losing the battle against the deepening darkness, foretold nothing good. Their hearts gave up on the possibility that the ride would end well.

Or maybe it was the look in Silvana's mother's eyes. Her gaze was double: it faced the world, and at the same time demanded that the world face it. It reflected a cheerful teasing, like a boy flashing his buttocks to police officers coming to arrest him. This duplicity made Silvana feel split: on the one hand, she wanted to identify with it, and on the other hand she hoped it wasn't prophetic, hoping her mother was foregoing, just this once, her startling ability to tell reality from illusion, that the outwardly humane behavior of the German and Italian soldiers wasn't concealing some harsh, cruel reality.

The truck rode on. The wind mocked what little protection the green tarp provided its passengers. Silvana's father put his arms around her in an attempt to warm her body, and her mother brought her mouth closer, wishing to warm her heart: "*Ma t'hapish, ya binti*, don't be scared, my daughter." After twenty minutes, Toni asked to switch seats with her mother so she could be closer to Silvana. "Silvi," she said, resting her head in her older sister's lap. "*Che facciamo?* What are we going to do?" It had been years since she'd called her that. "Silvi." That was Toni's nickname for her sister when they were little, and even then she used it only on those rare occasions when the competitive component was taken out of their relationship. Silvana didn't answer her little sister, only stroking her curly black hair, the hair that filled Silvana with glee whenever Toni teased her, because everybody knew that Toni didn't make do with her blue eyes, her slender body and her glowing olive skin—features which caused many to nickname her *La Bella* Toni—but envied her older sister's long straight hair. Silvana stroked Toni's hair enthusiastically, suddenly yearning to stretch it and smooth it out. Tears rolled down her cheeks and landed on her sister's hair. She began singing, silently at first, and then in a meek voice:

I shall tell you children
Of the redemption of the Land of Israel
Acre after acre
Hill after hill
The land of the people is built
From the north down to the Negev

[handwritten margin notes: nation destroy nation b/c / form empty land]

She almost didn't notice the words leaving her throat. She was surprised to hear herself singing to Toni. She'd never liked that song. Whenever they sang it at Talmud Torah, she did so with express lack of desire, and only her fear of the teacher, Roberto Kachlon, made the words emerge from her throat at all. Toni squeezed her hand and joined her on occasion. The more Silvana sang, the more she wanted to keep singing. When she finished the last line it was like she'd spat it out whole only to go back and start singing it all over again. This time, Toni joined her in the very first line. Silvana knew her mother was now listening to the sound of her life: her two daughters, her two lungs, singing a song of hopeful vision in the midst of one of the hardest moments of their life. She knew her mother was now thinking that the upbringing she'd given them, which she viewed as her life's mission, was bearing fruit during the greatest test of their lives. She knew that, though her mother wasn't so attached to the Zionist vision, she was happy to see them use it to express their withstanding of this test, not because she wanted her daughters to adopt the Zionist vision more than she had, and not because it was something she wanted to instill in them; after being humiliated only for being Jewish, she felt that this vision alone could serve as something to lean on, so that she didn't collapse and shatter. didn't really wasn to leave Lydia behind - complex engad w/ Zionism.

From the corner of her eye, behind her mother's shoulder, she saw Yona Hachmon, who sat silently at the edge of the bench, staring at them with wonder, as if looking at a picture that was still being painted, and waiting longingly for more characters to appear in it before it froze forever. But her daughter Yolanda and her son Nissim, called Simo by all, did not join the singing. Not only did they not make any gesture of hope, but Yolanda cried ceaselessly, leaning her head on her father's shoulder, and Simo, a strong twenty-five-year-old, trembled and cried alternately.

The five soldiers sitting across from them all witnessed this vision, but only one of them paid attention, watching intently. His dark face merged with the darkness almost completely. His uniform was a few sizes too big, making him look unlike most Italian soldiers Silvana knew, who, even at wartime, tried to look stylish ("It's important to look nice when you die," she heard many of them say, possibly joking). He spoke a Sicilian dialect and his legs stretched ahead, as if trying to liberate his body from the boundaries of this place. Silvana watched him. She strained her eyes to cross through the dark and see his. She hoped to have some sort of conversation with him, to glean a hint of information about their destination. The moonlight filtered into the truck from time to time to help her out. For a moment, the light was so strong, almost like a flash of lightning, that she thought the moon was hovering on the floor of the truck, rolling around between her and the Italian soldier. But even the strongest light couldn't free her from darkness: the Italian soldier's glances didn't disclose any information. His eyes seemed to chatter, but remained expressionless. When she tried asking him with hand gestures where they were going his response was an affectionate mimicking of the way she stroked her sister's hair. Shortly thereafter, when she motioned to the German officer with her head and signaled with her hand that she wanted to know what he wanted, the Italian soldier answered with a surreptitious gesticulation, insinuating that he couldn't stand him either.

Regretful, she continued to sing. The words formed the image of the Hebrew soldier before her. She wondered again what had happened to him. Had he managed to escape with his friends and meet the British army? Was he killed? Perhaps he was captured by the Germans? The more she considered these options, the more she realized how pointless the thought was.

Her pondering came to an abrupt end. The truck suddenly shook violently, rattling not only its passengers, but everything that was going on in Silvana's mind. The thoughts that had been filling her brain did not remain whole, and neither did they shatter against its walls, but rather completely evaporated, as if they'd never even existed. Her terror shook her entire being: it seemed that anything that had ever occupied her mind now abandoned it forever, turning it into a dark, empty cave, even the strongest memory too weak to shift the enormous rocks of oblivion from its door.

"*Ya rabi hen!*" she heard her mother yelling. "Oh God!" Normally, when her mother spoke the name of God, it gave Silvana a start, but today she remained indifferent. Perhaps because of the crack in her faith, which formed after she heard Salvatore

Sarusi speak of the Germans beating Jewish girls during Kristallnacht, or perhaps because this cry was no longer enough to rattle reality. Her mother wasn't the only passenger who began speaking due to the bumpiness of the ride. Even the Italian soldier, whose blurry eyebrows Silvana could now see in the moonlight, finally muttered an answer to the question Silvana tried to answer him earlier, regarding their destination: "I don't know. *Veramente non lo so.*"

Her father, on the other hand, veiled himself in silence. While the horror that had taken hold of her, her sister, and her mother was cloaked with a layer of mystery for not knowing the way, he began acting coolly because he had an idea about where they might be headed. When, early in the morning, they reached Ajdabiya, his eyes showed an old confidence, as if his past authority was returned to him.

The small city on the coast of the Mediterranean greeted Eliyahu Lilo Hajaj warmly, as if they were old friends who reserved a special affection for each other in the time since their previous meeting. Ajdabiya presented the possibility of showcasing his clear advantage over the Italian and German soldiers. Those tried in vain to find a place to rest and have some water. Silvana's father led both captors and captives authoritatively toward a large stone house with a large well in the yard and a water spring nearby. The landlord, a tall Arab whose many wrinkles were revealed by the morning light, walked out to greet him with a strong hug. The hug seemed to strangle the German officer. Rather than the rough orders he'd delivered thus far, now all he could offer were long silences broken by mumbled bits of sentences as their host gave them a tour of the three stories of the building, advising them which rooms to choose. "We shall rest here," Silvana's father suddenly declared assertively, pointing to a large green room on the second floor with a large window facing the sea. Everyone was shocked and obeyed mindlessly. The Italian soldiers, Silvana's mother, and her sister each stuttered in their own language, "Yes… here… this is fine… good." Even the German officer repeated after them. He stared into the room, nodding and mumbling a few syllables that quickly died down. Eliyahu Hajaj couldn't believe his eyes and ears. For a moment he was taken aback, stunned by his own orders. He repeated himself, quietly this time, making sure he was the one to speak the words that still echoed in his mind.

The members of the two families collapsed, exhausted, on the blue floor tiles, holding the clothes, blankets, and sheets they'd brought with them close to their bodies. Two Italian soldiers wriggled into green sleeping bags after depositing their guns in the hands of another Italian soldier and the Italian truck driver. The German officer and soldier sat down with their weapons and equipment in the long hallway, expressly avoiding staying in the same room with their captives. The insult burned the flesh of the German officer. He wasn't able to share a room with what was now its main tenant.

This tenant was no other than the statement Silvana's father had made. It was present in every corner of the room, disrupting the sleep of the families, whispered from one to the other, and filling their hearts with immense pride. It imbued their aching souls with renewed faith in the world and the possibilities of existence within it. Silvana's father wasn't seen as a man who retrieved his authority with force, but as authority itself, returning to its natural dwelling following a period of forced exile.

"*Wach auf, lass, wach auf!*"[10] They were awoken by the German officer's shouts. Silvana didn't know where she was, not even when the sea appeared beyond the wide window, taking over her fuzzy field of vision. The sight of the smooth sea let her continue the dream she'd had: she and Nassarin were playing *giran*—jacks—by the Wall of Dreams, then descending the twisting staircase, hand in hand, to swim at Jeliana Beach. She quickly got a hold of herself because the order of the German officer wasn't directed only at some of them: his order did not distinguish between the prisoners, the Italian soldiers, and the other German soldier, but was meant for them as one unit, and they all had to obey.

---

[10]From German: Wake up, let's go, wake up!

This amazed Silvana and also encouraged her. She now believed that the Italian soldier with the fuzzy eyebrows and the foreign dialect truly didn't know where they were headed.

The family members placed their clothes, blankets, and sheets in a pile in the center of the room and convened around it. After they shoved them into a large sack they received from the Arab landlord, they made their way outside. When she walked down the stairs, it occurred to Silvana that not only that one soldier did not know their destination, but that the other Italian soldiers and the German soldier didn't know either. For a moment she thought maybe even the German officer didn't know where they were headed, and that the obsessive repetition of his wake-up call, "*Wach auf, lass, wach auf!*"—he screamed it at them several more times as they packed their things—was clear proof. But as they left the house, her body was scorched by the sun and her hopes were wiped away. The German's officer's elegant appearance in the sizzling desert heat and the dusty roads—his feet in tall shiny boots, his shirt buttoned all the way up, a cap perfectly positioned on his head—did not allow her imagination to wander any longer.

The heavy heat provided her with partial relief. It blurred her thoughts, and therefore blurred her anxiety about the future. In each and every one of them, the heat blurred the fear that had died down at night and was revived in the morning.

The Hajaj and Hachmon families got on the truck, using each other's help and the help of the two Italian soldiers. They sat on their bench, now no longer two separate families but one cohesive unit. Silvana held Yona Hachmon's hand. Yona's hand was soft and pleasant to the touch. Staring at the faces of the German and Italian soldiers, Silvana thought of her beauty ritual. She thought of how she took care of her prettyhands, and how before special events, or when joining her father on business meetings, she always took special care of her outfit. She also thought of something else, something she'd never allowed herself to admit before: the main reason why she never agreed to her mother's pleas to get more dolled up. She wondered why now, after her father's old authority was restored, she allowed herself to admit that her refusal stemmed from her wish to please him. She didn't wonder why now, sitting across from the soldiers and their erect guns, she admitted to herself that on occasion she'd tried to be the son he never had.

Nothing interrupted her thoughts, they simply evaporated like the clouds of dust that were disappearing behind the truck. The ride became rougher. The road from Benghazi to Ajdabiyahadn't been pleasant, but now the road had many potholes due to so much bombing. Every so often, the truck had to ride directly on the soft sand. The driver, who was very skilled, kept going around faulty patches that looked like quicksand. After about thirty minutes in which they'd only advanced a few kilometers, he suddenly stopped the truck. He got out of the driver's cabin and whispered with the Italian soldier with the thin mustache and the briliantined hair, who translated for the German officer. Though she'd considered it many times, Silvana couldn't figure out why the German officer told them to get off the truck immediately, and why he screamed like mad, "*Aussteigen!*"[11] It occurred to her that he might be doing this to compensate for the silence and limpness that had taken over him in Ajdabiya, but the thought was pushed back again and again, shifting in her consciousness with no purpose or direction, until it finally faded away. Even the thought that the German officer had simply gone mad didn't last long.

The vision they saw wasn't enough to explain the officer's screechy "*Aussteigen!*" About five meters ahead of the truck were twenty bodies of local children, about six or seven years old, some of them headless, others missing their limbs. A little behind them was the body of a young woman, her breasts chopped off, her arms and legs spread apart, her face staring up at the sky, her eyes open in eternal wonder. Toni fainted immediately. Silvana harnessed all of

---

[11]From German: Get off!

her mental energy. She couldn't collapse. She helped her parents carry her sister to the truck. The moment she stood behind the truck, where she couldn't see the horrifying vision, not even from the corner of her eye, she got down on her hands knees and threw up. The remains of her innocence were spat out along with what food was in her stomach. Even as a child she was aware of the wars that covered every piece of land in her country with terrible visions, but until that moment she'd never seen cruelty for the sake of cruelty. She'd never thought that being human meant being evil, and man's world view could be painted with a murderous gaze just as it could be painted with a compassionate one.

One of the Italian soldiers brought her father a jerry can so that he could sprinkle some water on Toni's face. Her father refused to do that, and instead tried to wake up Toni with light slaps to her cheeks. Toni quickly began regaining her senses. Silvana's heart ached. She hoped it would take longer. She hoped her sister would get a chance to rest for a bit before returning to the reality that had knocked her down so violently. Her father helped Toni get on her feet and held her close to his chest, which appeared more impressive than ever to Silvana because it was devoid of the war insignia that decorated the shirts of the German officer and one of the Italian soldiers. Toni wept into her father's chest, saying, "*Sha ka'ed yetzir pi had a-dinya?* What is this world, Daddy?"

The Italian soldier, whose hair had lost some of its luster and seemed like mush clinging to his skull, ordered them to get back on the truck with a pale face and a limp tongue. Silvana couldn't do it. His order sounded like a foreign, indecipherable language. She could do nothing but get down: get down on her knees and lie on the ground, get down to the depths of his soul and ask the great question embedded in the face of the woman with the chopped breasts. Her mother, the only one of the two families who was able to contain herself, grabbed her hand and led her to the truck. She pushed her up the metal stairs of the truck, and Silvana was able to climb them only because suddenly, out of any context, she compared them to her dreams. But it wasn't only her dreams she was stepping on as she walked slowly to the back of the truck; she also left her closest friends, her thoughts, to die in the scorching sands of the desert. From the moment she sat down in the truck she stopped thinking. Her mind was a kind of selective traffic tunnel: thoughts and imagination were forbidden, and the tunnel was only open to feelings, which slid through it as fast as racecars, as if marking it as their natural habitat, rather than the heart, as common wisdom had it. Her feelings clashed and slammed into each other mercilessly: her love of life with her hatred of war; her self-pity with her cruelty toward herself and her anger for having collapsed like a little girl at the sight of one terrible vision, while others had survived much worse; her pangs of conscience for not demanding that the soldiers find out the meaning of the horror they'd seen clashed with her acceptance of her own helplessness. More than anything, desperation shattered all of her efforts to nurture hope, and after a while she began fearing she would never feel it again.

The truck got on a smooth road. It appeared straight as a ruler, clear of any evidence of bombing. The atmosphere inside the truck became a little looser. The Italian soldier handed everyone large pieces of pita bread and listened, along with his two comrades, to Eliyahu Hajaj's eloquent explanations as he told them, his tone softer than usual, that the company he worked for, Fratelli Capone, had helped the Italian government build the coastal road. He glanced at Silvana and mentioned that she worked with him too, and began explaining, without considering that his listeners might already know the details, that the road stretched over 1,822 kilometers, from the Egyptian border to the Tunisian border. In conclusion he added, louder now, that Mussolini himself had come to Libya to christen the road, which was known as the *Strada Costiera*, the National Coastal Road.

The Italian soldiers listened carefully, as did the Germans, though they did not understand it. His confident tone, and especially Luigi Hachmon's comment, "*Yamel lu kabud*, he's honoring him," in light of the German officer's attentive expression, awoke a hope that they were headed somewhere better, or at least nowhere worse.

In the early evening, as the sun illuminated the sea with all its glory as if primping for the last hour of the day, as the land lent the sky some of its color, the relative ease within the truck reached its climax, along with the sense of security felt by both families. The clearest expression of this was when Silvana's mother rested her head on the tarp and said, "*Che fortuna che siamo inglese*, we're so lucky to be English."

Silvana watched the sea, which, as always, indulged her, comforting her for the difficult ride. She revived the images that had seemed to be crushed under the truck's tires in the beginning of the ride, but this time didn't make do with staying at the Zaruk house on Lido Beach, being welcomed by Governor Rudolfo Graziani, or taking shelter at the home of her father's good Muslim friend. This time she added a fourth image: they would stay at the Ottoman fort on the Tripoli coast with four other Jews of British citizenship, in excellent conditions. Within three or four days, they would be joined by other Jews who were not British citizens, such as her friend Liza Genish, whose tortured face as she boarded the truck was engraved in Silvana's mind. A few days later still, they would all return to Benghazi.

This image shattered her reality, and Silvana constructed an alternative universe, made of tiny particles that had nothing to do with what things were truly like: the German officer looked at the beach with moist eyes, gripped with longing for his homeland; the Italian soldier whose pants were too big contemplated the state of his favorite soccer team; Luigi Hachmon was lost in thought, his head resting on his palm, as if calculating something, perhaps the monetary damage caused by war and the compensation he would demand from the Italian insurance company, Assicurazioni Generali, which also insured her father; Toni was recovering from the shock she'd gotten from the horror in the desert; the green tarp suddenly detached, floating away in a cloud of dust; and she, Silvana, looked at the sky with a wide smile on her face.

The barricade three kilometers up the road put the shattered reality back together again. Two German soldiers—their heads pinned deep inside their helmets, as if they hadn't removed them since leaving Europe—signaled for the truck to stop. They walked to the back hatch and conversed with the German officer. Wonder spread over their faces at the sight of the German soldiers sitting together with their Jewish captives, and this wonder did not fade even after the officer explained apologetically that he and his soldier were merely using the opportunity to get a quick ride to Tripoli.

Silvana was gripped by terrible anxiety and all her attempts to fight it off were for naught. Evening hadn't come yet, but every few moments her eyes went dark. A dark void and flashes of light took turns in front of her eyes. She wanted to avoid the next moment of darkness and looked to her family. They looked back at her, also requesting their own comfort. When they realized that such comfort would not be provided, they made do with knowing that she felt like them, all climbing together up the tree of anxiety that was growing within her, holding on for dear life.

After checking the Italian driver's papers for a few moments, the barricade soldiers allowed the truck to keep going. They only rode for twenty minutes more. Now it was completely dark. The German soldier ordered the Italian driver to pull over and the other soldiers to prepare for bed. The driver pulled nine sleeping bags from the cabin, but no member of the Hajaj or Hachmon families took any of the bags that remained after the soldiers took theirs. They preferred to use their own blankets and sheets, which were imbued with the memory of their households.

They walked to the beach in a row. The senior Italian soldier led the way, frantically rubbing his head, as if trying to wipe away the gleam of the product. The German officer walked at the end of the row, fumbling slowly, looking distracted. Two of the Italian soldiers started a fire. Silvana walked closer to the flames. Her anxiety was burned off at once, like a piece of paper. The fire that warmed her body ignited her recollections from her trip to the desert.

She watched the busy preparations for bed with a mixture of relative calm and curious expectation, as if watching a play from the plush seats of the Teatro Berenice.

The words "*Schlafen*," "*Dormire*," and "*Yarked*,"[12] were sounded again and again, blending into one. Silvana spread a sheet between her mother and her sister, covered herself with her blanket and closed Toni's eyes by running her hand over them. Toni didn't move and her breathing was imperceptible. She seemed to have found the perfect sleeping position. Ever since they were children, Silvana believed that beneath her sister's constant pampering lay a dormant monster that was nothing but a death wish, which would be awoken once Toni became released from religion's control. Whenever Toni heard statements such as "And you shall choose life," or "In death, they ordered us to live," she insisted that she wasn't devoutly religious. Nevertheless, deep inside she was still entirely bound by the chains of religion. Sometimes Silvana thought that Toni's constant yearning toward death didn't lie beneath her tendency toward indulgence, but had rather created it. She wondered if her sister's inability to delay gratification, her expectation that people would quickly fulfil her wishes and indulge her every whim, treating her friends as means to an end, might have

---

[12]From German, Italian, and Jewish-Libyan Arabic: To sleep.

been the result of a profound intuition that told her she would end her life at a very young age, long before anyone else. This is why Silvana was so surprised to see Toni's behavior at the shelter in Benghazi and after leaving it. She now recalled with wonder Toni's devotion, her ability to put the distress of others before her own. She asked herself again how she could reconcile this with her pampered personality and the death wish that motivated her.

For a moment, she remembered one of those piping hot nights when they slept on the roof of their house in nothing but underwear. Toni had told her then, distractedly, that there was no such thing as personality, that any talk of it was idle chatter, and that people could change with every passing moment, never becoming enslaved to their personalities.

Now she stared at Toni, as if trying to find an answer in her face for the mystery of her character. Her sister looked dead, and it occurred to her that the terrible stress that had accumulated within her, the sadness for their circumstances and the joy for not having been taken on the trucks with the others, might have mixed together to form a mighty storm of emotion that her heart had trouble withstanding. Spent, overcome with messy thoughts about her sister, Silvana closed her eyes and quickly sunk into a deep sleep.

In the middle of the night, as she dreamt about making love to the Hebrew soldier behind one of the large rocks at Jeliana Beach, Toni shook her awake, panicked. "*Dove siamo?* Where are we?"

Silvana, still enthralled with her fading dream, answered absentmindedly, "*La spiaggia*, the beach." She woke up, got a hold of herself, and found that they were indeed at the beach, but not the one she'd yearned for. The scene of her lovemaking with the Hebrew soldier was overtaken by other visions: her family, in rags, lying by her side; the Hachmons, their faces tortured masks; three exhausted Italian soldiers, and two semi-alert German soldiers. She put her arms around Toni and Toni hugged her back. Silvana looked at the sky and whispered in her sister's ear that they would be in Tripoli in two days, and after taking care of some matters regarding their British citizenship, they would stay with the Zaruks at Lido Beach, and then return to Benghazi.

Even in the dark, she spotted the spark that appeared in her sister's eyes. She thought that Toni, just like other people who had a death wish, yearned for death as long as it wasn't readily available, and escaped it whenever it became a concrete possibility. She was amused by the thought that war was able to remove anxieties the way you rip a band-aid off a wound.

Toni's affirmation of life wasn't the only good thing to happen to Silvana that night. She also heard the short, mustachioed Italian soldier, who looked better now that his hair was free of brilliantine, telling his friend while warming his hands by the fire that the German officer had told him these Jews were British and would be transferred to a camp for British prisoners of war. She would never have imagined that the prospect of imprisonment would make her feel so liberated. She never imagined that prison would become her escape route, but the thought that she might run into the Hebrew soldier in the prisoners' camp made it just that. There, between the walls of the camp, among countless imprisoned foreign soldiers and traditional Jewish families, there, within that human chaos, she would be able to consummate her passion for the Hebrew soldier, and rid herself of the customs of her community.

Her good mood continued through the morning. To her surprise, they were not woken by the German soldiers, nor by the Italians. When she opened her eyes to the sun, which was warm in spite of the early hour, she saw the soldiers still curled into their sleeping bags, and only one Italian soldier was guarding them, holding his rifle in a pose that bespoke slumber.

She stretched, sat up, and looked at the sea. The sight of it still pleased her. She continued to enjoy the hope that she would soon see the Hebrew soldier, and occasionally looked over to her sleeping family.

She felt an urge to go in the water before everyone else woke up. She wanted to arrive at the camp fresh, having washed away what remained of her foul mood. The Italian soldier that guarded them read her mind from within his sleepiness, gestured with approval, and said, "*Ma solo per due minuti*, only for a couple minutes."

It was a very long couple of minutes, in which her hunch that they would be put in a privileged prisoners' camp in Tripoli only intensified. She believed she would meet her soldier there, and that the war would soon be over. She got out of the water, the sheet wrapped around her body clinging to her with wetness.

The moment she sat down, her mother, who had just woken up, looked at her unhappily, tossed over her tattered brown dress, and muttered, "*Ya rit'ha akemt*, if only your mother had been barren." Her mother had rarely used this expression. Only when her daughters drove her out of control. Silvana didn't answer, but she was insulted by her mother's words, which had put a damper on her light confidence.

She walked, confused, behind one of the rocks, this time with the approval of the German officer, who had woken up as well, removed the sheet and put on the dress. Then she took off her slightly wet underwear so she could go to the bathroom. She wiped herself with a piece of paper she found behind the rocks and put her underwear back on. She stood up, smoothed her tattered brown dress as best she could, and walked back to the sea to wash her hands.

Everyone washed their faces and mouths with water from the jerry can. Julia Hajaj and Yona

Hachmon used the toothpaste and soap that Julia had in her bag. Then they walked back to the truck. On the backdrop of the infinite space, the truck looked like a toy. Silvana watched the road, looking for bomb damage but finding none. The road was endless. This cheered her up and she thought they would be in Tripoli sooner than expected.

The place of the broken road was taken by scorching heat, which now dictated the course of their ride. Unlike the broken road, the heat was tyrannical, allowing no one to undermine its control. Whenever anyone tried to say anything, they were lashed at by the heat, which prevented them from finishing their thought. Therefore people only sounded hums or the buds of thoughts, requests for water or pieces of dried pita. Even when they got off the truck to go to the bathroom, no real conversation dwelled in their mental space. In fact, without the shade of the tarp the heat beat down on them, and they couldn't produce much more than exhausted body language. The ride went on languidly for the next few hours, with none of the passengers breaking the silence that filled the truck.

Only in the early evening, when they arrived at the village of Sirte, did things change. The heat began to break, and they sat beneath a blue shed in the center of the village. Silvana had no clue why the German officer decided to spend the night there, rather than in one of the white stone houses offered by the head of the village, a skinny man with a long beard, dark face and bouncy green eyes that seemed to want to pop out of his head. For a moment, she thought the officer made his choice because of the unpleasant memory of their night in Ajdabiya, and that he was trying to avoid further humiliation, but later she thought he might have simply wanted them to stay close to the truck, since, once the weather improved, he became fully alert and prepared to continue the ride at any moment.

Either way, when evening filled the air, three veiled women approached them, under orders of the head of the village, and served them fresh pita bread placed flawlessly on a silver tray, mounds of olives in emerald colored dishes, long and narrow water pitchers, and an assortment of cheese on a large wooden board. Silvana completely forgot that they were divided into conquerors and captives, even as the German officer signaled that they may begin to eat. This information was swallowed within the excitement they all felt at the sight of such delicacies.

Silvana ate with a vengeance. Forgetting their lowly status as prisoners had overshadowed her recollections of the past few days. Oblivion seemed to be filled with vitality. It also took over the souls of her family and the Hachmons, who appeared more at ease. The change was especially visible in Toni, who suddenly appeared refreshed and renewed, as if all of her tears and her "*Che facciamo?*" had never even occurred. Their place was taken by occasional smiles and statements such as "*Questo e unbel paese*, this is a beautiful country."

This state of mind brought back Toni's old appearance. Though her white linen dress was stained and her hair messy, she was beautiful again, the same *Bella Toni* she'd always been. In addition to her thick lips, her fair eyes, and her symmetrical face that seemed to have been chiseled by a sculptor, the spark of fresh mischievousness in her eyes afforded her body with a quality that could not be quantified, an ephemeral layer that escaped any specific anatomical description.

The veiled Arabs cleared the olive dish and the cheese tray and brought out two silver pots of black coffee and two white porcelain bowls filled with dates. This was the first time since their journey began that Silvana saw her father at ease. There was almost nothing that gave her father as much pleasure as drinking black coffee. This simple action was his anchor. As he slowly sipped the beverage, it seemed that all his bothersome thoughts just melted away. Silvana loved the black coffee her father poured her from the *finjan* in his office, though this love was somewhat forced, a habit her father had gradually trickled into her soul.

Dates, on the other hand, were something she loved most naturally. She'd often imagined that the tall palm trees scattered around Benghazi had

(handwritten margin note: dates come from palm trees?)

brought her up. As a child, she watched with wonder as people climbed them, lithe as street cats, to reach the fruit. She often joined her father's employees on the date harvest, unable to wait for them to return with baskets overflowing with dates.

Now, as she took some of the dates served to them, she felt she was cupping a precious childhood memory. She rolled the dates between her fingers. Her mother noticed it, and Silvana thought she spotted tears pooling in the corner of her eye. Her mother's gaze was more loving than ever. Did she want to repent for her "if only your mother had been barren" comment from that morning? Or perhaps she recalled how Silvana used to dance around, a free and cheerful little girl, around Eliyahu's workers, before they went on the date harvest? Silvana returned a modest, appeased smile. Her mother's caressing eyes pushed away the hurtful words of that morning.

Twenty minutes later, with the flavor of dates still lingering in Silvana's mouth, they began preparing for night, following the orders of the German officer, who avoided getting involved in the argument of the Italian soldiers over who should go on guard duty first. Silvana, on the other hand, decided to intervene, pointing out that on the previous night the truck driver was the first guard. The soldiers were so surprised by her comment that they stopped arguing and quickly divided the guard duties to everybody's satisfaction.

Silvana slept soundly through the night, but was unable to continue her dream about her future meeting with the Hebrew soldier. She used reality to help herself complete it, bending it in order to paint a clear ending. After she woke up, she recalled the Italian soldier telling his friend that the captives would be transferred to a British prisoners' camp, and immediately pictured her meeting with the Hebrew soldier. She daydreamed from the bottom of her heart, almost able to feel her dark arms wrapping around his white neck as they stood, surrounded by soldiers who cheered for their embrace, as well as for the war's imminent end. A grating thought sliced through her: in her vision, she did not see the fences that would surely surround the camp. She awoke from her reveries, shooting upright as if she'd been bitten by a snake.

The passengers boarded the truck. To Silvana, the truck was no longer a vehicle transporting people from one place to the next, but rather a place in its own right. Before boarding it, she noticed the activity all around—the Italian soldiers swarmed around the truck with unending industriousness, as if they were its slaves. They put air in the tires, filled the truck with gallons of gas, wiped dust off mirrors and tires, carefully arranged the trunk, and beat the tarp with dedication until they'd cleaned all the dirt and dust off it. The soldiers seemed to be doing their work automatically, in a pattern that had been predetermined, as if all of their independent thoughts stopped existing when they were around the truck.

The road seemed to stretch to eternity once more. But unlike the previous days, this time her eyes were deceiving her. After a short ride, they arrived at a point where the road ended. They stopped. She was afraid they would have to view a similar image to the one they'd seen two days before. She was glad to find this wasn't the case.

The truck driver examined alternative routes for the rest of the journey. The passengers remained on the truck, awaiting a decision that was never made. From the exchanges between the Germans and the Italians, Silvana gleaned that the driver was debating whether to go down to the beach and ride on the sand, or make a bigger detour to be able to ride on asphalt.

Unthinkingly, she turned to get out. She wanted to tell the driver he couldn't drive on the beach. She couldn't bear the thought of the truck getting stuck in the sand and their arrival in Tripoli being delayed; the thought wrapped around her neck like a noose. But the moment she stretched one leg out of the truck, the German soldier, who'd been complaining of the heat, stood up, cocked his gun, and pointed it at her while shouting, "*Halt!*"

Silvana froze in her tracks. The German officer told the soldier off and gestured for Silvana to sit down. She remained in place. A few seconds later she got a hold of herself and walked back to her seat by her father, who held her and said, "Don't worry, my dear girl, we'll soon be in Tripoli."

Her mother moved to the seat across from her so she could kiss her and wipe away her tears. Her sister reached her arms from her seat on the other side of her father and grabbed Silvana's hand. The sound of the engine that had started again slowly subdued her turmoil, filling her with peace. She gave herself into it. It was the only sound she heard. The more she listened, the more all the other rustles of the passengers became swallowed in it, and so did the silence that filled the endless space between sea and desert. After a while, still upset and angered by her own helplessness, she dozed off at intervals. She imagined that the road was a creature with a long head, eyes and an endlessly erect neck that was watching her and pondering her—a human who is only visiting this world for a short time while the road is here to stay. It didn't see her as someone leaving her own place, but as someone whose goal was to go nowhere.

By noon even the truck itself seemed to be dripping sweat. Julia Hajaj suddenly mentioned Rita, her husband's Muslim sister. It had been years since Silvana last heard that name. She never imagined that her mother, of all people, would be the one to break the family code of silence. She knew how attentive her mother was to her father's complete intolerance of his sister's name, and how aware she was of the pain that came with it. But now her mother had broken the rule, as if pushing through the locked door by force. "*Ma tkulish Rita la Suha,*" she heard her repeating. "Say Rita, not Suha." She had no idea why her mother had brought her up now, and why it was at this moment she insisted on erasing her Muslim name—Rita, not Suha. She thought her mother might be angry that Rita had been saved of the terrible distress they were going through, but she wasn't convinced, because her mother's tone was hard to interpret: anger at the delinquent Muslim sister became mixed with self reproachment for following her husband's attitude so blindly.

Silvana's father's response to her mother's repeating mumbling was to continue to slowly chew on a pita given to him by one of the Italian soldiers. His face was crestfallen, staring into empty space. Lilo Hajaj had always been good at disguising his emotions, sometimes even from himself. But now his emotions seemed to be disguising him. The gloominess that took over him erased the remnants of his confident, strong, and charming image. Silvana turned to appease him, as if they'd switched places, beseeching him to stop worrying, and promising him that they would soon be in Tripoli.

The truck rode on. Rita's name put a damper on the pleasant expectation for Tripoli. Silvana didn't eat the pita that one of the Italians gave her. The threat of the rifle and the mention of Rita's name both clamped down on her throat, and she couldn't swallow a thing. Only when they stopped at an oasis in the afternoon was she able to shake it off and get some food down. She walked with the others behind a cluster of tall palm trees and drank some clear pond water. When she looked at her reflection in the water, her mind was emptied of the self-image ingrained in her. She no longer thought of herself as somebody who was able to get out of any situation and get along easily without the help of others. Now she saw herself as a lone leaf blowing in the wind. In the water she saw a submissive, lowly, wilting figure, her eyes lacking confidence, her hair wild, her body small and weak.

From somewhere, Julia Hajaj's reflection appeared in the water beside her. The reflection appeared much farther away than the immediate sight of her mother in reality. The watery figure's eyes did not shine with affection. They were piercing, distant, and cold. For a few seconds, Silvana thought she saw accusation in those eyes, as if she were accusing her flesh and blood mother for neglecting her children, reproaching her for her powerlessness. Her mother gave her a handful of olives she'd pulled out of her dress pocket and said, "*Kuli, ya binti*. Eat." Silvana realized her mother had been saving the olives for her all the way from the village of Sirte. She ate them slowly, taking pleasure in the wonderful flavor of her mother's care and devotion.

When she finished eating the German officer ordered them to get back on the truck. Silvana and her mother walked with their arms around each other. Silvana yearned to see their embrace from behind. It felt virginal; it was the first time she and her mother held each other as equals. Not the soothing embrace a mother gives her daughter, not the loving embrace a daughter gives her mother, but an embrace of two grown women who love and appreciate each other, an embrace of two women giving each other wordless strength. Even after they let go of each other and sat back down in the truck, their embrace continued to hold them together, and a thread of warm silence continued to tie them together for the rest of the ride. The subtle gusts of wind invading the truck at dusk caressed their silence. The vision of the desert's crimson carpet imbued the silence with majestic beauty—two women, mother and daughter, daughter and mother, their faces tired, their mussed hair dusted over, their aching souls wrapped around each other, listening together to the quiet beating of their hearts.

The next morning, after everybody awoke from sleeping on the side of the road, the truck continued at a turtle's pace. Silvana was filled with alert anticipation. Tripoli, oh Tripoli, she thought, recalling how on hot summer evenings they used to sit on the roof or in the yard while her father compared Tripoli to a mysterious, enticing woman.

He aroused her mother's jealousy, who repaid him by commenting that he'd had too much arak and that he was all exaggerations.

A few hours later, as they got closer to Tripoli, he showed no signs of excitement. He sat on the bench, his face crumpled and his body tired, not fighting back against the deep sorrow that took hold of his soul. But a little while later, as more and more trucks and horse-drawn carts appeared on the road, and as rows of refugees walked alongside it, Silvana thought the hustle and bustle was shaking her father awake.

Her mother and sister were certainly shaken up. Her mother's face lit up at the sight of all those people. She said some of the refugees looked familiar, and in a moment of jubilation claimed insistently that she recognized Abed and Gino, the two famous cobblers from Benghazi. Toni came back to life, speaking excitedly about their anticipated reunion with the Zaruk family at their home near Lido Beach, and Silvana was sure her sister would tease them all by claiming the bedroom overlooking the sea. The Hachmon family also looked excited. Silvana followed their lead, beginning to believe that she truly would soon meet the Hebrew soldier at the camp.

The truck maneuvered its way deep into Tripoli. Alongside areas that resembled ghost towns were other, very lively neighborhoods. Bomb damage was apparent everywhere, ruins having popped up both in the busy and in the deserted areas. Italian soldiers filled the central crosstown streets. The Hajaj and Hachmon families were alert. Silvana's mother was the first to break the tense silence in the truck, saying that even in her wildest dreams she never thought she'd view Tripoli as a home. The others mumbled their agreement, other than Eliyahu, whose silence persisted.

They arrived at the house of the Libyan governor, not far from the center of town, and got off the truck. Silvana saw a very wide, very white three-story building flanked on every side by palm trees, three huge white concrete domes surrounding one copper dome at the center of its roof. The windows were long and arched, and a path led from the driveway to the door, a few dozen meters away. A group of six people appeared, led by a tall Italian officer wearing dress uniform adorned with honorary insignia and a beret, his gait powerful. The excited whispering of the Italian soldiers, who hurried to smooth out their uniforms, told Silvana that this man was the governor of Libya, Rudolfo Graziani, in the flesh. He exchanged salutes with the German officer and soldier, looked at her father and Luigi warmly, as if they were his colleagues, rather than prisoners, glanced at the Italian soldiers in a way that instructed them to salute with awe, and was swallowed with his entourage and the two Germans in two long black cars, the likes of which Silvana had never seen before.

Civitella del Tronto

Evenings fell. Now, alone with the Italian soldiers, they felt somewhat relieved. They spoke to the soldiers more freely. Silvana tried to glean any kind of information about what was to come, but her attempts were futile. She only learned that they had to stay close to the truck and eat the food provided by one of the governor's employees. As she ate, she saw a short Italian officer walking briskly out of the building. When he came closer, he told the senior Italian soldier decisively, "*Andate al porto!* Go to the port!"

Silvana was glad to hear the order, assuming there were several possible reasons for them to travel to the port, all of which pleased her. She hoped the camp they would be placed in would be the camp for British prisoners, including soldiers from Palestine. Another possibility was that their captors had received orders to put them on a ship back to Benghazi. Her curiosity to see the Tripoli port bubbled below those two options. It looked a lot like the port in her city. At the Benghazi port, she often felt her privacy invaded by the glances of sailors, both local and foreign. The

Benghazi port wasn't a foundation for the nurturing of great private dreams, and yet she loved spending time there, because it gave her the illusion of living in a big city enveloped in a cosmopolitan aroma, to which people flocked from all over the world—not only soldiers of the many armies that wanted to force themselves upon it. She loved seeing boxes and crates spew out of the belly of ships like babies from their mothers' wombs. She also liked to watch the small boats maneuvering industriously among the large ships, coming closer and overtaking their courses, and pictured them as little girls vying for their mothers' attention.

A little while later the senior Italian soldier ordered them to get on the truck, which began to travel to the port. Its exhausted lamps lit the way. Complete peace took over Silvana. The anxiety she felt during a considerable part of the journey and the joy that had come upon her when she heard they were headed to the port seemed to cancel each other out. She was far from any kind of emotional turmoil. Explosions in the distance did not startle her, and neither did Toni's panicked grip on her hand. Even the relaxation she felt when she traveled alone in the desert did not resemble the peace she was in right now, because it had always been limited—she knew that the moment she left the desert, that peace would leave her. For a moment, when she noticed the relief on her mother's face, she thought the peace she felt now would never end. They had made their allegiance to each other.

The buds of this eternal peace wilted as they arrived at the port, which was intensely busy. Powerful lights illuminated the entire area, making it easy to forget that it was close to midnight. Military trucks and civilian cars rushed along the dock, a ship blew its foghorn restlessly, Italian words were shouted from all directions, police dogs barked, dragged along on their leashes, the engine of an airplane buzzed above—these all created emotional chaos in some of the truck's passengers. Silvana's father was the first to react. He wanted to say, "*Ma Inharash bahi*, this doesn't look too good," but choked the words down as his eyes fell on his daughter. Her sister and mother exchanged panicked looks; the Hachmons huddled in the corner like fugitives avoiding a sudden beam of light that threatened to expose them; and Silvana fixed her eyes on those of the Italian soldier, silently asking for an explanation. The soldier just kept watching the activity outside.

The truck pulled up by a black fence. "*Scendere!*" the harsh order was heard from below. "Get off!" a large Italian soldier with a mole in the center of his forehead walked to the door of the truck, pointed his powerful flashlight inside, and urged them: "You're sitting around here like you're at the opera!" When he noticed Silvana's mother taking too long to pack up her bundles and blankets, he yelled at her, "Leave it and get off!" Her mother quickly grabbed what she could and got off, but the Italian soldier continued to rebuke her slowness.

The prisoners stood in a line. A low ranking soldier counted them, pointing at them indifferently, as if they were items in a storage space. Silvana was degraded to nothing, a continuation to all the previous humiliations of their journey, no less than being called "*Afrikaner*" by the German soldier in Benghazi, or being urged "*Schneller, Juden*" at the Italian school, or by hearing "*Juden raus!*" shouted at el-Masjad. She lowered her eyes, trying to control the shuddering of her body, to no avail. She knew everyone was looking at her, and that they were witnessing her being publicly bereft of any human identity, becoming an object for all to see.

They walked through a white iron gate that was embedded in the black fence. Thus, the gates of Libya closed behind Silvana. Her trips to the desert, playing below *Heit Lehlamat*, swimming at Jeliana Beach, visiting the big synagogue, going on business meetings with her father, Sabbath and holiday dinners, Nassarin, brief encounters with merchants at Souk Delam, nightly walks along the Lungomare and plays at Teatro Berenice—Silvana's heart told her that from now on these would be nothing but dusty memories. She couldn't read the emotions of her relatives. Her heart ached to think that even her father might not suspect what was to come. She wished to penetrate beyond his eyes, but couldn't detect any alarm. He wasn't trying to conceal anything. Her heart sank and she was plagued with a horrifying sense of loneliness, along with the realization that her father, her progenitor and her protector, had no inkling of what she already knew.

They walked into a spacious warehouse. Silvana couldn't bear the noise inside. About two-hundred adults and children crowded in there, screaming and moaning like caged animals. In spite of the noise, she heard her mother's shaking voice as she said, "*Hadoni qulhum min reyrna trabelsia*. Other than us, they are all Tripolitan." Even now, she could detect in her mother's tone traces of the condescension of Benghazi Jews over their Tripoli brothers for being the more cultured and educated ones. She saw her father recognizing old acquaintances. A wide net of insult stretched between them, people of their stature in this kind of situation, and upon it spread out their shared memories. Her sister said nothing, as if beaten by her own mood swings from the moment they'd left the shelter.

After two hours of a weak guessing game, the possibility they'd all tried to forget came true. The doors nearest the dock opened with a bang, and dozens of Italian soldiers burst into the warehouse with their dogs, yelling, "*Avanti*, let's go, *salite*, get on!" They urged the prisoners on with their long rifles. A young, skinny, short man who stood about twenty meters ahead of them began running like mad. He made it no more than ten meters before he falling to the ground, shot by dozens of the soldiers' bullets.

In those moments Silvana didn't see herself as part of the scenario. She was watching it from the outside, a sort of living camera. She felt herself being dragged along with everybody else, climbing the ramp of the ship not by force of the soldiers' orders, but as if an invisible cameraman was working her with her hands, making her document the events. The ship they were led onto was entirely different from the gleaming white vessels she liked to watch at the Benghazi port. It was a long ship, and though its walls were painted dark, she could still see how dirty they were. It was hard to identify the original color of the deck due to coal residue, and the flagpole was much shorter than the ones of the ships she loved. The ship was so neglected and ugly that it seemed to Silvana even the sea refused to accept it into its endless space, pushing it back toward the coast.

When the deck was filled with people, the calls of "*salite*" were replaced by calls of "*Scendere! Scendere!*" Silvana, her family, and the Hachmons were pushed with everyone else toward the iron steps leading into the belly of the ship. They were all stunned and nobody dared resist or speak out. The belly of the ship was divided into three large storage areas separated by iron walls. Other than pipes stretching along the walls and straw on the floor, these storage spaces were empty. The entire place was filled with gloom even before it was filled with the exhausted bodies of people.

After their initial shock subsided, people began hazarding guesses regarding their destination. Even after the many hardships they'd suffered, many still believed they would be returning to Benghazi. Some thought they were being taken to a camp in Tunisia, and one persistent rumor even had it that they were being transported to Palestine.

As they walked down the metal steps into the belly of the ship, Silvana's father mumbled, "They're taking us away from our country." Then he added weakly, "They're taking us to Italy."

At first Silvana ignored him, too preoccupied with shielding herself from the harsh cold. She clung to her mother, but felt that her mother wasn't clinging back, rather curling into herself. When she put her arms around her, she knew her mother was thinking about her own life—not necessarily about what was going to happen, but about what had already happened. Her eyes, which narrowed whenever she was disappointed with herself, her weak grip on her daughter, and her repeating mumbles about how they should have escaped to the mountains or the desert— these all told Silvana that her mother saw the notion of being exiled from her country as something she could have avoided if only she'd acted differently.

Silvana clung to her father, but his embrace was also lacking. She pulled away and went to the more crowded area of the ship. The fact that her family and the Hachmons had been pushed into the central storage area, which was slightly smaller than the others, made things a bit easier for her. It seemed that a greater number of people had been pushed into the two other areas. After standing near three older men whose emotional turmoil was very obvious, she embraced one of their daughters, whom she met a year earlier at the Zaruk house. The girl, friends with the Zaruks' eldest daughter, was about Silvana's age. She had black hair, rabbit ears, and large, wise brown eyes. After pulling away from each other, the girl said Silvana's name, reminded her of her own name, Regina, and they hugged again. The perfect balance of their first hug was gradually lost, until finally Silvana was leaning and Regina was her support. Silvana dragged the hug out as long as she could.

She wasn't just leaning on Regina now. She tried to reach the future, to see it beyond the thick fog that was encasing her life. But the future could barely be seen, a tiny dot inside a mighty cloud of uncertainty. Her imagination planted comforting visions in her heart: a trip to a neighboring country, perhaps Tunisia or Algiers, a short stay in a prisoners' camp for British citizens, and a swift return to Benghazi at the end of the war.

This future offered no role for the Hebrew soldier. During their desert journey, she'd often encouraged herself with the thought of a future reunion with him, which gave purpose to her terrible present. Now she gave up this idea in order to allow her comforting thoughts to more easily come true.

She returned to her family. The ship set sail. The illusion that they were headed for Tunisia dropped anchor in Silvana's mind, but only for a short while. Whispered rumors quickly redirected her thoughts. Almost everyone was saying they were going to Italy.

Of all people, Silvana's father was the one to say nothing, thus saying everything. His eyes narrowed into slits for practical use only. His robust arms hung from his shoulders like pale sausages at a butcher shop. His legs bent and then froze. She'd already seen him in recent months in situations that had undermined her image of him, but never like this. His appearance in that moment caused her tremendous pain. She couldn't take it and tried to cling to the familiar image of her father. Her imagination took her to all the many times when her father's behavior was the antithesis of the way he acted now; the times when she heard him speak of his life with confidence and satisfaction but not smugly; all the times when not only was weakness not in his character, but when he was able to aggressivelypluck it out of others, as well. She remembered especially well how he locked Toni in the shop's storage for two days without food because she refused to help them with work during an especially busy time, claiming she didn't feel like it.

The intense cold forced Silvana to let go of her reminiscing. It seemed to freeze her in the present moment. Her mother wrapped her in the only sheet she managed to take with her when they got off the truck, but it served no real protection. Silvana lay down on the straw and made room for Toni under the sheet. Toni lay against her and Silvana felt her shivering and heard her teeth chattering. There was no sign of the brave Toni, the one who cheered up all the adults, her little sister who took the reins back in the shelter. Now she was part of a herd. "Silvana, what am I going to do?" she whispered. "I don't know where fear is taking me. It's leading me down unfamiliar paths. It's going to leave me in a place I can never return from, even if things work out and we go back to Benghazi."

Silvana was once again impressed by Toni's words. She wondered how it could be that for so long she saw her sister as nothing more than a spoiled, superficial girl. She was angry with herself, and angry with life, for having led her on for so many years, disguising whole layers of her sister's soul.

She didn't answer Toni; didn't promise her that everything would be all right, didn't tell her not to worry. She knew if she said those things, Toni would know for certain that she was actually trying to soothe herself. There was no point in it. Instead, she drew herself closer to her sister. Silvana noticed that, just like them, no one else in the storage was speaking. In the silence she was able to hear the sounds of the sea: the bow of the ship slicing through the water, the rumble of the engine, the crashing of distant waves, and the occasional call and beating of the wings of birds circling above. The sounds submerged her thoughts in silence. She fell asleep, giving into an awful exhaustion, the likes of which she'd never experienced before. Neither the piercing cold nor the rocking of the boat woke her. She slept soundly.

Silvana woke up into a dark morning. Her sleepy eyes slowly recognized the fallen faces of dozens of people, and the petrified faces of others, unmoving. The fog that came in from the sea covered everything like an enormous prayer shawl. Her mother, who had her back to her, was clutching a tiny book of Psalms she'd kept in her bra the entire journey, and her father was continuously repeating one mumbled statement, of which the only word she could fully comprehend was "Italy."

Toni was still asleep. Silvana carefully pulled away from her. She wanted her to sleep for as long as possible. She hoped that, with the passing hours, the gloominess of the storage would also evaporate, and that Toni would awaken to a different atmosphere.

That did not happen. Even as the light of day penetrated the storage, the room remained dark.

Depression filled it, solid and undefeated. Luigi Hachmon, of all people, who'd been a pale shadow of himself until then, tried to encourage the passengers and plant some optimism in them, perhaps because he'd sailed many times in his life and felt comfortable at sea. At first, his words sounded like hollow statements, but with time they made more and more sense and were heeded. He confidently determined that they were indeed being taken to Italy, but only so that the Italians and Germans could trade them for prisoners held by the British. The British citizenship of the Jews imprisoned on the boat, Jews of Benghazi and Tripoli alike, slowly became a mantra that automatically relieved any anxiety or uncertainty.

This was the case when a fat woman who, for some reason, was dressed festively, adorned with many bracelets and golden necklaces, sobbed with panic and mumbled that they would never see Libya again, or when a little boy with kinky hair and fair skin barked at his mother that he was afraid. "*Ma t'haposh*, don't be afraid, *henan nigliz*," people called from every direction. Silvana tried with all her might to believe what Luigi said, but her common sense wouldn't allow it. She saw it more as a superstition. She was worried that the Libyan coast, slowly moving away, would become a haven only for her dreams, and that she would never see it again.

The more people believed Luigi Hachmon, the less Eliyahu Hajaj believed in himself. Luigi's new status among the prisoners gnawed at his self-esteem. Silvana directed her attention to this, so she may forget herself and focus on her father instead. She wanted to encourage him in new ways she'd never even thought affective. She held his hand tightly, pressed his head against her shoulder, rubbed the back of her neck, kissed his forehead and even gave his chest a single rub, all the while repeating, "*Ma t'hapesh, inta twili saltan fi Benghazi.*"[13] Her father squeezed her hand wordlessly.

Her wish to forget herself didn't come true. Each time the ship rocked she recalled her situation. Her fear returned to her, telling her that the farther they moved from Libya, the less chance she had of ever seeing it again. Nevertheless, once in a while a frail hope crawled into her soul, telling her that things might still work out for the best. Her faith did not lessen even as she saw adults and children throwing up, or when two old ladies fainted before the eyes of their sobbing children.

Her mother gathered courage from her behavior. She compensated her for her husband's lack of communication. "Silvana, *ma nitsened kan elik*, I trust you," she said, bringing tears to Silvana's eyes. For years, she'd waited for a sign that her mother trusted her, not merely acquiescing to the freedom

---

[13]From Jewish-Libyan Arabic: Don't worry, you'll be the king of Benghazi once more.

her father allowed her. Ever since she was a little girl she waited—first hopefully and alertly, then impatiently, and finally with disappointment and a hint of pain—for the moment when she was big enough in her mother's eyes. And now, of all times, with the storm and the shock battling over her soul, her mother's words carried that much more weight, because this trying time brought out pure truth.

This truth intoxicated Silvana. It provided her with the strength necessary to float above these difficult circumstances. "*Ya emi, ma t'hapish, etitki ela Allah*," she told her mother, stroking her hair, the way her mother did for the poor and needy, though without the patronizing flourish her mother always added to her gestures. "Mom, I won't let you down."

Silvana no longer needed an external grasp to distract her from her situation. The promise she made to her mother was enough. This promise afforded her the role of sole leader of the Hajaj family. Deep inside, she was glad to have this role. Thus, a few hours after they were squeezed into the boat, she pushed her way among the other passengers to get some food for her family from two Italian soldiers who appeared at the door. She elbowed people who tried to push ahead of her, and crawled between the legs of a tall and skinny man who never stopped calling out, "*Habeza!* Bread!" She bit hard into the shoulder of a short hunchbacked woman who dug her nails into Silvana in an attempt to push in front of her. Even the Italian soldier who gave the food was impressed by her determination, and before Silvana could even demand portions for her entire family, the soldier put ten slices of bread and a block of butter in her hand.

This was not the end of it. On her way back to her family, she had to protect the food from the hands of strangers that lunged at it like vultures. She placed the bread and butter in her mother's lap and told her to divide the food equally. After giving each of them their portion, her mother hid the rest of the bread in her clothes and winked at Silvana.

Now Silvana turned her thoughts to one single concern: how to get her hands on some sort of cover to protect them from the persistent cold. This was no simple task; there were no blankets to be found, and her mother's thin sheet provided only weak, ludicrous heat for one person at a time. Those who had blankets clung to them at all costs, carrying them around and glancing threateningly at anyone who came close.

After looking around her, Silvana walked determinedly to the front of the storage. She pushed her way through the crowd to the door. Two Italian soldiers who stood in the doorway called for her to stop, the shorter of the two pointing his rifle at her. She paused, looked into the eyes of the other, tall soldier, ran her hand briefly through her hair and stood up tall. The tall soldier told the short soldier to lower his weapon. She walked closer to the tall soldier, her chest rising and falling in front of him with each breath. He asked politely what she wanted. She pointed to her exposed legs and ran her hands over them in a quick heating motion. He said in a northern Italian dialect that he would get something to warm her up. Stretching her neck as far as she could, she signaled that her relatives also needed some cover. "*Vedrò che si può fare,*" he told her, having glanced quickly at her legs once more. "I'll see what I can do."

He returned a few moments later, carrying two blankets, and saying, "*E tuto qvalo que chec'è,* that's all I could find."

"*Grazie,*" she said and returned to her family.

The blankets she brought them further established the new power dynamic that was forming within the family, covering the old hierarchy like a shroud over a dead body. It was clear to her mother, and somehow to Toni and the Hachmons as well, that Silvana was now the head of the family. Her father's reaction only strengthened the new structure in their minds. He remained hunched and folded within himself, staring glumly into space, into a faraway, invisible place, avoiding his family's eyes.

Silvana gave her mother the blankets and told her to give one to the Hachmons. Her mother looked at her unhappily and stayed put. Silvana repeated herself, this time more sharply: "*Ateyhem ali yechbu!*

Give them what they want!" Then her mother quickly gave Yona the shorter of the two blankets. Yona looked up to Silvana and said with a shaking voice, "*Allah yahfed li ela Silvana*, God save you, Silvana."

Loyal to her new status, Silvana skipped her turn in the blanket rotation. All her mother's pleas were useless, but her cold ears told her several hours later that her concession was taking a heavier toll than she'd thought. Toward evening, she felt as if they would fall off her head. Nevertheless, she still did not take the blanket from her mother and sister, who shared it without offering it to her father. Instead, she rubbed her body with her hands and hugged Regina, who moved between her own family and the Hajaj family, unable to find her place. But these techniques were insufficient. The cold crawled up Silvana's body, taking hold of one part after the other. Silvana imagined herself walking through the Sahara on an especially hot day, desperately searching for a bit of shade.

At night, when the cold reached its peak and Regina's body no longer provided protection, nor did her most elaborate imaginings, she let go of the role of leader who sacrificed herself for the benefit of her flock. Silvana took the blanket off Toni and her mother, waking the two of them up.

"*Che fai?*" they asked almost unanimously, "what are you doing?"

Silvana was surprised by how quickly the two of them had grown accustomed to the duties of her new status; she was especially surprised by her mother's reaction. She was so stunned that she could only assume her mother acted as she did in order to toughen Silvana up. After some hesitation, and against her better judgment, Silvana returned the blanket to them, refusing their invitation to squeeze in with them. Even when her mother suggested that the three of them only cover their legs, Silvana turned them down. Her mother and sister did not look guilty at all. The cold was more powerful than anything else.

She shivered for the rest of the night. Only when morning came and the sun filtered into the storage, bypassing the "Roman blockade," as everyone called the Italian guard on duty, she finally stopped shivering. She rose to her feet and looked up, trying to see beyond the ceiling. She wanted to patch the crack formed between her and God on the day she heard the tale of little Rachel Rosenzweig who'd escaped the terror of the Nazis, but the crack only grew wider. She consoled herself that now, when it wasn't so cold anymore, she'd be able to play the role of family leader more easily.

And indeed, toward noon, when the weather was practically warm, she even allowed herself to go beyond her duty, running around the storage in an attempt to encourage other people. Her efforts were successful. The situation not only challenged people's sanity but also—to her inexplicable joy—their world view. Even older men, who would normally refuse to take the advice of a young woman, listened to her as if she carried the word of God. The statement "The Jews are a strong people," which Silvana repeated without knowing if it had any truth to it, resonated with some of the storage dwellers, who began whispering it to each other. A one-eyed man with a stern face and an exceptionally long mustache, who spoke somewhat poetically, took things one step further: he began recounting Jewish history, lingering on events in which the Jewish people demonstrated its strength. When he began telling the myth of Masada, Silvana quietened him, worried that instead of cheering people up he would scare them with the idea that they were facing ruin, and imply that they should follow in the footsteps of Elazar Ben Yair and his contemporaries. At any rate, the general mood seemed to have improved.

Late in the evening, a group of three young men even broke into a rendition of *Carry Your Flag toward Zion*, the anthem of the Libyan Zionist Youth Movement. But at night the level of fear rose once more. All real and imagined sounds that had given voice to the familiar, the noises to which they held on tightly, slowly died, and instead came a silence that even the crashing of waves could not break.

Then a loud explosion sounded from the sea. A wailing began in all directions, spewing broken sentences and shattered nightmares. People ran around, searching for cover, children and elderly covered their ears with their hands, orders cut through each other, coming from the deck, which seemed about to collapse at any moment under the stomping of Italian soldiers' feet. Endless barrages of gunfire were aimed toward the sea, and a cannonball shot out.

In complete contrast to what she'd heard people usually did in such situations, Silvana did not act out of any instinct. Instead she thoughts things over, quickly. She concluded that she urgently needed some real information about the source of the explosion, which she would use as a basis for a story to calm the nerves of the people around her. She ran to the doorway, which was now unguarded, and climbed the steps to the deck. Italian soldiers screamed at her from every direction.

"*Mina!*" She heard one of them screaming. "*Una mina è esplosa!* A mine exploded!"

Then she heard another explain that it was just an old British mine that didn't cause much damage. She hurried back down to the storage and explained what she'd heard to the people who gathered around her, telling them there was nothing to fear. Her news was supported by the gradual lessening of the screaming on deck. She repeated the story again and again.

The more the screaming subsided, the more people gathered around her, and she had to explain herself again.

Suddenly, an involuntary shift occurred within her. Rather than calm the people into going back to their places, she wanted to continue to fascinate them and keep them close. She no longer stuck to the dry facts, but began spinning intricate tales regarding the reasons for the explosion. She loved being seen as an agent of calm and wanted to earn people's looks, even if she had to stretch the truth to do so. In those moments, she became enslaved to her newfound power, and even felt an intense urge to take revenge against truth itself, which more than once had slapped her in the face, like the time when she was ten years old and wounding words appeared on the blackboard in her classroom: her father, the words said, sold goods to the occupying Italian army.

People settled down. The soldiers stopped shooting. There were no further explosions. The chaos subsided. Silvana's status became established, and with nothing else to hang onto, many people awaited her prophecy of the future.

Many people could not fall asleep that night, either because of the explosion, or because they all already knew, based on information leaked to Silvana by the Italian soldier, who seemed to like her, that they would be reaching their destination the next day. They didn't know where the destination was, but they knew it was close.

The next morning, they found out. Two burly men who were taken up on deck to help the soldiers with some physical tasks reported they'd seen Naples in the distance. The notion that every child in Benghazi was raised on, "See Naples and die," now received horrific new meaning. Silvana said nothing. She stood still, gauging people's reactions. Some of them stared back at her, awaiting her words, but she kept silent and still.

After a while, the silence broke, replaced by many questions: "What are they going to do to as at the port?" "Why are they taking us to Naples, of all places?" "Are they going to take us somewhere else from there?" On the backdrop of these panicked question, Yona Hachmon's complaint stood out: "Why Naples? Couldn't they have taken us to Milan? I've always wanted to see the shops on Via Monte Napoleone."

The uncertainty was broken at once by a soldier who appeared at the doorway and ordered them to prepare to get off the ship around noon. They didn't understand how they were expected to prepare. They barely had any belongings with them, nor any idea of what was to come. But the order was so decisive that they all tried to prepare anyway. Women smoothed their clothing, men tucked in their shirts and fastened their belts, mothers ran their fingers through their children's hair, and families stood in neat rows.

Silvana did not protest this bustle, but neither did she join in. She knew anything she did would be construed as the result of knowledge. She waited to see what happened, and things happened quicker than expected.

Dozens of policemen and soldiers arrived in small boats, their attitude making the captives yearn for the treatment they'd received from the soldiers on the ship. They pushed them roughly onto the boats, beating them and yelling, "*Avanti Israeliti*, go on, Israelites." ~identity. Internal vs. External

Silvana looked at the red roofs of Naples and imagined that the city was looking back at her compassionately. She'd waited her entire life to see Italy, dreaming of the places her father had described to her, places that had become part of her memory. Anticipation was now pushed out of her dreams, its place taken by one single desire—to see Libya again. The knowledge that she was about to step for the first time in her life onto land that wasn't her own awakened an unbearable yearning. The idea of being in another country defined her as belonging to her own country more clearly than ever; she longed to be swallowed by her homeland. She'd never envisioned Benghazi more tangibly than in those moments. The Lungomare, Via Calanzzo, Souk Delam, Piazza del Municipio, Jeliana Beach, Teatro Berenice, the synagogue, el-Masjad, their shop and their home—they all spun around her like horses on a merry-go-round, each in turn inviting her in.

The merry-go-round of her mind was cut through by the horrid scream of an old lady announcing she wouldn't leave the boat, even if that meant immediate death. Silvana approached her and tried, uselessly, to calm her down. From the jumble of words the old lady blurted Silvana was able to glean that she'd promised her husband on his death bed that she would never set foot in Italy. She didn't mention the reason for her promise, only repeating it over and over, weeping. A few people approached her, including a man who stroked her hair as if she were a little girl and told her he'd known her husband, and that he would not have objected to her disembarking. The old lady continued to weep, put her head in the lap of the Tripolitan man, and repeated once more that she wouldn't be getting off. Silvana was surprisingly pleased that the man's efforts to calm the lady down had failed. In spite of the great stress they were under, she didn't want another man's success to illuminate her inability. Eventually, two Italian soldiers came over and simply carried the shriveled old woman away. Moments before they stepped on Italian soil, the old lady expired in their arms.

Stunned by the death that had taken place before their eyes, the Jews got off the boat in perfect order. They were welcomed by a new group of Italian

soldiers who set a course for them toward a soccer
field. In spite of the light rain, the cold, and their new
circumstances, Silvana couldn't help but marvel at
the field, which was entirely different than the one
they had in Benghazi. So different, in fact, that she
wondered if it wasn't intended for a different, more
noble and elegant game. It was made of fresh grass
rather than sand, its goals had thicker nets, and its
size was almost twice as that of the Benghazi field.
For a moment she seriously considered fleeing along
with her family; but only for a moment, because an
order spoken by a soldier to line up on the sixteen
meter line set her straight. She knew the moment she
took a step that signaled an intent to flee she would
be shot on the spot. She stood behind her father,
stretching up to her full height, thus preventing her
sister, standing behind her, from looking at anything
but her own back. She even took a step back for this
purpose.

Now she spotted a long line of trucks outside the
fence. They did not resemble the Mercedes trucks
or the ones owned by Titanic, a trucking company
owned by Pio Nahum, a friend of her father's. They
were long and wide, brand new, with very large tires,
and a front bumper that resembled an animal's face,
a kind of distorted dog and bear hybrid. They were
covered with brown tarp. She thought they might not
be so cold inside those trucks. The othershad the same
idea, and when ordered to walk over to the trucks,

did so willingly. In fact, they all walked over quite quickly, their faces growing looser, more relieved. Later, Silvana realized they'd done that because they longed to be in motion, choosing uncertainty over certainty; as long as they hadn't arrived in their permanent dwelling, their hope of returning to Libya was still alive and breathing.

The Hajaj family and the Hachmon family were separated. The former was put on the third truck of the convoy, while the latter was put on the first. Julia Hajaj and Yona Hachmon managed to sneak a quick hug that contained the full scope of their emotions, and then the trucks were on their way.

The racing landscape the captives saw from the moment of their arrival in Italy planted a sense of threatening foreignness in their hearts. They drove past low houses with red-tile roofs, buildings four or five stories high, small and large churches, sprawling meadows, streams and flowing rivers, and yellow fields of wheat. Though these sights were all new to Silvana, none of them were as foreign as the snow that appeared when the truck began climbing the mountains. A customer at the shop once told her that some mountains in southern Libya were often covered in snow, and her father had told her now and then about the snow in Italy, but she couldn't even fathom the reality of the word. The sight of actual snow didn't change this. The carpet of white spread in front of her covered her consciousness, and now she seemed to see nothing but random flickers and sparkles, as if all images were gone from her mind.

Only after digesting what she'd seen was she able to tell herself: I'm seeing snow. The longer she stared at the snow falling and piling all around, the more flashes of the desert she saw in her mind. In her imagination, the desert appeared at noon, with the sun beating down on it, revealing it in all its glory, the dark dunes mixing together with the lighter ones. Then it appeared in twilight, when the setting sun dresses the sand reddish brown and the animals begin emerging from their burrows. When the convoy reached close to one of the peaks the snow was no longer that thick, and Silvana saw nothing but desert.

Almost all the passengers watched the white mountains as if seeing a metaphysical phenomenon, divine extensions visiting the real world for a brief moment. Only Silvana's father wasn't watching, having seen such visions before. The sight of snow rescued him from his lifeless, inner fort, sending him back to the not so long ago days when he went to Italy as a well-connected merchant. Silvana hoped that the piercing look that now appeared in his eyes was a clear sign of his regaining his composure, returning to life, and that he would quickly return to be the same old Eliyahu Hajaj, a fearless man that, even in his darkest moments, always noticed glimmers of light and led others to them.

But a moment later his gaze landed like a snowflake atop the accumulation of desperation that had piled within him, and his eyes went hollow once again. Silvana contracted with pain. The expressionless look on her father's face burned her soul. She didn't move even when one of the women, who, unlike anyone else, was wearing a long raincoat, said she thought they were in central Italy, not far from Umbria. In those moments, Silvana had no interest in her new role as family leader. It felt like a pointless load she was forced to carry on her back down a dead-end road. Desperation and helplessness once again consumed her.

She couldn't afford to keep sinking; within three hours, some of the passengers began voicing their concerns, while others seemed to have been released from the amazement of seeing the snowy mountains, filling the space of the truck with questions that remained unanswered, hanging in air. Silvana stood up and walked over to a scared elderly couple, ran her hand over their heads, and clamed them down: there was nothing to be afraid of, being in Italy was like being at home. She left all other question marks hanging in the air of the truck. She let them evaporate by themselves following her calming words, but they continued floating over the heads of the passengers in the next hours. Most people fell asleep and only woke up five hours later, when the truck pulled up at the bottom of a snow peaked mountain.

Toni, who hadn't slept a wink, put her face in her hands, but couldn't stop her teeth from chattering, and her mother curled up, as if to make it harder to remove her from the truck. Silvana hugged both of them. Three Italian soldier ran over to the truck, their large flashlights illuminating its contents.

Silvana, her sister, and her mother all stepped off the truck as three quivering petals of the same flower. They didn't leave each other's side. The darkness swallowed the gaze of the world, and nothing could be seen. They walked across the muddy ground along a line marked by the soldiers' flashlights, huddling together against the cold, but the cold was so intense that any attempt at warming up was destined for failure.

Silvana recalled having once seen one of their neighbors, a young man named Hasan, working out in his backyard. When she asked what he was doing, he said it was a Chinese martial art. He taught her that the main principle of the art was not to resist an opponent, but to use his movements to one's advantage. She decided to utilize the same method against the cold, letting it pass through her rather than cling to her body. She stood with her legs slightly apart and focused on that thought. It might have been an illusion, but it caused her to suffer less than others.

They were taken into a huge Italian military tent, in which dozens of blankets were spread, and were reunited with the Hachmons (suddenly, as if outside of space and time, her mother told Yona Hachmon that she was jealous that they had the faster truck, and put her arms around her).

After some time in the tent, Silvana felt the chill abating. She took advantage of this relative comfort to focus and think. From the behavior of soldiers and their conversation she learned that the tent would only serve as temporary lodging, and that they might be moved elsewhere as early as the next day. She moved among the people and encouraged them to take anything from the tent they could use. And indeed, the moment no Italian eyes were watching, some people collected everything the moon shone over: Italian military food dishes that were scattered on the ground, torn knitted hats hanging from wooden poles, tattered socks cast aside unthinkingly, broken plates, unsharpened pencils, torn paper, and even stones. Some of them shoved the objects beneath the blankets spread on the ground and fell asleep beside them. Silvana only used the blanket to cover up and was instantly asleep.

In her dream, she saw herself as a little girl climbing into her parents' bed in the middle of the night, lying between them and wrapping her arms around her father's body, then around her mother's belly. Her mother whispered for her to go back to bed, but prevented her from doing so by holding her tighter.

When she woke up, her mother's hand was wrapped around her waist, just like when she was a child. Silvana removed her arm gently and looked around the tent. The morning light that filtered in crawled along people's frozen faces. They slowly began opening their eyes, their first rheumy glances directed at the tent's door, as if trying to guess what the new morning had in store for them. The snow that piled a few meters away undermined their glances: its complete foreignness seemed to announce that any attempt at interpreting the true picture forming before them was destined for failure.

After most people had woken up, an older officer appeared behind the shoulder of the guard at the doorway, and calmly and pleasantly asked them to be ready to leave shortly. Everyone tried to use the remaining time in the tent to wash their faces and mouths with warm water from two large pails. The bathing was done in silence.

Silvana wondered if they would ever be a community again. The question filled her head, leaving no space for any other thoughts. She wanted to shake it off, but the question continued to mercilessly peck at her brain. Only when they left the tent in rows did it leave her be. Her mind was now filled with the castles that appeared on the snowy peaks before her amazed eyes. They were taken right out of the books she read as a child, where they always rose on arid mountain peaks. She looked up at the castles with the odd premonition that she would spend a long time in one of them. She took a few steps, directing her feet to the harder parts of the muddy dirt, and toyed with the question which castle she would choose— the one made of brown bricks, or the one with the red tiled roof, or perhaps one of the two that featured towers rising above them like sentries.

Submerged in this dilemma, she walked across a tenth of the kilometer that separated them from the castles. She smiled briefly and her heart was filled with joy, joy for not having forgotten how to smile; though she hadn't done so for a while, it was still possible.

Suddenly her mother stared at her with hopeful wonder. Her own smile reflected at her from her mother's eyes, and her mother seemed to be guessing that her daughter knew something positive that she herself could not see. Exhausted, her mother didn't ask, and only kept watching her, as if hoping she continued to smile.

They walked up the mountain, hunched, their legs faltering and their faces tired. After walking about two-hundred meters, a bloodcurdling scream sounded behind them: "*Mat, mat*, dead, *ma dayem kan rabi*,cruel fate, *mesa, baruch dayem emet*." Silvana turned back and saw an old woman in a torn dress and a green headdress kneeling beside an old man and shouting, "*Raz'li mat*, my husband is dead!" Silvana only knew what she mustn't do in that moment: she mustn't get involved, she mustn't use this opportunity to assert her leadership among those who already viewed her as a leader. Against her will, she could see clearly that her desire to lead had nothing to do with her wish to help others. She burned with shame, and shame, along with fatigue from the long climb up the mountain, forced her to take a break from leadership. She felt that everyone expected her to approach the old woman and support her, but chose not to do so, instead remaining in place and following the events from there. She didn't move even when two soldiers carried off the body of the man and his sobbing wife to the side of the road, shouting at the others to move on. One of them blurted, "*Benvenuti*, welcome, to Civitella del Tronto." His cold, ironic tone told the more perceptive in the crowd that a death like the one they'd just witnessed was a daily occurrence in this place.

Silvana noticed very subtle signs of apathy gradually taking over many of the faces around her. She could even recognize them in her mother: her eyes, which only moments ago smiled back at her, now looked hollow, and her lips, which had always been full of life, now looked withered. Silvana knew that similar changes were taking place in her own face as well. It grew limp, her mouth hanging open, her eyes staring ahead. That recent smile, the sudden joy, energizing her spirit and sharpening her mind— these all seemed like fictions, empty promises, small frauds her mind had employed in the battle for her soul.

She continued to walk through the mud, which grew more traitorous the farther she advanced. Entire stretches of ground that appeared stable turned out to be quicksand. From time to time she heard stifled weeping over the kindness of the deceased old man. They were brief, coming and going, cut short, playing a terrifying tune over a wilting heart.

After faltering about a hundred meters more, when the peak could be clearly seen in the distance, Silvana made up her mind to settle down in the southernmost castle. Its red roof led her to think that life there would resemble a fairytale. The sight of the castle held the most sublime promise of the moment: the castle would wipe away the present. She pictured herself walking down long, narrow hallways, glinting chandeliers hanging from the ceilings, biting into ripe fruit carefully arranged in silver bowls, stepping into vast, heated rooms, and bathing in a large tub, her beloved Italian Trozzi soaps carefully lined on its wide edge. She imagined herself brewing Lavazza coffee in the kitchen, making rich sandwiches and hot soups, sleeping in a wide bed on fresh, fragrant sheets, thick comforters and soft pillows, staring out at the snowy landscape beyond wooden shutters.

Not a moment went by before reality slapped her in the face: an Italian soldier pierced the air with warning shots. "*Vi ho detto più veloce!* I told you to hurry up!" he screamed.

Silvana quickened her steps and watched the soldier. He seemed to have a reason for his behavior. He moved with express speed back and forth along the parade of captives, trying to make his commanders notice the fear he planted in them. Right after shooting into the air and filling it with screeching syllables, he glanced at his supervisor, anticipating acknowledgement. Silvana didn't quicken her steps any farther. She refused to serve as a stepping stone on the soldier's way up the rank ladder. She didn't urge her relatives to walk faster, either. Fear did this for her.

Her mother encouraged herself to walk quicker by humming an old Italian tune, repeating the line "*L'uomo deve sempre continuare a sognare in qualsiasi situazione*, man must always continue to dream, in any situation." Her sister began lifting her knees like an accomplished athlete, no longer trudging along.

Silvana knew they were wise to quicken their step and that she was foolish to refuse to do so. But wisdom was never the most important quality in her view. She was often told she was smart, but never took it as a great compliment. She preferred to be praised for her courage or her kindness. To her, these qualities were more important than smarts, and yet irrevocably tied to it. She always thought that kindness and supreme courage entailed a deep understanding of the heavy toll they might take on the person exhibiting them. She always believed that such understanding was a clear sign of intelligence. But now she wasn't acting out of either courage or kindness. It was pure pride that led her to disobey the Italian soldier.

Luckily for her, her relatively slow gait wasn't much slower than the quick step of most other walkers, and she blended right in. But they didn't blend into her: all at once, she felt the kind of estrangement she often suffered from among the Jewish community in Benghazi, plucking her out of the group, only to return her to them a few days later. She felt she didn't belong with the people walking around her, that they might all be headed to the same place, but not on the same path. But this time, unlike previous occasions, she returned to the arms of her community very quickly. When they were about a hundred meters away from the castles, four planes sliced the sky over their heads in a meticulously straight line. Their noise was petrifying. Silvana had never heard such a clear, sharp, rattling whistle before. The noise echoed loudly for a long time afterwards. She clung with panic to a woman with dirty red hair, who was standing behind her, asking, "*Sha yehabi yamlulna?* What are they going to do to us?" The sound of the planes did what even the Italian soldier's gunshots couldn't do—it crumbled Silvana's wishful imaginations into tiny flecks. She walked up the mountain with everybody else in dead silence, toward four ancient collapsing, threatening castles, awakening horror visions of dungeons that are just as dark in the daytime as they are at night.

She could maintain her calm no longer. With each further step up the mountain she felt herself descending into the cellars of her soul. The dark bile that lurked like a predator took hold of her, and she no longer had the power to shake it off. All she wanted was to reach one of the castles and sit down. But the road looked long, and the cold pierced her with burning gusts of wind, only exacerbating her desperation. She also felt indifferent about the snow. It no longer appeared like a giant piece of fabric that someone had tossed over the land to serve as a pearly white backdrop for her downfall.

Silvana kept walking forward and simultaneously retreating into herself. She noticed no one around her. She thought of nothing. But when she saw large bumpy brownish gray rocks that resembled the ones at Jeliana Beach, a painful thought burst into the emptiness that had taken over her thoughts— she missed her ability to miss things. This thought ignited for a moment before extinguishing. When they finally arrived at the castles, she wasn't thinking anything at all. There was no power of thought within her; she had no purpose.

The sight of the castles set her firmly in reality. Their presence forced her to gather her thoughts and decide which one she and her family would enter. Though it wasn't their decision to make, they could influence it indirectly. Silvana realized that if they walked to the head of the row, there would be a better chance of them being directed to one of the farther castles, which had towers sprouting from their roofs. She preferred the tower with the red-tiled roof, the one closer to them. Her preference seemed to break through the fogginess of her vision. She directed her family to the end of the row. Her mother managed to embrace Yona Hachmon, speaking to her in archaic Arabic, assuming, wrongly, that her daughters wouldn't understand. She told her that if they were to die here, she wanted Yona to know she'd always loved her.

The people who marched ahead of them were indeed directed to one of the two farthest castles by an Italian officer who had rough features and thin hair. From the corner of her eye Silvana noticed one group walking into one of the two closer castles. From a brief glance at their own group, which was beginning to be swallowed into the castle, like a line of ants into their underground nest, she realized their group had about the same number of people as the other group. She recalled hearing an Italian officer say there were three hundred of them, and assumed that about a hundred people would be housed in each castle. She held onto this number, not because it meant anything to her, but because she appreciated math.

The number reminded her of her own exceptional skill for calculation. The zeros were like rings she held onto in order to pull herself off the ground and revive herself from the darkness of her soul.

When she walked into the castle she was surprised to find that the whispers she'd heard during the climb had been correct—all signs pointed to this being an old hospital. Some of the iron beds arranged along the hallway with pristine precision had mysterious medical equipment hanging over them. White cabinets were installed in the walls, red crosses marked at their center. In the middle of the long hallway, inside a nook in the wall, were five abandoned wheelchairs. Some bandages were rolling around on the floor, some new and some used, and a picture of two nurses and a doctor, embracing and smiling at the camera, hung on the wall down the hall. Two stretchers stood on top of each other at the end of the hall, and piles of new scrubs rested on the floor. The sight of the remains of the hospital planted hope in Silvana that they'd arrived at a site that had been expropriated from the war, a place sealed against its horrors, far away from its foolishness, a place where they could remove their mask of misery and return to being just like anyone else.

For some reason, watching the medical equipment brought her some relief. For a moment she forgot her assumed role as family leader. Her mother acted in her place, leading them among the crowd. When they arrived at the end of the wall, she and Toni took hold of four beds. She pushed them close together, using the help of her husband, who seemed to have awoken from a years-long sleep, forming one giant bed.

They spotted a female Italian soldier who trudged along lazily, as if waiting with infinite boredom for something to finally happen. She was giving orders as an afterthought, not seeming to care at all about whether they were carried out. "*Andare a prendere le coperte e lenzuola dalla stanza che è dietro questa porta.* Go get blankets and sheets from the room behind that door," she said, scratching her head slowly. Silvana turned toward the door, but her husband blocked her way and announced, "*Ana mashi,* I'll go," as if embarking on a dangerous mission. [handwritten: family dynamics in a patriarchal society]

He returned a few moments later, carrying some blankets and pillows. "I got us the best stuff," he said with ostentatious pride, like a child yearning to prove himself. Silvana's mother wrapped blankets around her daughters. With the wool around her body, Silvana realized how cold she'd been. She yearned for the desert, a brief chill climbing up her back. She let Toni and her mother make the beds and walked to the window. A screen of snowflakes fell on the mountains before her. The premonition she'd wished to nurture was now raging within her: staying in the red roofed castle would be an unrealistic experience. This time the sensation lingered for a longer time, and at the moment nothing happened to return her to the dire reality. This time, the sensation disappeared gradually, being sucked out of her by the confused looks of the people around her.

By the afternoon there was no trace of it. Neither the red tiles, nor the snowflakes, nor the dark skies, the likes of which Silvana had never seen, nor the sweet exhaustion that took over her—these were no longer colored by the comforting tones of imagination. People's lost looks and their meaningless scampering down the hallway were revealed to her in all their wretchedness. Her ears absorbed the ongoing sobs of the old lady who'd lost her husband and the shuddering cries of little children. The unequivocal knowledge that she had no idea what would happen next kept pecking at her thoughts.

She tried to preoccupy her mind by making herself useful. She walked among the adults, asking if they knew anything about this place. Almost nobody knew anything about Civitella del Tronto, other than a man of average height, whose expression disclosed nothing of the trouble they'd been through so far. He introduced himself as Meir Luzon and immediately began explaining that all these castles used to be public establishments, and that the area was known for its fine schools. This piece of information was Silvana's Archimedean point, a foundation for a new image of reality, whose pieces she slowly together by intently listening in on the guard from the partial answers given to her by the lazy Italian soldier.

The more information she gathered, the more the possibility of returning to Benghazi appeared like the delusions of a feverish woman. This was the case two days after their arrival, when she heard from one of those guards that, being British captives, they would probably remain in the castle until an exchange was carried out; but the way things looked, he added, the war wasn't going to end anytime soon. Silvana quickly learned that all her knowledge of outside reality would not help her one bit. She stopped pondering it and decided to think of the castle as the entire world. She began arranging her life there as best she could: she showered as often as she could without complaining about the cold water, washed the sheets and her few clothes, volunteered to be part of a group that cleaned the bathroom, and made herself more clothes from a wool blanket she got from one of the guards. She began exercising regularly, repeating the routine she'd learned from Nisso Zuaretz, a fellow captive and gym teacher at the Tripoli Jewish School. She played with stones she found in the yard they were allowed to go out to once in a while, scattered optimistic statements in her conversations with her family and everyone else, and tried as best she could to form friendships with the guards, especially the female ones.

More than anything else, she tried not to think of the future. She gave that up almost entirely. Whenever a thought of getting out of her castle of captivity began forming, she nipped it in the bud. She was stretching the present time to infinity, turning it into a period whose ends were too far to be seen. Her mind was filled with the here and now, which became her only world.

But sometimes the tables turned and it seemed that present tense was stretching her out, threatening to overflow into the future. Thus, one unseasonably warm morning in March of 1942, less than a month after arriving, Red Cross ambulances appeared at the castle gates, and five people got out. Their faces projected such natural good will that the prisoners had a hard time believing they were human. A rumor quickly spread among them that these people were there to liberate them. When Silvana heard this, a strange thrill rushed through her, making her shudder. It was apparent when one of the delegation members, a young, fair skinned woman with freckles and reddish hair, who spoke English with an unidentified foreign accent, stood before her. She asked Silvana some questions, mostly about the Italian soldiers' treatment of them. Upon hearing one of her answers, the woman placed her hand tenderly on Silvana's cheeks. Silvana wished for the hand never to leave her face. The woman noticed her pleasure, left her hand on her cheek and ran it softly over her face.

Silvana thanked her silently, wishing to tell her something, but her throat wouldn't obey.

Silvana never spoke to anyone else about so many things in so little time as she had during that moment of silence; not even during her long silence with Said, Nassarin's brother, as they rode home together in the *azuza carrozza* the day she first saw a German soldier in Benghazi. The feeling that rose within her awoke a yearning for something else—an honest conversation with someone. She frantically searched for it from the moment she saw the Red Cross woman walking slowly and thoughtfully out of the castle. At first she turned to Nisso Zuaretz, the gym teacher who was fifteen years her senior, but though he was quite an interesting man, who exhibited wise and sensitive interest in her situation, she couldn't help but think that he was trying to preserve the social hierarchy of Tripoli. He did his best to spend his time with the community elders rather than with simple folk. She got sick of this quite quickly, and after a short exchange by the water hose in the yard, she walked back into the castle to search for a new conversation partner.

Her eyes fluttered over what she saw: elderly people, all withering, their eyes extinguished, their arms dropped at their sides, their bodies giving in to exhaustion; men and women, some of them stomping their feet nervously, others silent, others yet moving frantically between rooms; young men and women, many of them attractive, their faces expressionless and their mouths pursed, paralyzed; boys and girls, only a few of them still preserving some of the charm of their youth, all standing or sitting around aimlessly, or pretending to be busy to regain some pointless hope. None of them seemed like a fitting partner.

Disappointed, she was making her way to the shower one day when her eyes fell on a young man about her age, sitting on a stool against the wall of the hallway. He was reading a Bible leisurely, his legs crossed at a refined angle. He appeared to be absorbed in his reading and completely detached from everything around him. She thought he was smiling lightly, an almost imperceptible smile, like the one on the faces of the serene men praying at the synagogue, uniting with their God. She liked him immediately.

His quiet confidence and gentleness reminded her of the Hebrew soldier. She stopped at a distance and watched him. The lamp over his head, which the prisoners had guarded carefully along with the three others from the moment they realized the castle had electricity, illuminated his face mysteriously. The light of the lamp seemed to duel with the faint sunlight that filtered into the castle, and the weak light on the boy's face darkened any possibility of deciphering his expression. She was surprised by the prominent wrinkles on his forehead.

Silvana walked over hesitantly, and before she could even open her mouth, the boy looked up at her and asked, "*Int binrazia binghazina?* Are you from the family that came from Benghazi?"

Silvana nodded weakly and answered, "Yes."

He cleared a spot for her on the wooden bench and introduced himself, "Tino. The prisoner trapped outside his country, Tino Sa'adon."

The moment she sat down, Silvana felt bitter. The realization that they were captive in a foreign land landed inside of her like a rock. This realization, which had been gradually advancing toward her awareness but always backtracking before it got there, now rooted inside of her mightily. Silvana sat down next to Tino Sa'adon and they began chatting, mixing together Arabic, Italian, and contemporary Tripolitan slang.

"Don't you think we'll be released?" she asked with a heavy heart.

"I do," he said. "But I don't know where we'll be released to."

"You think we'll ever see Libya again?"

"You know what's strange? I see it now much more than I did before. Ever since we've been here, in this detention camp, Libya keeps passing before my eyes, all the spots I always walked by without stopping… all those places, like the small bell garden behind the Tripoli market… I can see them now, in detail."

The words "detention camp" gave her a start. "But do you think we'll actually be there again?" she insisted.

"Anyone who promises that is a fool."

"So you don't think we'll be leaving here?" she asked angrily.

"I can't think about that."

"So venture a guess," she said, both impatient and alarmed.

He raised his eyes to her, then after a short pause said meekly, "Then no. I'm guessing we won't."

The fear that filled her after this conversation was alleviated sporadically by the clear knowledge of having a friend in the camp (from the moment Tino Sa'adon ventured his frightful guess, she began using the word "camp" instead of "castle"); not only because she knew she'd met someone with whom she could speak profoundly about many subjects, and not only because she felt comfortable around him, but mainly because she immediately felt that his most definitive quality was reliability. She was surprised to discover that his terrifying guess was what made her want to spend time with him. In the midst of the chaos inside of her, she yearned for a truth to lean on. She could not find this truth in someone who would try to console her because she was a family member. She needed a stranger whom she could trust. In Tino, both of her needs were met: the need for a grasping point, and the need for conversation.

With time, she wondered more and more at the essence of what she provided him. He didn't seem eager to talk to anyone, and preferred solitude. Had it been possible, he would have preferred to spend all of his time reading the Bible. She also didn't think he'd developed any feelings toward her. He didn't reveal a hint of enjoyment from being needed. A week after they met, they were already sporting the intimacy of close friends, and yet Silvana avoided asking him for the source of his need to speak to her. She was afraid to hear his answer, and couldn't bear the idea that he might tell her he felt no such need. His need for her was her grasping point. Thus, whenever she thought he wasn't requesting her support or assistance, she did all she could to make her want it.

This was the case in early April, when it was clear to all of them that the camp would have no daily routine, and that their only tasks would be the ones they chose themselves. Silvana stood in line for some dry pieces of bread and a bowl of soup— even food supplies had no apparent schedule and were distributed at random times—and saw Tino being pushed out of the line. To her disappointment, he did not ask her for help, instead making his way back to the end of the line. She called him over and pushed the woman in front of her in order to make room for him. He was alarmed by her behavior, but nevertheless quickly squeezed into the space created between the two women, acting as if he'd always been standing there. A few days later he told her about the guilt he still intensely felt over the death of his twin brother at the age of three, from a disease he'd contracted from Tino. He explicitly asked her not to mention it again, but Silvana still made him listen to her opinion, sharing a similar case that had happened to a family she knew in Benghazi.

Within the routine-less space in which they were trapped, the ability to meet Tino became no less important than the contents of their meetings. For as long as she could remember, Silvana always had a complex relationship with routine. On the one hand, she often felt stifled by it, and would release herself from it through a hasty trip to the desert. On the other hand, she often used routine to defend herself against the emptiness of life. Often, yearning for routine and the desire to free herself of it shared control over her soul. Now, in the camp, no one told them how to spend their days, and even lights out didn't happen at regular hours. Precisely because of this, her attitude toward routine became completely unequivocal: she missed it. She therefore established the desired routine through regular meetings with Tino, usually twice a day: first in the late morning, after washing her face and teeth in the frozen water that trickled from the rusty faucet in the front yard; then in the late evening, when her parents were folded into their bed like little children, near the door that separated the long hallway from one of the five giant rooms.

Their meetings usually had a recurring structure. They began with a prosaic question—*how did you sleep? Do you also spend all day waiting for evening?*—moved on to a mutual interest in each other's families, and from there to deep heart-to-hearts and discussions about the meaning of life. Their discussions quickly honed in on the question of belief in God. Silvana's questions emerged from within the crack in her faith, and Tino's answers tumbled down, firm as rocks, from the mountain of his. They were not enough to appease her. The crack that had opened in her soul when she heard the story of the Rosenzweigs had only deepened since, turning into an abyss that could not be filled by the devoutness of another.

But in spite of this, it appeared one time that the crack would close and that Silvana's belief in God would return to surge through her soul as it once used to. This happened in the end of March, as the noon sun illuminated the earth. The world seemed beautiful even from inside the camp, so beautiful that it must have been created by some directing hand. Even from within the camp, this hand seemed never to have left the world, continuing to provide it with its goodness for as long as necessary.

But the very next day the weather returned to its evil ways, and the crack in her faith returned with a vengeance. Silvana examined her surroundings and saw things she wished she didn't: children in rags constantly scratching their heads and blowing their noses on their dirty sleeves; adults dragging their feet through the rooms and hallways, besides themselves; hunched elderly staring at the world with amazement. Here and there a sigh of misery was heard, containing no grudge, but merely a submissive acceptance of the situation's absurdity.

Silvana couldn't avoid the thought that the image forming before her attested to the pointlessness and utter arbitrariness of life, to there being no directing hand, and if there ever had been, it was torn off long ago. With no real order around her, she yearned to at least experience the semblance of order, to recall the illusion of an organized world that was part of the past now moving away from her.

She approached her parents and sister. They sat side by side, leaning against the wall, and chatted aimlessly. She curled up between them, as she did when she was a child. She gave meaning to the authoritative look that finally appeared on her father's face and the hopeful words that escaped his mouth. Her mother had tears running down her face. She'd been waiting for this moment for days. It was enough to watch their family from the outside and catch the quick lowering of the eyes whenever she looked at her husband to know this. It was easy to detect a clear note of lament about the lost family hierarchy. Silvana was glad about the tears her mother now cried. Deep in her heart, she delighted in them, like a girl excited about the sensation of running water. Her mother reached her arm behind her father's shoulders and touched Silvana tenderly. Her touch contained almost everything: her endless love, her appreciation, her gratitude for understanding the state of her father, her attempt to relieve her parents, her hope that things would peacefully return to their normal order, and mostly her parental authority, which had been often broken as a result of Silvana's persistent independence, but still seeped through their lives, as her mother signaled with her gentle looks every morning.

Silvana rubbed her mother's arm, and her touch contained almost everything: her wish to restore the inner order of the family, the love she felt for her mother most days of the year, her appreciation for her mother's willingness to forego some of her desires for the sake of family unity, and mostly her yearning to feel a hope that would cancel out Tino's guess. The longer her mother continued to stroke her shoulder with confidence, the more her faith in one day returning to Benghazi was restored.

Even the terror of the mountains seen through the diamond shaped window did not break her faith. Her faith was based on a foundation of sharp blades, but when she feared she could no longer bear the pain, Silvana recalled what her father had promised her mother as they embraced: "We'll be back in Benghazi." It was enough to keep her faith alive, not only because her father spoke with his old determination, which was his identifying mark in Benghazi, but because of the expression on his face, which was identical to the one he had when he signed deals: his strong eyes were steady in their sockets.

She slept wonderfully that night. She'd lost so much sleep ever since they'd left Benghazi, and now she finally slept soundly with no night terrors—a sleep reminiscent of the peaceful harmonious slumber of her nights in the desert or of her afternoon naps on the roof of her house, in all aspects other than the place where she woke up. Though she awoke in the camp, there was nothing in it to take away from the pleasant feeling of safety she'd enjoyed that night: not the lost look of a young woman who'd woken up nearby, not the erect posture of the Italian soldier who guarded the gates, not the stained military jeep parked in the yard, and not the cold that took over the castle once more.

The next day was not the opposite of the night but its direct continuation. When she went to wash her face in one of the rooms, Silvana didn't feel the distress that had weighed down on her in previous days. Even her mother's thinness, which was suddenly revealed to her, did not change her feeling. She looked at her skinny hands and shrunken face quite apathetically.

The next morning she was filled with joy in addition to her sense of safety. The moment she woke up she noticed a group of sleepy people pouncing on open packages delivered by the Red Cross. She pushed her way through them, using her strength to get ahead of the old people, who were too weak to protest. A quick glance told her the packages contained food and hygienic products. She was the only one to choose toothpaste over canned food. She had an urge to brush her teeth. For days she'd dreamed of scrubbing them with toothpaste and removing the taste of humiliation. She often dreamed of Pasta del Capitano, the toothpaste she used in Benghazi in front of the mirror, overjoyed by refusing the swak—her mother and her friends' habit of whitening their teeth with green almond peels that turned their lips reddish brown.

Silvana walked over to the bathroom with a feeling she'd already forgotten. Just as the previous morning nothing could undermine her sense of safety, now almost nothing could impede her joy. She was so happy that for amoment she even allowed herself to be disappointed that the toothpaste delivered by the Red Cross wasn't Pasta del Capitano. She spread it carefully on her finger, as if the fate of the world hinged on the precision of her movements, and put her finger in her mouth. But her mouth rejected it. The toothpaste tasted like terribly faraway times, and it was as if her mouth could no longer contain anything that wasn't bland.

She tried to brush her teeth again twenty minutes later, and this time she was successful. She removed some of the grime that had collected on them, as well as some of the horrid taste that had made a home for itself in her mouth. She felt a light giddiness. She continued to brush frantically, foam dripping off her lips and her motions quickening, as if trying not only to remove the grime, but her teeth themselves. The wonder on the faces of the captives watching her only enhanced her cheer. She knew very well that where they were, the rational seemed irrational, and vice versa. She continued to brush more energetically, in a tizzy. Even the Italian guard's surprised look didn't discourage her, since she'd long realized that their captors were also slaves to the dictatorship of Civitella del Tronto. She continued to brush until her hand finally dropped down, powerless. The sudden joy that had filled her now seemed to drain her of her energy.

She faltered back to her bed but didn't lie down immediately, not because she couldn't get on, but because she felt that she herself was the bed, nothing but an object, something to sleep on or throw out. Now, of all times, when she was utterly exhausted, she could finally see clearly—below the glazed eyes around her and the arbitrary movements of the soldiers, beyond the smells of urine and feces coming from the bathroom, beyond the stifled cries rising at intervals, and the slow mumbled conversations of the elderly—a vision of a possibility.

Silvana saw the Red Cross shipment as a clear sign of the human order that still existed in the world, and therefore, of a real possibility that everything she'd been through since Benghazi was occupied by the Germans and until now was merely a delusion that would soon pass, and that she was the only one exacerbating the sensations, emotions, and disastrous prophecies that plagued her; that Tino was wrong and they were moments away from the end of this nightmare.

This delusion was quickly shattered; the echo of an explosion was heard in the distance. The soldiers rushed to an underground shelter outside the castle, urging each other with loud shouts, abandoning the prisoners behind.

The horror of danger did not skip Silvana. A shard of her previous pondering rose into her consciousness: we, as people, have free will. On the other hand, she recalled a statement she'd often heard in Benghazi: "*Lilt kabru ma yibtash bra*, man cannot escape his destiny," and quickly rejected it. That moment, she realized she was by no means prepared to end her life in Civitella del Tronto.

She immediately shook herself off and got up to chase an Italian soldier who ran to the doorway, calling back to Toni, "*Ta'ali*, come on!" Her sister watched her with stunned eyes, unmoving. Silvana didn't pause, running out of the castle, gathering what was left of her energy to catch up with the Italian soldier, who'd tripped and then immediately got back on her feet. She crossed the yard and ran through the wide open iron gate. The Italian soldier disappeared, only to reappear a moment later behind a mysterious shed, the purpose of which Silvana had wondered about many times. She heard the echoes of another explosion, and the barking of dogs rose from within the shed.

She saw the soldier disappear underground and hurried after her. She saw an expansive room containing chairs, army uniforms, rifles, civilian clothing, and even some musical instruments. A pack of cards, loaves of bread, sausages, dishes, water and beer bottles, cigarettes, and a bottle of red wine were scattered over a large table. Around it were ten half-naked soldiers. They gaped at her as if she wasn't even human. One of them pointed at her clumsily and asked the soldier, "*Che è questo animale?* What's this animal?"

Silvana fixed her eyes on them with determination, trying to push their glances back into their sockets and close their eyelids over them. Unbelievably, they accepted her presence in the underground, reinforced room, thanks to her courage. One of the female soldiers, whose breasts were covered only by a bra, addressed her politely, offering her a seat next to her. Silvana accepted, but could not stretch her world of concepts to contain the image before her eyes. She'd never seen a group of soldiers as wild and derelict as this. She recalled the Italian soldiers who used to spend their leave lying around on Jeliana Beach; those soldiers always made sure to fold their uniform, preserving their honor and the honor of their army, looking prepared to defend it and what it symbolized at any given moment.

One of the soldiers asked Silvana if she was thirsty, and before she could even answer, he gestured to a short soldier to pour her some water. Silvana sipped and was immediately filled with guilt; she didn't know how to deal with the realization that the moment she felt true danger she took care only of herself and forgot about her family. Even the fact that she'd called for Toni to join her as she fled couldn't compensate for such neglect, and she had to admit to herself that she had only done it to fulfil an obligation.

The echoes of explosions faded away. A few soldiers played cards, others sat around aimlessly, and another sang an aria in an impressive operatic voice. The soldier that Silvana had followed suddenly stood up, borrowed a small military jacket from another soldier, walked to the door and told Silvana, "*Vieni, torniamo al campo*, come on, let's go back to camp." The words were spoken softly and invitingly, and Silvana recalled her mother's peaceful voice whenever she invited her to join her in the afternoon at Signora Saban's spacious and elegant house, whose quiet nobility was praised among Benghazi women. Silvana got up and followed the soldier wordlessly.

Spring and Passover came even to Civitella del Tronto. The Passover Seder that year was like none they'd known before: there were no guests or hosts, no regular or surprise readers of the Haggadah; they gathered slowly, a group of hunched, lowly people. Tablecloths made of torn sheets, laundered by the women again and again in the hopes of returning some of their original glimmer, were spread over the long table set by Tino Sa'adon and a few other men in the center of the main hall. Each plate served three people. The utensils that had been scrubbed furiously were crooked. The bottle of wine was replaced by a bottle of water. The *maror*, the beets and the lettuce were nothing more than wilting bits of rotting vegetables they'd received from the soldiers. There was no matzah.

The Seder transformed the memories of its participants. It erased a few of the less pleasant attributes of their Libyan Seders from their minds. They could still imagine the outfits worn by guests around a Libyan Seder table, the pearly white tablecloths, the glasses that sparkled translucent, the fresh paint on the walls, the full wine glasses, the decorated silver goblet reserved for Elijah the Prophet, the chunks of roasted meat and other delicacies, the kisses showered by hosts and guests, and the cheerful human warmth that simmered through all homes.

They could no longer see the current that had always run beneath these pretty visions. They did not see, not even for an instant, the mutual loathing that guests and hosts often felt toward those who embraced them with roars of joy as if they'd just returned from lengthy captivity; nor the wretched maneuvers utilized by heads of families to lead venerable guests to choose their homes over others; nor the petty teasing and the carefully directed vengeful insults shot by the women while arguing on insignificant matters such as the quality of food or the seating arrangement.

After singing "The Four Questions" Silvana could no longer stand by the table. She was shaken up by her sister's trembling, stifled by her mother's tears. She had to remove them from her field of vision. She wrapped herself in a blue wool blanket she'd received from the Red Cross people, and went out to the yard. The weather was quite nice, and the meager light emerging from the castle softened the all-encompassing darkness. The world seemed to be bathing in eternal silence. Her closest friends, her thoughts, had turned their backs on her, leading her on. They evaded her, leaving her with no more than a hint of their existence. She wasn't able to capture even one full notion.

Suddenly, loud barks sounded from the mysterious shed outside the camp. Silvana jumped back, but was nevertheless tempted to go check out this place that was being guarded by such intimidating dogs. She overcame her trepidation, clutched at the blue blanket, and walked out through the iron gate, taking advantage of the guard's absence. She walked slowly to the shed. The barking grew louder but seemed to change. The closer she got, the shorter the barks grew, and when she was standing right beside the shed they sounded more like screeching breaths. She walked behind the shed, searching in vain for a window or opening through which she could peek inside. Then she paused, calculating her steps. Suddenly she heard human voices, sobs rising and falling, "*Non abbiamo tradito*, we are not traitors." She quickly turned back. She didn't want to investigate what she'd heard, didn't want to understand what she nevertheless did, against her will: that the barking had come from human lips. She was unable to face the cruelty that demanded her recognition.

She returned to the Seder table. Her face gave nothing away. The people standing around the table continued to imagine faraway places. She addressed Toni: "*A-teliyana hama mush kif ma hsebnahem.* The Italians behave differently when they're away from home."

Toni made a face, signifying that she did not understand what her sister was talking about, and continued to sing Passover songs meekly. Silvana looked around the table, and her eyes fell on Tino Sa'adon.

His brown eyes were shifting in their sockets, as if trying to escape his smooth hair, which fell over them. They looked at her as if they too had seen what she'd seen. She lowered her eyes. His all-knowing gaze reminded her of his guess—that they would never return to Libya. She couldn't accept it. She couldn't imagine never seeing her homeland again. The borders of Civitella del Tronto became the borders of her world, but she needed to believe she'd go back. This thought was not trapped in Civitella del Tronto. It hopped over its walls. Silvana looked up to Tino, and his eyes elevated her spirits, because she thought she recognized the shadow of doubt. He looked more hopeful than ever. But within only a few moments she realized this was only an illusion.

Tino walked passed her and muttered, raising the subject himself for the first time: "Silvana, do you remember what you asked me? *Di el-hin ana damen ili ma naraush el-hush*. I'm certain now that we won't see home ever again."

She didn't answer, trying instead to cling to the optimistic world view she'd inherited from her parents. In spite of her father's dark mood, she continued to believe that at his core he was still an optimist. This wasn't easy. She had to rework the images that appeared before her. In her mind, she stripped people of their filthy rags and dressed them in fresh clothing; she painted the faded, dirty walls of the camp with glowing brightness; she polished the sad lamps that dangled from the ceiling like tailless snakes; removed the fences that surrounded the inner structure of the camp; peeled the uniform off Italian soldiers. More than anything, she forced herself to see a horizon that did not contain a war.

This horizon was not available for long. The very next day it disappeared within the smoke of battle that rose from all fronts. At dawn, a group of three senior Italian officers walked into the castle with a German officer. They stood in a row at the center of the hall. The most senior Italian officer growled at the soldiers in charge of captives, announcing that the war was exacerbating on all fronts. Silvana realized this meant a deterioration in their conditions, but had no idea what to do about it. She tried to help her family by telling them encouraging things. In an attempt at reliability, her father said, "*Ya binti, ma t'hapish ali, ana hali bahi.* Don't worry my daughter, I'm fine. Take care of Mom and Toni."

Toni had no reaction, but her emotional state seemed to have balanced out. Her mother leaned against the wall, nodding at the encouragement. Only after asking for her thoughts several times, did her mother respond: "*Sto guardando il tempo.*"

Watching time. There wasn't much more they could do. Silvana considered her mother's words;

she knew very well that only an unrealistic act would help them comprehend this unrealistic reality, and perhaps help them fit in somehow in the place and time within which they were forced to exist. In spite of this, she made a concerted attempt not to act irrationally. Once more, she adopted the role of the responsible adult, this time with a vengeance. She turned to the Italian soldier she'd followed once to the shelter outside the camp, and asked to act as mediator between the soldiers and the captives. The green eyed soldier looked at her apathetically, not acknowledging the fact that the prisoner before her had been exposed to the underground room, then said drily: "I'll take care of it."

The next day, Silvana wordlessly announced her appointment as a prisoner liaison. Her gestures became sharper, her footsteps more determined. Some frowned upon her initiative, but most people supported her, which thwarted any attempt to undermine her authority. She arranged a more equal distribution of the food portions received from the Red Cross. Gone were the days when some people received canned meat or tuna, while others had to make do with fruit and vegetables. She also made sure to distribute biscuits, chocolate bars and cigarette packs equally. Only one man was not subjected to this policy: her father. In her heart's battle between justice and her father, she chose her father. Not only because she wished to build him up and return his old status in the family, but also because she wanted to show him that she, his daughter, had the power to provide benefits to certain people as she saw fit.

But her father's response was the opposite of what she'd expected. He explained to her that if she'd been appointed by the Italians to liaise between prisoners and captors, she had to do her job properly, without discrimination. He nevertheless devoured the two chocolate bars she'd given him, not before muttering with his good old smile, "This is nothing like the chocolate they sell at Piazza Navona." He also sucked gleefully on the Extra cigarette she gave him as if it were one of his fine cigars. At this point, Silvana knew he'd somehow become truly accustomed to their new life. He didn't give up much of his pride, but he'd stretched out his frame of reference, no longer complaining needlessly about how he'd been wronged.

She missed the things she used to do with her father in Benghazi, not out of a wish to restore their relationship of authority and resuscitate familial hierarchy, but because she missed the joy it had brought her. She mostly missed the days when her father decided to cut the work day short and took her in the late afternoon to Via Roma or Via del Municipio, stopping at the rolling carts to buy her some *torrone*—white almond candy—or *crocante*—peanut candy—and wandering the streets till evening, foregoing his rough exterior for the sake of tenderness.

The deeper they moved into summer, the more her longing seemed to evaporate into the hot air, and August 1942 went by without hardly missing a thing. In her mind, this month was deemed "pudding month." One morning an Italian soldier who'd just arrived in the camp with a noble air about her told them that from now on, once a day, one of them would be able to leave the camp for the nearby town to buy food, soap, and toothpaste. Silvana's father, Luigi Hachmon, and three men from the Tripolitan group consulted, and decided to entrust Tino with the shopping mission. Each morning Eliyahu Hajaj gave him some silver coins—even in the camp he seemed to have an endless abundance of them—and sent him to buy food, vegetables and cheese.

These foods established Tino's status. They bought him power, which he used lavishly. He tended to the requests of some people while turning down others, all according to one single criterion—his mood. Only Silvana's requests were not subject to his whims. He believed he'd stripped her of her power as liaison, and therefore made sure to meet all of her needs.

Silvana, who was entirely indifferent to Tino's new position, abused his guilty feelings without hesitation, requesting pudding every day. From the moment she first tasted it, she wanted more and more.

She ignored the issue of kosher, which might have set its sweetness out of bounds. Its pink and yellow colors shone like a single colorful item in a black-and-white world. She delighted in it as she used to in the gelato she bought at Itzam's ice cream stand between the Lungomare and Jeliana Beach—with incredible slowness, telling herself again and again: don't let it end, just make it last. She shared her pudding with no one. Whenever she noticed anyone watching her covetously, she gripped the pudding cup in her fingers and returned a threatening gaze, as if the pudding was her ticket out of the camp.

Pudding month came to a close at the end of August. One night the scorching weather suddenly subsided, and Tino invited Silvana for a short walk in the yard. She obliged. In the hand farthest from her he held a pudding cup with the same certainty and softness he'd held his Bible when they first met. She unwillingly recalled the Hebrew soldier again. She yearned for his image and the night they'd spent together at the Hachmon house, which seemed eternities away.

She walked a few steps ahead of Tino and wordlessly beckoned him to follow. She sat down on a rock that was only slightly revealed by the moonlight, and Tino sat at her side. She dipped her fingers in the pudding, licked them, and then put them to Tino's lips, almost forcing him to taste the residue of pudding, and said, "*Gibtlek*, for you." He hesitated before licking her fingers, and suddenly Silvana kissed his lips, searching his face for the blue eyes of Amos Rosman. She put her hand on the back of his neck and thought: *Amos Vered... Amos Vered...*

When Tino pulled away she kept thinking of her soldier, silently speaking his Hebrew name, the name he wanted to take. She kept wondering: *what would Amos Vered think if he were here? What would he think of our situation?* As they stood up and continued to walk around the yard she wasn't considering the embarrassment she might have caused Tino, nor the possibility that she'd aroused him. She only thought of Amos Vered's answers to her questions. They were unequivocal: without ignoring the complexity of the situation, faith in the victory of the British and a return to Libya shone beneath everything else like a polished gem.

In the following days she clung to this faith as if to a ring from heaven. She did all she could so as not to drop back down to the earth, which was stained with the shattered dreams of Civitella del Tronto. This was the case one morning, when she saw Yona Hachmon sitting alone, her naked face watching the world through eyes that could not see any kind of future. She did nothing to release Yona from her despair. In fact, she turned her back to her, holding on for dear life to her faith in the Hebrew soldier. This was also the case when an Italian soldier told her they would soon be transferred to a much worse camp, led by uninhibited German officers. She held on to the ring of faith once more, trying as best she could not to shake it.

The kiss she gave Tino gradually dissipated, and by fall there was no memory of it, perhaps because the strong winds blowing into the camp emptied it of anything that wasn't crucial, leaving its dwellers with nothing more than the realization that they would face their destinies alone. Silvana often wondered what would come of them, if she would ever see the streets of her beloved city again, its people, its boulevards, its town squares, its beach.

More than anything, she kept wondering if she'd ever see the desert again. This thought was unique in its purity. Not a hint of another thought invaded it. Only when she'd milked the question for all it had did she turn to think of other things, and especially one other thing—the seasons. Benghazi didn't have real autumn or spring. The summer and winter switched quickly, and no separate, independent season could be recognized between them. Here in Italy she'd witnessed the notion of autumn, which she'd heard so much about from her father, for the first time. She didn't experience it in the alleyways of Naples or the avenues of Rome, as she'd always dreamed, but even the bars of her soul could not keep autumn out.

But this autumn had nothing to do with what she'd imagined. It was quickly swallowed by winter, going almost unnoticed. Their misery, which she'd sporadically managed to push aside in the past six months, took hold of her at the beginning of winter, and wouldn't let go. Until now, the prisoners had somehow blended in with the Italian soldiers and Red Cross people, but now they looked like the remainder of creation, emaciated and derelict. Silvana couldn't bear it, but had no ability, and, truth be told, no real will, to change it.

Until one afternoon, as she watched snow piling up once more on the mountains outside the camp, she was filled with sudden energy, and began a conversation with herself: Why shouldn't we run away? *I don't know if there's any place to run to, and I don't know if running would improve anything.* But perhaps running is a goal in its own right, a worthy destination? Perhaps the sheer act of running would be able to transform our circumstances?

These questions plagued her even at night, illuminating it. In the sea of darkness pouring from the cold sky of Civitella del Tronto she could suddenly see a few flashes of light. The idea of escape wouldn't leave her alone. She wondered how to go about planning it, considered who to share it with. There were no natural partners, but the distinction between natural and artificial had long ago been lost on her. She decided that other than her family, she would include two or three other people in her plan. The right time to escape would be at night, after gathering everything that would help them survive winter as they fled to the south of Italy, where her father had close friends.

First she approached Tino, who looked at her with a vagueness about to become clarity, rubbed his beard, and after a long moment said that escape wasn't out of the question. Next she approached a young woman named Zala, who always found the time to offer help to all the prisoners and never begrudged any task she was charged with. Other than her strong spirit, her lithe, muscular body persuaded Silvana that she should be invited. Zala fixed her big brown eyes on Silvana with a silence that erased all background noise, and said, "I'm with you."

But when Silvana shared the idea with her parents, her escape plan took its final breath. Her father said he didn't think it was a very wise idea, and wasn't swayed even when she suggested they could reach his Italian friends in Rome or Naples. Her mother looked at her as if she had no idea what she was talking about, and her sister announced gravely that winter was not the right time for escape.

Her initial plan might have resulted in nothing, but the idea of escape continued to fill her mind from time to time, usually when she was terrified to think that the war might never end. Then she felt a strong urge to take a step that would release her from the repeating pattern of life in the camp. This cyclical thinking always took her a step back from what she wanted to do. After waking up in the morning, she removed the wool blanket, washed her face and spent hours doing nothing, chatting a little with some people, eating, staring at the exposed snowy peaks, and waiting indifferently for lights out. Then, at the end of the day, she had no more desire or power to take any practical steps to release her of this depressing routine. One night she tried to outsmart her own lack of initiative: she wouldn't escape, but rather annihilate all desires completely. She would choose the lack of will to live.

This was at the end of December. The darkness that invaded all corners of the camp was unbearable. Silvana leaned against the wall as usual, turning her back on her mental spine—her optimistic spirit—and was filled with a deep yearning to die. She'd been dizzied by suicidal thoughts once or twice before, wishing to spare herself from some pain or another, but this time her death wish was pure impulse. It filled her guts. Her entire being longed to disappear, to fade into an eternal, unconditional sleep.

She got into bed without any preparation. She stretched out her legs, spread them apart, stretched her arms to the sides and covered herself from head to toe. She slept like a rock. When she awoke the next morning she saw her mother's aching face, the prisoners faltering into the bathroom, and the despair that took over the Italian soldiers who walked in and out of the camp with no defined purpose. She was terrified to recall the previous night. She was glad she was still a part of this world. She remembered she had a world, even if she didn't love it anymore. She stood up and went through her morning routine with unusual speed and vitality, as if this would erase the impressions of the night.

But as the days went by, it dawned on her that that night was constantly seeping deep into her thoughts, enforcing the painful knowledge that it cannot be extinguished. After lazily crawling into her mind, it conquered it with violent determination.

This happened a short while after the world entered the year 1943. February was almost over. The cold reached its apex. The snow that knocked against windows melted her thoughts. Now she could feel nothing but impulse, wanting or not wanting things. She wanted. Not to fade into the fog of being or evaporate into endless sleep; this time she wanted to pluck herself out of the world at once, as an infected organ in the heart of the earth.

Her mother, who sensed her state of mind immediately, isolated her from the others and encouraged her with her faith that it would all be over soon and they would return home. Silvana broke into tears. Her mother held her against her chest, reminding her that even as a little girl, she'd always been the strongest, withstanding difficulties that caused other children to collapse. She rubbed her head and added that her crying emptied her of weakness, and that it would help her deal with things later. Indeed, within a few days her wish to disappear was gone, dissipated into the fog of existence.

In spite of what her mother said, Silvana stopped waiting for the end of the war. Instead, she waited for spring. A thin rain fell almost unceasingly, and the wait stretched out like a sea overflowing and submerging everything in its path. The days didn't pass, replaced instead with one long day that repeated itself over and over. Whenever she tried to take action, a voice inside her praised passivity.

When she stood up to join a group of people exercising under the guidance of the gym teacher, Nisso Zuaretz, the voice told her, *Let it go, Silvana, save your energy for a time of need, the time will come*. This was also the case when her father asked her to take over Tino's role as shopper, claiming that Tino was no longer able to get his hands on quality products. Immediately after accepting the job, without discussing the matter with herself or with Tino, the voice took hold of her again: *Let it go. Why would you do that? Stay inside this camp until true liberation arrives. A daily outing will only confuse you, making you think you're in control of your life*.

Sometimes she obliged to the voice, and other times she refused to cooperate. Either way, it was her permanent companion until spring, when it began to fade away. In the middle of May, when the sun governed Civitella del Tronto, lashing out at any intruders, the voice went mute, and Silvana was revived. Her faith that they would soon go home was restored, and she did all that was in her power to block its way out: she spoke less to Tino and to the Italian guards. Whenever she inevitably got wind of bloody battles in this front or another, she plugged her ears and her soul. She gradually became less sensitive even to matters not concerning the war. She didn't even notice the new distress that seeped into Toni's heart until it could no longer be ignored. Only then did she realize that Toni was completely indifferent to their life in the camp, that she no longer cared whether or not they would be released. Silvana didn't know how to deal with that. She thought that even if she shocked her sister she wouldn't be able to release her from this emotional muteness. She began speaking to Toni privately, mad at herself for having been so blind. Toni didn't cooperate, only occasionally saying, "*Lasciarlo perdere*, let it go." Silvana stopped after a few attempts, but only as a means to let her sister gather her strength and realize that she wouldn't be giving up on her.

Indeed, shortly thereafter, when she saw Toni standing in the yard and staring at the setting sun, she approached her and started a new conversation. This time she chose a different tactic. Rather than a series of questions, she began reminiscing about their childhood. She mentioned the days when they rode together on a red bicycle loaned by a neighbor, old

Yasser. She mentioned how Yasser always said the world was more beautiful when seen from a moving vehicle, because it was easier to sift through the bad. Toni said nothing, but a hint of a smile twitched on her lips. Encouraged by this, Silvana mimicked old Yasser as he admonished them whenever they returned his bicycle with a dent. At the sight of her punishing finger, Toni's mouth stretched into a naïve smile. Silvana did not leave it at that. She wanted her sister to speak. She asked her why she liked old Yasser so much. Toni gave her a long look, knowing full well that Silvana was trying to get her to speak, then said, "*Una persona per bene*, a good man." Silvana said this was certainly a good reason, and then wondered aloud about Yasser's health. Toni fixed her with tired eyes, as if telling her she'd exhausted her word quota for the day and would not be fooled, but then couldn't stop herself from saying, "If he's still alive, he would die right now of pain, because he couldn't help us."

Silvana let her be. She sensed that if she pushed her, her sister would retreat back into silence. Toni continued to watch the dying sun, not noticing Silvana turning back into the castle. Her mother waited in the doorway with one question on her lips: "How's Toni doing today?" Silvana said she'd be fine. It occurred to her that her mother's worried tone didn't match her expression. For a moment she entertained the thought that her mother's face had fixed in a permanent expression since arriving at Civitella del Tronto, and remained unchanged regardless of what took place in her soul. This seemed to make no sense and total sense all at once. This was an enigma, and she determined to track her mother's face.

Summer was in full swing, subjecting the camp to its whims. People failed in their attempts to fight off the heat. Long silences gaped between conversations. The soldiers exchanged sleepy glances. One day, Silvana followed her mother, focusing on her face and making note of every twitch. Her mother's face seemed to have molded into one expression: her eyes were sunken, her cheekbones protruding more than ever before, taking over her entire face. Her wrinkled forehead made her head seem bent, and her nose poked out at the world in a final act of defiance. Her face didn't shift even as a young man ran amok right past her, screaming that he had to return to Tripoli immediately for a relative's wedding. After a long observation, Silvana concluded that her mother's face was indeed fixed in one expression and that there was no point in continuing to watch her. But just then, her mother's face changed. Without any apparent reason it stretched out, as if below the layer of acceptance was an opposite one, vitally searching for a way out.

Silvana stored this vision in her mind. Whenever she felt herself about to collapse, she took comfort in it. Even the rumors that the Germans would soon take over Italy did not drain it of its power. It only began to crack when the rumors became fact, as summer left Civitella del Tronto and autumn was knocking on the doors of the castle.

On the second week of September, German soldiers replaced the Italians. They were completely different. Their uniform was black, they wore black caps on their shaved heads, with a symbol of cross and bones; on their lapels they had insignia in the shape of an eagle and a pair of crossed lightning bolts. The biggest difference was in their treatment of the prisoners. Everything changed once they arrived. The prisoners were no longer allowed to send someone out for food, and had to make do with meager food portions. The soldiers beat them whenever they wanted, for whatever ridiculous reason. If they didn't like the way a certain prisoner walked, they dragged him violently across the ground, letting gravel leave its marks on his body. They took the watches off the wrists of the few men who still wore them and tore off earrings from women's earlobes. Silvana's mother had removed her earrings back on the ride to Tripoli, but she still wasn't spared the pain of yanking—the sight of Yona Hachmon's torn ears made her soul bleed.

To Silvana's astonishment, the presence of the *Tedeschi Nere*—the black Germans, as the S.S. soldiers were called—also had a positive effect on her family: her sister was released from her haze.

In light of the *Tedeschi Nere's* treatment, Toni rebelled against her own apathy. She acted against her familiar indifferent self when she saw one of the guards, an S.S. man of average height, dragging an old woman across the ground. Toni pounced from her corner, screamed at the soldier in Italian and Arabic, and tried to release the old lady from his grip. The soldier slapped her face, throwing Toni back against the ground. The blood that trickled from her nose removed whatever was left of her apathy. She muttered into the dirt of Civitella del Tronto, "I'll kill his heart." She'd never spoken this curse before. She knew that saying it required real action, causing the cursed man to grow so angry that his heart gave in. And so, after promising her trembling mother that she wouldn't confront the Germans again, she shared her revenge plan with Silvana.

Silvana felt split in half. On the one hand, she identified with Toni and wanted very badly to make the S.S. man suffer. On the other hand, she was horrified by the possibility that the confrontation would actually take place. She was glad to find Toni attentive to her thoughts. Toni hugged her and whispered that she had nothing to worry about. She would be very careful and make sure that her revenge disclosed no one.

But Toni wasn't always able to conceal her hate for the man. Silvana and her parents always carried out orders perfectly, keeping their faces to the ground, but Toni defied him from time to time, pretending not to hear his orders or responding with a slight smile in the corner of her lips, mocking not only the events, but life itself. The soldier didn't always respond to her teasing. Sometimes he was so preoccupied that he seemed to be engrossed in inner conflicts that threatened to take over his soul, not even noticing what was going on outside. And yet, once he kicked Toni in the stomach after she refused to carry a bucket of whitewash from one side of the camp to the other, announcing proudly that she didn't work for the *Tedeschi Nere*. But even this occurrence had a silver lining. As Toni lay on the ground, folded into two with pain, her mother rushed over, wanting first of all to make sure that her daughter's childbearing abilities hadn't been compromised. Silvana realized that her mother was still hopeful.

But in late October hope left her mother's body like a dead fetus. Civitella del Tronto was so cold that even the memory of summer heat was forgotten. In the middle of the day, with no prior warning, three soldiers gathered all the men together, and before the women could even wonder at what was happening, the men were put on trucks and separated from their families.

Since the Germans arrived, vague rumors of a plan to send the men to forced labor camps had made the rounds through the camp several times. But none of the women truly believed the men would be torn

away from them with the same swiftness that their
earrings had been ripped off their ears. *camp people to objects*

Once they realized their men were being taken
away, the women began crying at once. Their cries
were varied, no two were alike. A woman with a flat
neck named Yehudit released a screech that sounded
like a funeral lamentation; an endless scream
occasionally broken by the words "*Ya rabi*"; an older
woman whom Silvana stayed away from, forcing
herself to forget her name because of her deviant
behavior (she once stole a small piece of cake Tino
had brought for one of the camp's children) screamed
ceaselessly "Eliyahu, Eliyahu!" Silvana's mother
screamed a broken "No… no…" The screams blended
together, rising and falling for a fraction of a second,
only to return, ear numbing. Silvana's cry was also
unique. Without breathing, she screamed one single,
meaningless syllable. All her pain joined together to
form a raging wave of torment. After crying she was
no longer the same Silvana. Now she knew she had
to escape from Civitella del Tronto no matter what.
That was the only way to regain her humanity.

She knew she had to plan her escape cold blooded,
and so she first wished to dull the pain of seeing the
men taking away. This cost her. Wherever she turned,
she saw the absence of men. It was so tangible that
she almost felt she could touch it. The image of her
father lorded over this void, allowing no other figure
to cast a shadow. In the short periods of time when

Silvana was free from his image, she planned her escape. At first she considered the direction. She weighed all the factors and concluded she had to go south. There were villages at the bottom of the mountains to the south of Civitella, and she assumed she would be able to get some food there. Her father always told her how they were just like the people of Southern Italy, and so she assumed that the farther south she went, the more likely she was to meet friendly faces.

After choosing her direction, she made up her mind to go alone. She realized that the Germans might punish her mother and sister more harshly if she went alone, but also that leaving together would make them more likely to be caught, since her mother's agility was limited. The idea of leaving her mother behind and taking Toni with her never crossed her mind.

Now all that remained was to find the right time. In the three weeks that had gone by since the *Tedeschi Nere* arrived at the camp, she often followed their guarding routine, and decided to spend a few more days observing it. She noticed that each night between ten and ten-thirty, the guards languidly changed in a small opening in the back fence. She realized that the tall soldier with the chiseled nose always left his post about ten minutes before his muscular friend arrived to man it. This time gap gave her hope, bridging between her fear and her wishfulness, and in the four nights that remained before her set date she swung between those two emotions.

The day of her escape had arrived. In the previous days, doubts kept plaguing her, and sometimes she wasn't sure she still had any of the spirit that had created the plan. From the moment she awoke of her disturbed sleep that morning she couldn't put one question to rest: if she ran, would she ever see her family again? Images of their life in faraway Benghazi passed before her eyes: sitting on the wide balcony adjacent to the yard, laughing wildly over one of her father's jokes or a bit of her mother's gossip about her friends; having a festive Sabbath dinner; walking to the synagogue in formalwear, taking their time, making it last. These images coalesced into a kind of pendulum in the center of her body, moving it from side to side. When her eyes met Toni's, this hurling became unbearable. Toni realized that Silvana was preparing to emerge from the camp. Silvana couldn't bear to keep this secret from her sister, and finally decided to tell her only right before setting out.

But in the afternoon her mood miraculously transformed and all fears and hesitations left her. She could see clearly the reason she'd decided to escape—the absence of men, which was felt strongly during the hours when they used to gather in a corner and discuss matters with gravitas, like heads of state who were calling the shots.

She shoved a few tin cans she'd collected in hiding when the Italians were still in control into a bag she'd sewed from a sheet, stuck a small family photo the Germans hadn't found down her underwear, kissed her mother and sister gently, careful not to raise any suspicions, and waited for dark.

It never got dark. Instead, a great light appeared. At dusk, all the men who'd been taken away a month earlier appeared at the camp like a divine delusion. Wearing torn work clothes, injured all over, skinny and faint with hunger and thirst, they fell into their wives' arms, mumbling one sentence over and over again: "We walked 180 kilometers."

Only after getting some dry bread in them and sipping what was left of the women's soup, they were prepared to tell their story: they were sent to build fortifications on the frontline by the Sangro River, and when a lethal attack of British planes showering fire and brimstone over the work camp began they ran for their lives, along with their guards. When the women asked why they returned to the camp rather than escape, they all said, "We wanted to come home."

Silvana's escape plan was forgotten, but a new, alert, vital emotion pulsed inside of her—an all-encompassing wonder at the order of the world. She couldn't tell left from right. In the next days she paced the camp dreamily, watching the returned men. She embraced her father again and again and still couldn't believe he was actually there with her. She asked him to tell her more and more about what had happened to him in the month that had gone by, to eliminate any doubt regarding the end of his absence. He complied with her repeated requests, never turning her down, even when he was exhausted. Over and over again he described patiently how they were transferred to the frontline by the *Tedeschi Nere*, who never missed an opportunity to abuse them along the way. Once and again he told her that the abuse in the trucks was nothing compared to the prolonged cruelty they'd experienced from the moment they arrived at Crocerta, the painful lashes on their backs and kicks in their faces whenever one of the Germans suspected they weren't working fast enough. Against all odds, they were able to return to Civitella del Tronto without being captured by any of the German soldiers they met along the way, thanks to a senior German officer they'd bribed with gold chains that two of them had kept on their bodies, and who escorted them throughout the 180 kilometers. The same officer even warned the camp guards not to hurt the prisoners, claiming there were orders from above to keep them safe and sound.

There was only one thing he didn't explain: why he demanded that she keep away from Tino. But after noticing that other men in the camp were keeping their distance too, she realized she didn't need her father to explain it to her. Once, while

Nisso Zuaretz demonstrated different stretches to preserve flexibility, she asked him and he finally told her what happened with Tino on the frontline. In short, breathless statements, as if trying not to hear what he was saying, he told her they knew for certain that Tino had snitched on four of his friends, saying they planned to escape and were therefore conserving their energy and not working hard on the fortifications. In exchange he received fresh bread, a plate of fine pasta, and some sweets.

Silvana mocked herself. She couldn't understand how she ever believedtrustworthiness was Tino's strong suit. Her mistaken perception of him undermined her faith in her own judgment. Now she thought she might have also been wrong about the Hebrew soldier; perhaps, beneath his trusty façade and pleasant mannerisms was a layer of traitorous malice. And as if to add insult to injury, she recalled that she'd initially liked Tino precisely because he reminded her of that soldier. But her doubts about the Hebrew soldier were short lived. They faded in light of her old thoughts, which were overtaking her heart once more. They fluttered through her mind like a flock of birds, coming in through one end of a tunnel and returning into the open air through the other end, then back again.

This time they included a brand new idea,a bird of a different feather: Silvana asked herself if after the war was over and she found him again, Amos

Vered would agree to live with her in Benghazi; were the words he whisper to her in their single night together—that he wanted to be where she was— stronger than his Zionist dream, the foundation to his sense of meaning?

She assumed her soldier would refuse to move his home from the Land of Israel to the edge of the Sahara. In spite of this, she continued to take solace in her imagination, envisioning herself and her soldier building their home in the field adjacent to her parents' house. The deeper they moved into a surprisingly mild winter, the more at home she felt in her imagined house. In the middle of February 1944 it became her true home. Whenever reality felt harder than usual, she escaped to it, and the house always waited for her with open doors and embracing walls. In her mind, she saw Amos Vered step out of it every day to manage her father's shop while she headed out to fulfil her dream of running a modern school for the Jewish sons and daughters of Benghazi. For this purpose she was willing to give up her old dream of establishing this school in Al-Jabal Al-Akhdar. She saw the two of them returning home at night, eating dinner together in their modest dining room, and chatting for hours in their cozy living room. She saw them making love in the bedroom that Toni had designed for them in return for never being treated like the little sister again. She didn't see the blindness that was evolving in her, she didn't see their dream house fall apart before it was even built, destroyed by the mightiest tractors in the world—life and death.

The winter of 1944 refused to leave Civitella del Tronto and invaded the territory of spring. The rain weakened but seemed to never end, and the cold persisted.

Bergen-Belsen

May 1944

One day in May of that year, the true winter of Silvana's life began. That morning, ten German Army trucks appeared at the gate of the camp, spitting out S.S. people. A sharp, screeching call was heard before things grew clear. "*Lass! Lass!*"[14] the soldiers shouted at the prisoners, directing them toward the trucks with gesticulations and the butts of their rifles. Silvana's instinct told her that from this point on she would no longer know what date it is, and that she must begin counting days and nights in her mind. She etched the date in her heart, May 6th. She didn't look back. She didn't want to give Civitella an opening through which it could snake its way into her mind in the future. She also didn't look ahead. She didn't want to see the sealed windows of the future. She focused fully on walking on the wet dirt, her footsteps crushing any possibility of thought before it became a thought of a possibility.

---

[14]From German: Let's go! Let's go!

Her family walked very close to her. She couldn't hear their breathing. They all walked the fifty meters to the trucks with held breath. Even the toddlers who'd spent most of their lives in Civitella made no sound. They also seemed to be waiting alertly to find out where they were headed. The trucks were on their way. At no point during their trip did their destination reveal itself. No German mentioned its name, no bit of landscape informed them about it. Once in a while, Silvana heard her mother mumbling, "*Bis ma yitalonash min Italia*, just don't let them take us out of Italy." A while later, she joined her in her mumbling. A quick glance at the other passengers confirmed her suspicion that they were saying a similar prayer. A few of them looked at the floor, others looked up as if trying to pierce the tarp above them with their pupils, and one fingered his *tefillin*, which had survived the whole way from Benghazi,

Not long thereafter, their prayers seemed to have been answered. The trucks pulled up one by one. None of the passengers recognized the place, but her father guessed they were near Modena. Even after they were taken off the truck, accompanied by the barking of two giant dogs, and looked at the view before them, they couldn't tell where they were, except that they were still in Italy. An hour later they were ordered to form rows. Then a rumor circulated that someone had seen a sign behind the building that read: "Fossoli di Carpi Transit Camp."

The news of arrival at a camp made Silvana deeply worried. "Transit" meant they hadn't reached their final destination. She was concerned they might be taken beyond the borders of Italy. She tried as hard as she could to hold back her fear, but within a few moments her restraint failed and fear began to leak out. Her mother came to her aid. She reminded Silvana that, so far, everything they thought would happen didn't, and there was no reason to believe that would change. Therefore, they shouldn't think that being in a transit camp would necessarily lead them to a permanent place. Silvana adopted this explanation. She expected the unexpected.

But a few days after arriving at Fossoli di Carpi, the most expected thing of all happened. The sun reached the center of the sky earlier than usual, and they were put on trucks and taken to a small, desolate station. This was the first time Silvana ever saw a train. It looked nothing like the trains she'd heard about from the Italian soldiers in Benghazi. At first glance, she noticed there was no seating car. A second glance told her she was right. Her father held her hand in his left and Toni's hand in his right, and Toni gave her other hand to her mother. Silvana ached to hold her mother's hand, wishing for her entire family to hold hands. She didn't do it. She was afraid it would involve turning her back to the train.

The train stood in solitude on the rusty tracks. An S.S. soldier walked by, removed his cap and asked, to the roaring laughter of his friends: *"Möchten Sie vielleicht eine fahrkarte für die erster Klasse?"*[15]

Though they couldn't understand his words, they understood the spirit in which they were spoken. Silvana recalled that moment in early 1937, when the four of them stood hugging and trembling in their kitchen, praying that the terrible noise heard from every direction would soon stop. She hoped wholeheartedly that this moment would end in a similar fashion, revealing itself not as a destructive earthquake, but merely a light one, causing little damage. The words another soldier spewed at them hinted at something completely different: *"Es lohnt sich. Es gibt dort sehr gutes essen."*[16]

Silvana felt an electrical current running a chill through their arms. She gripped her mother's hand. A scream was shot out of nowhere: *"Einsteigen!"*[17]

They got on the train. Silvana was at her lowest. The screaming, coupled with her terrible anxiety about their destination, scared her so much that she defecated in the underwear her mother had made her from a sheet in Civitella.

The view from inside was no help. The train car was almost entirely sealed. It had only two small windows that a man of average height had to stand

---

[15]From German: Would you like a first-class ticket?
[16]From German: It's worth it. They have great food there.
[17]From German: Get on!

on his toes to look through. The sight of the exposed car was only revealed to them for a few seconds before it was filled with people. People's frantic eyes spoke only of anxiety and helplessness, and their mouths gaped with shock and inability to decipher the vision. Silvana stood among them, desperate to remove her soiled underwear. The train began moving. Hours went by. Every once in a while they heard explosions, which seemed directed at the train tracks. One of the explosions, which occurred near their car, pushed the remaining feces out of Silvana's body. Her mother noticed this, pushed her through the crowd to the corner of the car, hid her with her body, helped her remove her pants and underwear, rolled them into a bundle, and placed them behind a broken wooden chair. From her large cloth bag she pulled out pants also made of sheets from the Italian fashion conglomerate of Civitella del Tronto.

After half a day on the train, hunger began demanding Silvana's attention. It wasn't the moderate hunger that had accompanied her ever since they arrived in Italy—to which she'd quickly grown accustomed—but an unbridled desire for food. She made her way through the crowd to Yona Hachmon, assuming she was hiding bread somewhere on her body. "*Zibi*," she said sharply. "Give me."

Yona understood her intention immediately, put Silvana's head to her palm and let her peck at a piece of bread she'd concealed in it, making sure no one could see what they were doing. When Silvana was finished, Yona buried half a slice in her hand and told her, "That's for Toni." Silvana made her way back to her family. Toni stood against her mother, her head resting on her chest, her eyes shut. Silvana wondered whether to wake her up to give her the bread, but decided it was best that her sister remained removed from reality. She nibbled at her sister's bread, hoping Toni didn't wake up before she finished it. Her mother, who realized what was happening, told her not to punish herself, that it was good she ate Toni's bread, because the *Tedeschi Nere* had allowed them to pack food and drink before they left the camp. This was only partly true. The S.S. did let them take food and water, but then confiscated some of it right before they boarded the train.

Another half a day later, the silence that had weighed down on the passengers began to lift. "*Ukfi!* Stop!" someone screamed from the end of the car. "*Henan nhabo ninzlo*, we want to get off," someone said from the other end, stifling a cry. The train kept going, alternately speeding and slowing down, successfully maneuvering its way among explosions near and far, passing by peasants, whose shocked expressions at the sight of a cattle train filled with people could be seen clearly even through the train's tiny window

Tino's voice sliced through the chorus of cries with an acrobatic scream. The other screams were irreversibly tangled in each other, burrowing into oneanother, while his was devoid of any other sound. It was distinct, a pure scream. "*Yasser!*" he yelled with all his might, stretching his voice to the limit. "Enough!"

Everyone heard his plight, but nobody responded. Muffled whispers began immediately: *if Tino is so hungry, let him eat himself. Perhaps he should ask his friends, the Tedeschi Nere, for a plate of pasta.* When the whispers completed their dizzying journey from throat to ear and silence returned, Tino began pushing people aside in a tizzy, carving through the human cluster left and right with a violence that had nothing to do with the old, gentle Tino Sa'adon, a man who only ever got excited about the Bible. He reached one of the corners, placed a wooden chair that had been tossed there against the wall, climbed on it, tied a sheet to a metal peg that protruded from the intersection of the wall and ceiling, wrapped the loop of the sheet around his neck, and kicked the chair away. No one rushed to his aid. His soul left him immediately, while his body remained hanging.

Out of the mélange of real hands around Silvana emerged two imaginary ones to grip her neck. She swung her head wildly, but it wasn't enough to release herself. She felt the meager air of the car skipping over her. Only after her mother leaned her against her chest did the imaginary hands slowly let go, and air gradually returned into her lungs.

The death of Tino Sa'adon seemed to revive some of the men who'd built fortifications on the frontline with him. They didn't try to conceal their joy over his death. Moreover, their exposed glee seemed to prevent them from seeing themselves, their eyes blocking out their own wretchedness. When the train slowed down, two men walked over to Tino's body and lowered it roughly, as if removing a hunk of meat from a butcher's hook. They wrapped the body in a sheet and tossed it in the corner. The image of the body didn't leave Silvana's mind, weighing down on her heart. Whenever she wanted to speak to someone, the body came between them. Silvana didn't listen to the words of consolation that were spoken into the air, such as "At least he died on Italian soil." She recalled Tino's guess, that they would never see Benghazi again. In death, Silvana gave him more credit than in his life, asking for his advice on many issues, such as whether she should try and plan another escape. There was only one subject she didn't discuss with him—faith. This subject remained off bounds in their imaginary conversations. Whenever it tried to seep in, Silvana conjured the image of Tino's body to impede the conversation. The image of the body made her cry rather than converse.

The first morning on the train was dark. Strong rays of sun invaded the car and illuminated Tino's death in a new light. Even the men who hated him, never forgetting his betrayal, were closed off.

Melancholy and horror covered people's heads like two giant domes. Nobody yelled. Nobody spoke. The smell of feces filled the car.

Silvana's father used this roaring silence to announce that from now on any food they had would be divided equally. For this purpose, he cleared off half a square meter where all food and water they managed to bring on the train was collected. They didn't know how long this ride would last, and Eliyahu Hajaj decided to distribute food sparingly. Each person received a full slice of bread for lunch and half a slice for dinner. Water was a bit more flexible. Children who asked for a sip were always granted it. Everyone assumed what they had would suffice.

But they were wrong. The train kept going even after two whole days, stopping only a few times for undefined stretches of time. More and more people approached the slightly bigger window, which people began referring to as "the most important thing in the world," for a sip of air. Some people even stood on Tino's body for this purpose. The sight of this was more than Silvana could bear.

On the third day the thirst began taking its toll on everyone. "*Meya*," people sobbed. "Water." Silvana avoided looking at people's faces as much as possible. Everyone seemed much older than they were. Even Yona Hachmon, whose fresh features everyone always gushed about, seemed old and faded. Silvana didn't want to see this, and suddenly she missed Civitella del Tronto. She wasn't the only one. Children begged their parents to take them back, women praised the place. But others were convinced they were headed to a much better place. David Halfon, whose long white beard gave him the appearance of a sage, announced they were headed to a fancy sanatorium in the Alps called San Pietro, where they would stay in excellent conditions so that they may be returned, safe and sound, in a prisoner exchange transaction. For some people, his words were a lifeline, and they held on to them for the rest of the ride. A few even asked for his source, and when he said he was told this by one of the *Tedeschi Nere* who guarded the camp, a man whose relatively pleasant demeanor was well remembered, their grip on the imaginary lifeline was renewed.

Silvana, on her part, was doubtful, but she was too exhausted to express her opinion out loud. When she felt herself choking, she leaned on Toni to lift herself up and peek beyond the most important thing in the world.

The farther they traveled, the greener the landscape became, providing fertile ground for her nightmares. As long as she saw Italian signs outside, her anxiety remained bridled. But on the third day she noticed signs in an unfamiliar language, and her nightmares broke through, the worst possible outcome knocking on the doors to her soul. As if to worsen the blow, someone behind her cried, "*Henan mush fi l'Italia tfikina minha*, we're not in Italy anymore!"

People tried to assess the situation, pushing up to the window on tiptoes, trying to look outside. No one could say where they were. The adults yelled, "*Eti l'Lilo yara*, let Eliyahu see!" Eliyahu Lilo Hajaj rose to his tiptoes and determined that they were either in Switzerland or Germany. Piercing looks were directed at David Halfon, accusing him for leaving Italy. Even his readiness to give up his water portion for the others didn't appease them, and many mumbled in rage mixed with unbridled frustration through dried throats, "San Pietro… San Pietro…" The pressure they put on him made Silvana fear he would follow in the footsteps of Tino Sa'adon, and for a long time she looked back and forth from David to the metal peg, the scene of Tino's horrid act. She only stopped when she saw a young man, whose name she couldn't recall, peering into a small water bottle and mumbling, "Who needs Eliyahu Hajaj's water." Her relationship with the indifferent submission reached the height of intimacy. Hopelessness wrapped slowly around her body, tempting her to merge with it, pushing her to see the will to fight as an ancient remnant of an irrational world.

She acquiesced, closing her eyes. Everything was quiet and nice, even the repetitious sound of the train's wheels, chik-chik-chak-chak, served as a pleasant soundtrack for their lovemaking. Even the stench rising from Tino's body could not disturb the pleasure that filled her. Silvana fell asleep. She dreamed of the Hebrew soldier, envisioning their marriage in a gorgeous ceremony, held in a place that neither of them had ever seen. A moment before the rabbi welcomed them into holy matrimony, they each went their separate ways, announcing their refusal to live in the other's country. When she awoke she thought only of him. Immersed in sleep, she didn't realize the train had slowed down and couldn't hear the conjecture of those around her. A few moments later, the third or fourth time she pictured her mother chasing her in her dream, pleading with her to go to Palestine with Amos Rosman, she heard the train stop.

They seemed to have finally reached their destination. "Saxony," said Eliyahu Hajaj. "We're in Saxony." None of them wanted to be there. They all moved their eyes between the most important thing in the world and the heavy sliding door. In spite of the thirst and heavy heat, none of them seemed to look forward to the door's opening. For the moment, it remained closed.

"I don't want to get off," announced Toni. Her father looked at her. Beneath his loving, anxious, and fatigued gaze, there was a hint of rebuke. "I don't want to get off," she repeated.

"*Binti*, there's plenty of water here," said her mother. "And I'm with you."

A while later, the door opened just a crack, as if someone outside had paused in their tracks following a sudden command. The crack between the door and its frame gave Silvana an angle on the outside world. It looked less threatening than she'd imagined. Even the barks she could now hear took nothing away from it. She even detected a happy tone in them, a kind of enthusiastic affection for the new guests. Silvana noticed that other people on the train looked less afraid too, and that a tentative relief was beginning to spread over their faces. Now the door also marked a way out of this situation. They seemed to favor this opportunity over anything else. The possibility to get on and off the train car was the most they could ask for at the moment.

The door slid a bit further, then lodged and refused all further attempts at opening it. David Halfon stepped over anyone who stood in his path to the door, wishing to close it. Somebody outside, whose thick hands were the only part of him that could be seen, tried to open the door as David Halfon tried to close it from inside. He didn't get the support he'd expected, not even from those who were more afraid of the outside than of the inside. Someone even mocked him, "*Yasser ya David*, leave it, we're at San Pietro. Let's get out." A moment later people outside the train called, "*Schwerer, schwerer.*"[18]

---

[18]From German: Harder, harder.

The door remained in place. Silvana's father suddenly said, "Look at that, the Germans aren't as strong as we thought." Silvana noticed a smile twitching on her mother's lips. It was no small feat; it was a sign that the train journey hadn't broken her spirit. In Silvana's eyes, this was testimony to the fact that her soul was still with her. She smiled.

The next attempt to open the door was also a failure. Loud voices were heard from outside, the Germans called for help. Minutes passed. Nobody came. The thick hand that had opened a crack earlier was gone. Silence spread outside the car. Inside, people ventured different guesses. Silvana was lost in thought. It occurred to her that even if she returned to Benghazi one day, she would always be sorry for Tino, for having guessed wrong.

It started to rain. A few people pounced on the crack in the door, trying to push their hands out and collect some drops of water, but were bitterly disappointed. The rain didn't return the gesture. A flock of planes was heard in the distance. The dance of rumors was in full swing. Now many believed that the Germans had left because of a British aerial attack, and that people on the train were left alone. Nobody knew how to react to this conjecture. It was neither compelling nor upsetting. A few suggested trying to open the door from inside, but nobody tried. They continued to wait and listen.

The rain grew stronger, the dogs barked angrily outside, as if incensed at the rain's invasion of their territory. "*Dahin!*" someone screamed outside. "Over there!"

A thunder of foot stomps grew louder. The people outside seemed to pass by their car. A woman standing by Silvana, who could no longer take the crowdedness, the thirst, the stink of urine and feces and the stench of Tino's rotting body, screamed, "*Henan hnaya!* We're in here!" Three pairs of hands and a large instrument were shoved through the crack in the door. This time the door opened at once, and the outside world spread before them.

"*Raus!*" called a tall, big framed soldier whose gesticulations preceded his words. "*Raus! Raus!*"

A few of them tried to lean against the wall of the car, but eventually everyone got off without taking a beating from the tall soldier's bat. Everyone managed to evade it except for Tino's body, which the soldiers beat wildly before finally throwing it off the train. They weren't able to hold a bat for long without fulfilling its purpose. About thirty seconds later, as the prisoners stumbled along the iron rails, their eyes to the gravelly ground, the bat landed again and again on the backs of slow walkers. Silvana's mother was one of them. It was the first time in her life that anyone had beaten her. She'd always boasted that no one had ever dared raise a hand to her, even as a child. As she took the blow, she grunted briefly and said nothing more. She seemed to be making every effort to carry her scrawny body with pride.

Silvana looked at Toni, who did not react, but just kept walking and mumbling that this is how their British citizenship has served them, her eyes burning holes in the tracks, as if wishing for redemption. After walking for a few hundred meters, an S.S. officer screamed at them to stop.

Suddenly, as if from another world, Silvana's father laughed and said, "Why do we have to walk? Don't they have a *carrozza*?"

On their right was a fenced camp containing long sheds and people lying on the earth like rocks. Silvana sensed what she later learned to be true: this camp would be the canvas on which her world would be painted. She looked left: a wide field with only a few trees blocking the horizon. The field was much livelier than anything she could see to her right. She'd already begun nurturing a relationship with it. She wished to view it as a source of comfort, of power, of resistance to everything inside the camp. She wished to see it as a door back to life. When they were told to turn right, she fixed her eyes on the field, her neck stretching to the left. As they moved farther away, it never left her thoughts, even as her body advanced right through the gates of Bergen-Belsen.

"Welcome to hell, black woman!" Those were the first words she heard at Bergen-Belsen, coming from the lips of an older, long-faced man. "We are all

Jews here." Had he not looked like a man eaten up by despair, Silvana might have thought he resembled one of the Rosenzweigs she'd met in Benghazi. Unlike her and the other Libyan Jews coming out of the cars, the prisoners at Bergen-Belsen were all white. The moment they walked intothe camp Toni said, "*Tima yehud taneyn ma yeshabhulnash*, the Jews here don't look anything like us."

The Germans led them to the central shed, shed 210. The number flickered in Silvana's mind. She recalled hearing a sage in Benghazi say that redemption and the end of exile would arrive in 210 years. Now this number was burned in her mind for a completely different reason: the fear that she might get lost on the paths of the camp and walk into the wrong shed. She didn't know the other Jews and had no reason to trust them.

The shed where she was housed with her family and the other Libyan prisoners was long. It was reminiscent of the gym at Talmud Torah. The moment they crossed the threshold, Toni quickened her steps and announced she was going to save them a good spot. Silvana walked behind her, pulling her mother, who was dragging her father, who was looking around anxiously. An S.S. man signaled for them to climb onto the bunk beds at the end of the shed.

The bunks were small and covered with two gray blankets. Silvana and Toni gave their parents the one against the wall, which was a few centimeters wider, and got on the other bunk. There was no way to get a proper night's sleep on those things. Even when the sisters pushed up against each other as tight as they could, the bunk was still too small to contain them. They didn't move, knowing they must be careful: the smallest shift by one of them would push the other to the ground. Silvana wanted to erase the memory of cold nights in Benghazi, when she crawled into Toni's wide bed. She tried not to recall the game of *Bicicletta* they'd played in those long lost days—how they held onto each other, pretending to pedal their feet. Toni also avoided remembering their bedtime games. Silvana lay straight as an arrow all night long, facing the ceiling, and chatted with herself about their childhood play without uttering one word about the games, in which they used blankets, pillows, and sheets.

From time to time Silvana carefully and slowly turned her head toward her parents, making sure their bed was indeed wider, and that they were sleeping better than she and her sister. A few times she even wished for them to shift a bit so that she could be sure they had enough room on the bunk she'd given them. "Everything's fine, go back to sleep," she told her mother whenever she thought she was awake and about to address her with a question. Only the next day did she realize she'd been speaking into the stifling air of the shed, her brain devoured by delusion, seeing as how her mother had slept through the night.

Silvana, on the other hand, spent a significant part of the night crying over the death of Tino Sa'adon, and yearning for his presence.

Dawn penetrated the shed like an uninvited guest. To see it in full Silvana had to turn to her side, but she couldn't do this without pushing Toni off the bunk. Instead, she lay still and waited for the light to come to her. A woman in a nearby bunk mumbled that even morning was afraid of this place. Muffled barks were heard from outside. Silvana thought of the roosters that awoke her for a moment in winter before she curled up in her red blanket, a gift from her grandmother in Tripoli for her fourteenth birthday. It suddenly dawned on her that they were lucky to have arrived here in summer. The thought of Bergen-Belsen in winter annihilated all other thoughts. She could feel nothing but terror.

Thirty minutes later, morning spread through the heart of the shed and her mother woke up. She reached for Silvana and Toni, saying nothing about their tiny bunk. Instead, she signaled for them to keep quiet so as not to wake up their father. His face was serene. Silvana envied him, suddenly infuriated. She couldn't bear the thought that he was sleeping soundly while she'd been awake all night. She even pondered waking him up, but a soldier in the doorway beat her to it, screaming "*Raus! Alle raus!*"[19]

---

[19]From German: Out! Everybody out!

"Roll-call!" They all rose urgently to their feet, adjusting their striped uniform, patting it for something invisible before they walked outside. "*Haf!* Hurry!" people called from all over. Silvana gripped her father's still sleepy body to help her make her way out to the yard. Her mother, who dragged behind, took a beating from a man who urged her to hurry up.

As it turned out later, the man was a Capo and had spoken Yiddish. He had some sort of conversation with Yona Hachmon, who demonstrated a sudden courage. "*Rirt zich schoin, vaibel! Rirt zich!*"[20] he said, and she answered, "*Tayeb*, all right," and so forth until they were finally outside. A few junior S.S. soldiers were waiting for them, holding giant, proud, fine looking dogs on leashes, waiting intently for some sort of go-ahead. The go-ahead appeared within minutes in the form of a two-horse wagon, on top of which stood a fat officer. "*Was sind das für Menschen?*"[21] the officer asked, his expression a mixture of grudge and wonder, turning to one of the S.S. men who were holding the dogs. "*Was Machen die hier?*"[22]

The soldier choked up, then said, "*Sie sind schwarz Juden. Sie sind aus Afrika hierher gebracht.*"[23]

---

[20]From Yiddish: Move it, woman! Move it!

[21]From German: What are these people?

[22]From German: What are they doing here?

[23]From German: They're black Jews. They were brought over from Africa.

Silvana's father, who knew some German, whispered a translation to his daughter. Silvana giggled quietly. For a moment she dared to think the officer would realize a mistake had been made and let them go, but she stood corrected. The officer, whose rank was *Obersturmführer*, whipped the horses lightly, and they pounded their hooves against the gravel rhythmically, allowing the wheels of the wagon to say their part too. When the wagon was behind them the officer yelled something to the soldiers and the horses galloped away.

Then a soldier whose simple uniform, bare of insignia, made him seem lowly, stood at attention and ordered them to form rows of five, saying, "*Ein langen tag wartet auf euch. Eine lange Woche. Ein langes Jahr. Eine lange Leben und eine kurze tod, hier in Bergen-Belsen.*"[24] Two higher ranking soldiers tried to hush him, but he wouldn't stop. Silvana couldn't understand his words, but easily recognized their cruel, mocking tone. One of the soldiers who hushed him began counting heads. After the third count, he left, leaving them at the mercy of their crushed hopes.

They didn't move. By the power of some unspoken order, they knew they weren't allowed to move. Silvana stared into the air, which was so

---

[24]From German: You have a long day ahead of you. A long week. A long year. A long life and a fast death, here in Bergen-Belsen.

thick she thought it might break. The screaming of a woman sounded in the distance, followed by a burst of gunfire. The prisoners planted their feet into the ground. Utter silence. It started to rain. Silvana looked up and opened her mouth to get some hydration, but the raindrops seemed to trick her, landing in front of her, behind her, and to her sides. She gave up and dropped her head. Thirty minutes later, when thirst was already prickling her throat, she looked up again. This time she was able to capture a few drops.

She looked at her mother and was stunned once again to see how small she'd gotten. Her clavicle seemed to be pulled out of her body, her eyes filled her entire face, her cheeks were sunken. But the sight of her mother also gave her pleasure, imagining what she must have looked like as a young girl. The older people in her town had often told her it was a shame she hadn't seen her mother when she was young. She'd heard her aunts say many times that Silvana only believed she took after her father because she hadn't seen her mother as a girl. Now, for the first time, she realized what they meant. When her mother stood up straight and whispered that they would keep standing for as long as necessary, that they were strong, Silvana hoped that their resemblance was more than just physical.

Though she wanted very badly to leave the row, go off somewhere and scream her heart out, she remained in place, still as a sculpture. From time to time she spotted someone in the row ahead of her twitching an arm or a leg, and held back from mimicking the movement. She took her mother's words to be a general instruction, though no punishment could be expected for moving a limb. She felt that good exercise now would allow her to withstand more difficult scenarios in the future. Someone behind her whispered that they'd been standing for over an hour. Silvana had no doubt the woman was right. It was the same woman she'd heard counting out loud earlier: "*Alpin hams mia uahad*, one-thousand five-hundred and two…" —Libyan Jews (mayor iauy) just 1 bunk

The rain stopped and the sky began to clear up. Deep in her heart, Silvana nurtured a hope that the fickleness of the weather would also inform other things, but a few moments later she received a clear sign of this camp's consistency. A short S.S. soldier with a wide face and longish hair appeared before them. He looked at them wordlessly. Twenty minutes later he turned around and left them alone again. Silvana was surprised to find herself yearning for his return. Standing alone was much more difficult than standing before him. His authority formed the illusion that she wasn't alone in the world, that there was order to things, that chaos was nothing more than a passing impression.

Her legs began to hurt; her knees buckled. She glanced at the heavier people around her, wondering how their knees were able to carry their weight. No one whimpered. No complaints were heard. The prisoners all continued to stand and listen to the eerie quiet, as if it would be the source of their redemption. But no redemption appeared on the horizon, Yona's whispered song rising in its place, breaking boundaries in this moment, of all moments: "*Samra ya samra ya camla faz'zin*," she sang. "Black, black, epitome of beauty."

Everyone slowly joined in. Toni's voice overtook others. She loved this song. Even Silvana, who hated the song and often mocked Toni's love of something so maudlin, joined the group, and for a moment, her voice and her sister's voice were competing. She recalled the German soldier who urged her on in Benghazi, calling her "*Afrikaner*," and wanted her singing to be so loud that the words "*Samra ya samra*" broke through the walls of Bergen-Belsen and spread, confident and echoing, throughout all of Germany. For a fraction of a second, she wanted Africa to shake the land of the S.S. But no German soldiers were around to listen, much less to understand or respond.

The singing slowly died out. People fidgeted more and more within their rows. Once in a while someone muttered something about not being able to take it anymore. Someone spat, "Tino Sa'adon *ando mazal* God help him. He doesn't need to stand here." A man standing behind Silvana kneeled on the ground, and soon many others joined him. Silvana's mother, worried that her daughter would see this as an opportunity to refuse orders, repeated, "Silvana! *Ma zilna wakfin!* <u>We keep standing!</u>"

Thirty minutes later an S.S. man finally arrived. It was one of the soldiers that had hushed the junior soldier earlier. He counted them with inconceivable slowness. When he was finished, they expected him to say something, give an order, but he only hummed, "*Gut*," and stood before them, as if waiting for an official to arrive and order him around.

The minutes ticked by and nobody appeared. They remained standing or sitting, watching the soldier who was watching them. It started to rain again, and more grumbling was heard from within the rows. The soldier didn't take his eyes off them, mesmerized. Only a while later, when the officer in charge arrived and said, laughing, "Was guckst du die so an? Wüsstest du nicht dass die Afrikaner erst zeit vier generationen aufrecht gehen?"[25] did his expression change. Other than Silvana's father, <u>no one could understand what the officer said, but they all knew he'd mocked them.</u> No one protested, not even to themselves. They only longed for some kind of order to let them move. But none came. The officer pulled the soldier away and whispered with him for

---

[25]From German: What are you looking at them for? <u>Don't you know that the Africans have only been upright for the past four generations?</u>

a long time. He lit a cigarette, making amused and serious expressions between puffs.

Suddenly, with no notice, Silvana's mother stepped out of the line, approached the officer, stood up as tall as she could, and said, "*Non possiamo più stare in piedi*, we can't stand any longer." Whether or not he knew Italian, the S.S. officer tossed his cigarette to the ground, stomped on it with his boot, and gestured with his head for the soldier to release the prisoners. The soldier approached them and gesticulated for them to split into two groups of men and women. This unified all shards of thought into a bullet that lodged in Silvana's brain: the men would be taken away again. She clung to her father. Her anticipated longing for him was so tangible, like a living blockade preventing him from being taken away. Only after she realized the men were being taken to do construction within the camp did she relax and let go of her father. Her mother, Toni, and she were taken with the other women to a nearby shed, where they were given jobs the Germans had deemed feminine. They were ordered to clean the bathrooms and to pull weeds that had grown wild around the shed.

Silvana liked this work. She lost herself in it. Work pushed out all memories. As long as she cleaned the bathroom she didn't think of Benghazi, Tino, or the future. But there was one thought this work could not push out of her mind—the image of the Hebrew

soldier. Thinking of him was like stepping into a
hidden tunnel and escaping Bergen-Belsen. A path
leading to a totally different world.

After several hours of work they were called
outside. Each woman received a bowl of soup and
a piece of stale bread. Silvana and Toni downed
their soups voraciously and gobbled down the bread.
Their mother didn't touch the soup. She said it
wasn't kosher, that it smelled like pork lard. Silvana
thought of her father. She knew he would refuse
to eat the soup too, making do with the bread, and
was worried that if he insisted upon this his power
would soon dwindle. At night, when they returned
to their shed, her worries only worsened. Her father
told them they'd been taken outside the camp to fell
trees, then declared he would never eat the Germans'
soup. Silvana didn't try to convince him otherwise.
She knew it was pointless. She fell asleep quickly, no
longer afraid to push Toni off the bed, so exhausted
that she'd lost the ability to move.

The next day was the same: standing aimlessly
in rows, being counted over and over, complaining,
knees buckling, splitting into men and women. But
when Silvana went to clean the bathroom in one of
the German soldiers' barracks, something happened
that made this day different: she met Rebecca.

Rebecca was in her early twenties (Silvana later
learned she was born on August 21st, 1920, the same
year as she). She was about 170 centimeters tall, her

legs strong and skinny, her face narrow, and her blue eyes slightly slanted. Her thick lips seemed to be borrowed from the American actresses Silvana saw in movies at Bendosa Theatre, her eyebrows expertly drawn. Even her shaved head took nothing away from her beauty. Silvana had never stood so close to someone with almost translucent skin before, not even when she met the fair Rosenzweigs back in Benghazi. She looked at her own hands, realizing for the first time how dark her skin was.

"Rebecca Rice," said the woman, dropping her rag into a bucket of water, and giving Silvana her hand.

"Silvana Hajaj," said Silvana, taking her hand. Her body loosened at once. For the first time in a long time she felt tension leaving her body rather than entering it. Silvana didn't know what language to speak, and finally asked, *"Parli Italiano?"*

"Un po," said Rebecca. "But I prefer to speak English."

After a few moments of perfectly comfortable silence, Rebecca told Silvana she was a Jew from Holland, and that she'd been brought to Bergen-Belsen with a large group of people. Her father owns a large publishing house in Amsterdam, where she sometimes works as a translator's apprentice. She emphasized the word "works," present tense. Silvana chose not to comment on the fact that she spoke of her job as if she'd just gone on short leave, instead asking her if her parents were with her. Rebecca said they didn't live in the same shed and lowered her eyes. Silvana was curious and wanted to ask more questions, but then they heard a German scream outside and returned to cleaning the bathroom. A few moments later a German soldier walked in. Something in the physical opposition between the two young women caused him to tell Rebecca, *"Wenn sie glaubst du bist anders als sie, nur weil sie schwarz ist, dann täuscht du dich gewaltig. Juden sind einen immer schwarz. Manchmal sieht man es auch von aussen, manchmal nicht."*[26]

The soldier went into one of the stalls to pee, singing to himself loudly. After leaving the bathroom in song and going out of earshot, Rebecca translated what he'd said to Silvana, rubbing her arm gently. Her touch imbued Silvana with renewed energy. She decided to use it wisely, not wasting it on unnecessary things. Rather than clean the bathroom vigorously she moved her hands slowly, chatting with Rebecca. The more they talked, the more impressed she was with the wisdom of the young Dutch woman, who analyzed each and every matter profoundly and soberly.

---

[26]From German: If you think you're any different from her because she's black, think again. [Jews are always black on the inside] Sometimes you can see it from the outside, and sometimes you can't.

Only on one matter did Rebecca's blindness persist: her job at her father's publishing house in Amsterdam, which she always spoke of in the present tense. Silvana decided not to say a thing, worried she might anger her new friend and ruin their budding relationship.

At night in the shed Silvana told Toni about her meeting with Rebecca.

Toni only said, "*Ma tinsayesh hiya mush kifna.* Don't forget she isn't like us."

Silvana was neither surprised nor disappointed by Toni's reserved response. What kind of disappointment could she feel in a place like Bergen-Belsen? This emotion did not pass the strict selection process that camp guards utilized for sensations that wished to enter its realm.

Silvana fell asleep quickly. That night, unlike the previous two, she fell from her bed, crashed to the floor, and woke up with alarm. The noise didn't even wake up Toni. A thought shot through Silvana's mind: that her sister might have pushed her off on purpose. When she got a hold of herself she realized that such a thought was a sign that this place must be driving her mad. She climbed back onto the bunk and tried every possible position that wouldn't disturb her sister's sleep within this tight space. Finally she lay down with her face near Toni's feet. This position gave her a new view of the shed. Everyone looked dead. Their faces and bodies were so utterly fatigued that they barely seemed able to breathe. From time to time she heard snoring, and the sounds of coitus came from one bed whose head posts were the only things she could see. She slipped her hand into her pants and fantasized about the Hebrew soldier. *masturbating? Bring num.*

The next morning the count was even slower than usual. This time they were counted by an officer nicknamed "Goebbels" due to his resemblance to the Nazi Minister of Propaganda. The man was short, limped slightly, and spoke a rather rich German. This Goebbels counted and counted, never finishing. When he got to around eighty, he cleared his throat and began counting again, limping around the prisoners. No one dared speak, but when he cut his third or fourth count short, a woman behind Silvana sighed with despair and began counting anew with him. He paused his count immediately and signaled for her to step forward. When the woman walked by, Silvana was surprised to find it was Yona Hachmon. She was astonished to realize, once again, how little we know the people closest to us. True, even when she sang "*Samra ya samra*" Yona Hachmon had broken through the boundaries of her personality as perceived by others, but this time she took a real chance. She walked confidently toward Goebbels, her back straight and her head held high, defiantly demonstrating the beauty of the black Jewish woman. She seemed to Silvana like the picture of beauty. All those times she was irritated by Yona's exaggerated tendency to get dolled up were wiped away from her mind. She now felt utter love for her.

Goebbels slapped Yona, and Silvana's cheek burned.

"*Ma titcharkish!* Don't move!" her mother ordered, knowing that Silvana was liable to speak up. But Silvana was unable to move. Her entire body was paralyzed with fear. In spite of the slap, Yona Hachmon looked up at the soldier with contempt.

Goebbels removed his hat, ran his fingers around it for a while, and then, to everybody's surprise, ordered Yona to return to her row. Though he'd never finished counting, he didn't pick it up again. Instead, he signaled to his subordinates to take the prisoners to work. Silvana prayed to be sent to clean the bathrooms again. She hoped to meet Rebecca Rice again, wanted to hear her soft speech and listen to her learned explanations. Though she made up her mind not to discuss Rebecca's blind spot, she wanted to experience it once more. It consoled and encouraged her, persuading her to believe that she could fool herself too, enjoying the illusion as long as reality allowed.

But this too was an illusion. Unlike Rebecca, Silvana was unable to lead herself on even for a moment. The instant after Goebbels ordered Yona Hachmon to return to her place, choosing not to punish her, she was convinced that Yona would be made to pay doubly later on. On her way to work she tried to get close to Yona, to give her a hug, but failed. A soldier walked by her side, preventing any chance of rushing ahead. Only when they got to her place of work—this time, to her regret, not the bathroom, but the officers' barracks—did Silvana manage to reach out and give her a quick hug. Her frustration worsened.

Silvana and Toni were put in a room on the floor of which was a mountain of army uniforms, rising to kiss the ceiling. A pile of civilian clothing towered beside it. In the corner sat an old man, quickly sewing pants. He didn't slow down even as the soldier spoke to him, and only looked up at the girls after the soldier left. He fixed them with a surprised look that emphasized a wrinkled face, and mumbled something in Yiddish. They couldn't understand him but caught a name he repeated, Moshe Katzman. The old man detected their embarrassment, rose to his feet with difficulty, and explained with gestures to Toni that she had to iron the clothing piled to the left, and to Silvana that she had to sew buttons on the pants to the right. Though they weren't very skilled in these tasks, the two went to work as if they were the Cyrenaica champions of sewing and ironing. After five hours of energetic work, during which they spoke as little as possible in order to avoid Old Katzman's glares, they went out to the yard, where they received soup and two pieces of bread.

The weather was beginning to change. The sun that burned the sky of Bergen-Belsen in the morning, allowing no one to hide—as if urgently trying to expose what was happening there—made way for a gathering of dark clouds galloping over from the north. Silvana ate her soup and bread slowly. She remembered how she used to take slow sips of *brudo*, the special chicken soup her mother made on holidays. She remembered the flavor of the soup, but couldn't recall the city in which she'd enjoyed it, Benghazi, her beloved hometown. The sea, the low houses, the sand, the synagogue, and the mosques were swallowed in the anxieties that drowned her mind. Benghazi became a nowhere in her mind. For the first time since she was forced to leave, she conversed in her mind with the absence of the city, rather than with the city itself. She wondered what it meant that she couldn't picture her hometown.

She finished her soup, leaned against the wall, and tried to conjure up the image of Benghazi from her imagination. This failed too, and even her deep breathing didn't help the image appear. Not only Benghazi was erased, Silvana's entire past was melting away in her mind.

She wanted to hold onto something to remind her of her history. To do this, she looked up at Toni, who sat in front of her with legs spread out, her face in the bowl of soup. Toni was thinner than ever, her fingers bending like knitting needles. Silvana could no longer imagine her outside of Bergen-Belsen. Though they'd only been there a short time, the place enforced the sense of having been there forever. The prisoners' blind obedience seemed to have erased the world outside the camp, their submissive feet trampling it.

Silvana stood up and walked toward the latrines, which were set in an open space at the edge of the camp. On the way over, her eyes searched for a piece of paper, but could not find one. When she was about fifteen meters away, she saw a small notepad fall out of the pocket of a German soldier walking ahead of her. She slowed down, and when he wasn't looking, bent down casually and picked up the notepad. The right pages had short statements that looked like a to-do list, and the left had long statements that seemed like a detailing of the tasks' performance. After making sure the soldier was far away enough, she shoved the notepad down her pants and continued on to the latrine. She found a corner that seemed hidden enough, lowered her pants, and crouched down. She peed easily, but could not defecate.

"Silvana," she suddenly heard a voice behind her. "Silvana."

She looked back. "Rebecca, Rebecca," she said, excited. She wiped herself with a page from the notepad, pulled up her pants, and ran to Rebecca. Since there were no German soldiers around, they had a long, uninterrupted embrace. Silvana didn't want to let go of her friend. All she wanted was to sink into Rebecca's body, to hear her heartbeat, to smell her hair and gain reassurance that they were only there for a short while and would soon return to their old lives.

Their embrace was not subject to the concept of time. It mocked the notion of quantification. Even when they let go of each other, the embrace lived on in all its tangibility, like an independent being that even they couldn't put to an end.

"Last night I slept, I really slept," Rebecca told Silvana, sitting down on the ground and pulling Silvana down.

"*Sha nitc?*" asked Silvana. Only after Rebecca stared at her questioningly for a moment, she corrected herself: "What do you mean?"

Rebecca looked beyond the fence of the camp and said, rolling a pebble between her fingers, "I woke up only five or six times."

The two of them continued to talk until they heard soldiers approaching. They hugged again and made plans to try and meet at the latrine at the same time the next day.

But the next day was torn off the necklace of days. The next morning the prisoners waited outside as usual, scared of the arrival of one of the officers. Thirty minutes later, Goebbels appeared and miraculously smiled at them politely.

"*Had el-Calb ma zal yadna*," Toni whispered. "Is that dog going to count us a million times again?"

Goebbels never finished counting this time either. When he counted aloud "*dreiunddreissig*"[27] Eliyahu Hajaj collapsed. Silvana, her sister, and her mother leaned down over him, crying, "*Baba*, Lilo, Eliyahu, *ya rabi*," their cries coalescing into one mighty wail. Within seconds her mother yelled, "*Hua mat!* He's dead! I'm dying!" The father died ?

Two soldiers lunged at her quickly and pulled her off her husband's body. She didn't stop screaming even after being punched in the face.

A horse-drawn wagon appeared a minute or two later. Two soldiers pushed the prisoners aside roughly and ordered two others to load Eliyahu Hajaj's body onto the wagon, which began moving out of the camp instantly. Julia Hajaj watched the wagon moving away, and her loud sobs continued. Silvana and Toni stood at her side the whole time, and then began following her like ghosts. Silvana remembered nothing from that moment until the end of the day. This period of time was completely erased from her mind, forever locked in the time and place of its occurrence, evading her memory forever.

She didn't see the camp in the following weeks, and her soul did not see her father's death. Everything

---

[27]From German: Thirty-three.

became horridly abstract. The shadows of bizarre visions and the distant echoes of pleas mixed together, carrying her like a cloud outside of reality. Even her mother's and sister's attempts to get a hold of themselves could not break the screen of inner fog that seemed to precede her like an industrious guide. Only her brief meetings with Rebecca threatened to rip through the screen, but they also failed. Whenever her friend's comfort and encouragement reminded her of the reality of her father's death, she conjured Rebecca's mantra—that they would soon return to their previous lives—to preserve the unrealistic state of her mind.

This went on until the end of August, when something happened to shatter the wall between her and the world, making her father's death real and alive. A prisoner named Carl Rott was appointed by the S.S. as head nurse and ordered to inject two-hundred prisoners with a sanitizer called Phenol, murdering them. This horrid act created a critical mass of evil. It charged Bergen-Belsen with a wave of horror and anguish, and rather than continuing to hover over Silvana like an ethereal balloon, her father's death crashed to the ground with a great explosion.

One of the people who were murdered was Rebecca's father. His death turned Silvana and her into sisters. From that point on, their souls were irrevocably intertwined, even when they were not physically near each other. Whenever they met they collapsed into one another, as if wishing to salvage from each other a replacement for the father they no longer had. Their tears mixed together. Silvana wiped Rebecca's tears with her drenched hands, and Rebecca did the same for her friend.

But crying did not compromise their ability to clearly see the suffering of others. The families of the murder victims, wallowing in their pain, appeared before them many times. Sometimes Rebecca even argued that they had to put their own suffering aside for the moment and try to help others. Silvana agreed, but had trouble translating words into action.

She therefore helped Rebecca help others, simultaneously helping her bear her burden. Thus, one night she snuck into Rebecca's shed to cheer up a girl named Marila Dolitzki, whose mother was one of Carl Rott's victims. Marila described again and again how a few years earlier Polish thugs broke into their house at night and her mother managed to convince them to rape her, thus sparing Marila, her only daughter. Marila kept repeating her wish to follow in her mother's footsteps and kill herself. Rebecca embraced her for a long time, held her face next to hers, and begged her in Polish and German, repeating that she should continue living precisely for her mother's sake. Silvana, who only later received a translation from Rebecca, stood aside, whispering to Marilla, "*Ma yikon kan h'eyr ma t'hapish.* Don't be afraid. It's going to be all right."

As she returned to her shed that night, she continued to repeat to herself what she'd told Marilla, but had trouble internalizing her own calming words. The sentence she said sounded less rational than all the German and Polish statements she'd heard and didn't understand. She lay on the bunk and looked at the adjacent one. Since their father's death, she and Toni took turns sharing a bed with their mother. Tonight was Toni's turn, her shriveled chest against their mother's body. The two of them seemed to be wishing never to wake up, remaining entangled in each other forever, frozen in their position. In spite of her exhaustion, Silvana couldn't sleep. For the first time she truly tried to think clearly of her father's death. The effort only further troubled her soul.

Among her thoughts, the realization that there was no chance she could ever return to her previous life came to her again and again. In the absence of her previous life from the future ahead of her, she thought, she only had to think of the present. Thus, each day, she had to use her meager powers to create an imperative for living. Only after she was completely taken over by inertia did this need subside. But most prisoners were not yet taken by this force. They asked themselves over and over why they did what they were doing, and whether it wasn't better to undertake an act of desperate courage that would release them from their lives at once. Luckily for Silvana, she still had her friend

Rebecca to help her find something to commit her to life each time anew. Thanks to her, she did not drown in the nothing and did not give in to despair. After her father's death, Rebecca's words mostly carried ethical meaning. She explained to Silvana repeatedly that they were serving as role models for many around them, and that even from their place of rest, their fathers expected them to continue to fight for their lives. Silvana mainly internalized the latter part of this message. She often felt herself enveloped in her father's expectation, which closed around her like a giant sack. In her heart, she spoke to her father's reflection with tearful eyes and a choked throat, promising not to put him to shame, never to break, to be a leader like he always wanted, to care for her mother and Toni, to return to Benghazi and reopen his business. She kept telling him how much she loved him. Whenever she spoke to him, she only saw the old Eliyahu Hajaj in her mind's eye, the one she'd known in her life in Benghazi. His new image, the one that appeared with the German invasion, was completely lost.

This received special articulation one day in September. That day was a day of celebration for her and the image of her father. She told him she had taken a part in the killing of the Capo Carol Rott. She described in detail how Rebecca, who knew the details of a plan formed by a few prisoners to take revenge on the criminal, had shared this information with her, telling her to wait behind the shed in exactly an hour. Only when they arrived at the meeting place did Rebecca explain to her that they were about to participate in Rott's killing. With tearful eyes and a shaking voice, Silvana told her father that in spite of her fear, she knew she was doing the right thing by helping Rebecca and another prisoner plug Rott's nose and mouth while others grabbed his hands and legs and beat him madly all over his body. One of them even sliced off Rott's penis with a shiv. When the Germans found out and couldn't get an admission from anyone, they shot ten people who were chosen at random. She also spoke of the shock she'd gotten after the murder, and of her left hand that hadn't stopped trembling since. She smiled at her father's image in the story's beginning and at its end, seeing them more clearly than ever, came closer and whispered in his ear: "I know you're proud of what I've done. I was a good girl, Father. I was a good daughter."

She felt better the next day. The trembling in her hand subsided. Though she'd barely eaten any solid food for days, she walked out to the morning roll-call with a spring in her step. For a moment she even had another forbidden thought about her anticipated reunion with her Hebrew soldier. The mental strength she'd acquired helped her carry the souls of her mother and Toni. During roll-call, she whispered words of encouragement to them. For the first time since her father's death, they seemed to have regained their will to live. Toni no longer whispered evil words about Goebbels, afraid he might hear her, instead standing at attention, prepared to carry out his orders. Her mother, on the other hand, spoke. She answered Silvana's whispers with her own whispers of encouragement, and continued to do so even after roll-call was over.

That day, Silvana and her mother were sent to pull weeds around the Nazi officers' barracks. As they worked, her mother told her that when she returned home the first thing she would do was pull the weeds that had surely grown wild in the yard, because Father probably couldn't bear to see the yard like that.

For the first time since they arrived in Bergen-Belsen, Silvana could clearly see their house in Benghazi. She held onto it with all her might. She knew the image would serve as a viewpoint from which she could see her city. As she leaned down to pull the weeds, the different parts of the city began to emerge. Though many parts of the puzzle were missing, one thing revealed itself: the special light of Libya, famous for uniting the hard with the soft in perfect harmony. This light imbued her with a warmth she hadn't felt for a long time. She wanted to indulge in it, to provide the abstract promise it contained with a tangible dimension. She continued to pull out weeds with stiff fingers, her heart singing a hope that one day she would see and feel the warmth of Libyan light again.

This music of her heart was short-lived. Suddenly, her mother collapsed before her eyes, crying her husband's name. Silvana lunged at her, and when she realized Julia's body hadn't been hurt, she lay on the cold ground beside her and put her arms around her, trying to console her, but to no avail. They both cried, and their crying did not bring them any relief. It only released their bodies from the meaning of their existence. They wished for their death, lying in each other's arms, curled together within the spirit of Eliyahu Lilo Hajaj. At the sound of an approaching engine, Silvana stood up and pulled her mother along. They went back to work.

That night, Silvana told Toni they had to take better care of their mother, not only sleeping by her side, but remaining as close as possible to her during the day as well. Toni nodded in agreement and suggested they tell one of Goebbels's soldiers, or even Goebbels himself, that thanks to the blind understanding between the three of them, they'd be able to reach full efficiency if they worked together, sewing or washing or doing any other task. Silvana agreed and climbed up to their mother's bunk.

That morning, their mother refused to go outside for roll-call. Silvana and Toni dragged her out by force. When Silvana stood in the freezing yard, hearing the hollow screaming of soldiers and seeing

Goebbels's conceited pose, any thought of asking
him for anything evaporated. She held her mother
close and hoped they'd be sent to work together
again. This did happen, but with one important
change. This time, Toni was sent with them.

Silvana's joy over this was short-lived as well.
She gradually realized that Toni was about to break.
She hoped that her sister would hold on, but couldn't
escape the feeling that this time Toni would fall
beyond a point of no return. This wasn't an immediate
conclusion. From that day on, she watched Toni sink
into herself under the double burden of their father's
death and the inability to escape her own fate.

Silvana, on her part, leaned on Rebecca more
and more so she could carry her mother and sister.
She did everything in her power to see her. For this
purpose, she snuck into the shed where Rebecca
slept more and more often, met her at the latrine
whenever she could, and even skippedout on her
randomly assigned work place to go to her soul
sister's randomly assigned workplace.

Her meetings with Rebecca almost always
recharged her with new power that allowed her to
also give faith to her mother and sister. Rebecca
almost never gave her the feeling that things were
hopeless; moreover, she almost always discussed the
good future they had ahead of them after the war.
One day, when they finished their business in the
latrine, Rebecca lit a cigarette she'd swindled out of

a capo, then translated into different languages a line from the Italian song Silvana's mother had sung as they climbed to the castles at Civitella del Tronto: "A person must keep dreaming." For some reason, Silvana remembered the German version best, and at night, as her stomach churned with hunger, she repeated to herself: "*Mann muss immer träumen. Mann muss immer träumen.*"

Still, there was one occasion when she felt despair latching on even to the strong and optimistic Rebecca. Silvana was worried that she might lose hold of her mother and Toni as a result. It was mid-October, and Bergen-Belsen was taken over by paralyzing cold. It defeated everyone: elderly, children, German soldiers, even hunger and thirst. Silvana and Rebecca sat in Silvana's shed, huddled together in an attempt to stay warm, saying nothing. There was no resemblance between their silences. Silvana's silence was full of anticipation for Rebecca's words that would help her deal with the cold, while Rebecca's silence now contained buds of life's negation.

But the very next day, as they met as usual in the open field, Rebecca told her excitedly that she was using her relationship with their capo, whose bad reputation as a cruel man earned him the nickname "Carl Rott the Second": he was infatuated with her, and she used this to get all sorts of favors. As if to demonstrate, Rebecca pulled a sandwich from under her shirt. Silvana leapt on it without considering the fact that her friend might want half. Only when she was more than halfway through, she asked Rebecca if she wanted any. Rebecca lovingly answered that it was all for her, but Silvana couldn't keep eating. She remembered how hungry her mother was. She only ate the sausage, licking the bread clean of butter like a starved beast, so that she could bring it to her mother clean of anything unkosher.

Rebecca, who knew very well that Silvana was gathering strength from her to support her mother and sister, said she would sneak out of her shed at night and come to sleep with them. Silvana's pleading, which was only for show, begging her not to put herself in danger by coming over, was in vain. That night, which was as dark as if God had ripped out the moon and the stars, Rebecca appeared at their shed. Upon hearing Silvana's name, some people thought a German soldier had arrived. People whispered, "A new German soldier!"

Silvana stood up and announced, "It isn't a soldier." The shed fell silent. Everyone tried to get a glimpse of the stranger, but it was just too dark. Silvana walked to the doorway and gestured for Rebecca to wait. She heard a new rustle traveling through the shed, a rustle of trepidation mixed with sorrow: this woman may not be a German, but she was certainly no Jew. Silvana tried angrily to stifle her voice as she muttered, "This is my friend Rebecca, and she's Jewish, just like us. She's from Holland!" She led

Rebecca to their bunks. Toni greeted her coolly, while Silvana's mother kissed her head and said, "*Sei mia figlia*, you're my daughter."

For about two hours, Rebecca gently coaxed Julia into talking about her husband and her life in Libya. Whenever Julia stopped talking, Rebecca put her hand on her shoulder patiently. Finally she promised her she'd be back in Benghazi, and asked Julia to take good care of her eyes so that she could see Benghazi for Eliyahu as well. Upon hearing these things, Toni got up and gave Rebecca's hand a long shake, the way Benghazi men did. Though it was Silvana's turn to sleep with her mother, Toni tucked in beside her, allowing Silvana and Rebecca to share a bed.

They lay down together, and soon enough Silvana could no longer tell her heartbeats apart from Rebecca's. They both joined in to form one melody. She woke up in the middle of the night at the sound of Rebecca crying, an ongoing, whispered cry. She didn't touch her or try to soothe her. An inner voice told her not to intervene in this moment trapped in her friend's soul. She also wanted Rebecca to stretch her crying out, letting it clean her soul and strengthen her resistance.

Silvana fell into a deep sleep. She awoke to a perplexing sight: the boys of her shed were dressing the older men so that they would make it to roll-call on time. Toni held her mother's hand like a mother holding her disobedient child, hushing her whenever she said she didn't want to go out. The morning light was nowhere to be seen. One thing still cheered Silvana up—Rebecca was no longer there; the Germans wouldn't notice she'd been gone from her shed. In her place were words written with mud on the wall: *Sono Tornata*.[28] Once again she was impressed by Rebecca's modesty. She'd never mentioned she knew how to write in Italian.

Silvana went out to the yard. There were no soldiers there, as if the Germans had forgotten the mandatory daily ritual, or had just decided to leave them alone. Nevertheless, none of the prisoners dared return to the shed. They waited outside, enduring the terrible cold. Some time went by and no German soldiers appeared. Everyone consulted. Some people suggested going to headquarters to ask about it. One person with an exceptionally large head suggested they take roll-call themselves and offered to do the counting. No one rejected the suggestion, but a few people objected to the man counting them himself. One woman even jokingly said he wouldn't be able to, because his enormous head would block his view.

The sight of her mother made Silvana the first person to break. She led her back into the shed and remained inside with her, protecting her and herself from the cold. People slowly followed, until

---

[28]From Italian: I've returned.

finally everybody but four people was inside. Toni was among the few who remained outside. Silvana wasn't sure if this attested to courage against the cold or to fear of the Germans. For the first time since they arrived in Bergen-Belsen, everyone complained about time not moving.

Everyone but Silvana's mother. She was mad that time didn't turn back, and so tried to turn it back herself; she lay flat on the bed, eyeing a group of three children playing *giran*, and began speaking of the early years of her marriage. It had been years since Silvana saw such spark in her mother's eyes, and she wanted to make it last, and didn't try to intervene in her mother's flow of words, the likes of which she'd never heard before. Her mother only paused once, when she mentioned Rita, her husband's younger sister who'd converted to Islam. Her face was suddenly alarmed to hear her husband's response, as if he were standing right behind her, listening in. She only tired of talking around noon. Silvana put her to bed, covered her in the torn blanket, and went outside. Everything outside remained as it was. Toni waited aimlessly with three other people for the Germans to come. They all stood there, trying to ignore the cold.

Children and adults called from the shed, "*Ana gian*, I'm starving." From outside, Silvana saw one mother put a boy's mouth to her wilted breast in an attempt to soothe him. She walked back into the shed, made sure her mother was tucked in, and announced that she was going to find out why the Germans forgot to do roll-call and ask for some food.

She went out to the German headquarters and walked by her Ashkenazi counterparts' sheds on the way. Some men were angry that she didn't return their greetings. From time to time she glanced at the tracks left in the mud by the German soldiers' boots. For the first time in a long time, they didn't scare her.

Near headquarters she saw a group of German officers, and one man among them in civilian clothing. He reminded her of her father: tall, confident, wearing a suit that resembled the kind her father had specially made for him in Naples and Tripoli. His appearance made her feel safe, and when she approached, Silvana addressed him, asking about the morning roll-call that hadn't taken place and the food rations that hadn't been received. He stroked her head the way her father used to, and answered in perfect English that she should go back to her shed, adding that he would see to it that they received food. The way the soldiers fawned over him promised her that he would deliver.

She made her way back to the shed. The impression of her encounter distracted her from hunger. When she arrived, she saw a surreal vision: the capo of one of the Ashkenazi prisoner groups got off a motorcycle driven by a German soldier, carrying two rolled fabrics from which slices of bread peeked out. The capo signaled to Toni, who still waited outside, to go in the shed. Inside the shed he gave Silvana a look of loathing, handed her the fabric, and ordered her to distribute the bread. Before leaving he muttered, "You are Herr Breitner's whore."

Silvana held onto the rolled fabric and ignored the starved eyes staring at her from all directions. Luigi Hachmon, who'd become a crumb of a man after Eliyahu Hajaj died, suddenly returned to life, pounced on her and knocked her down, shouting, "*Zibi l'macla, ya kilba*, give me the food, bitch!"

She protected the pieces of fabric as if they were her children and shouted at him to go back to his bunk. A few men came to her aid, pulling him off her.

She got back on her feet, pulled the slices of bread from inside the fabric and placed them on a nearby bed. A few men blocked the other prisoners. There were twice as many people as there were pieces of bread, and Silvana knew that if she cut each piece in half, chaos would ensue. She asked the men protecting her to think of a quick solution, and simultaneously tried to raise everybody's spirits. She didn't wait long. Suddenly she screamed, "*Achtung!*" followed by a demand in their own language: "*Ankatzmo l'zwaz!* Form pairs!"

Amazingly, everyone obeyed, forming pairs by the bunks. Each pair received a slice of bread to share. Silvana was left with three slices, which she saved for herself, her mother, and Rebecca. For a moment she felt guilty for having more food than the others, but only for a moment. She wanted to go to the latrine in hopes of meeting Rebecca there, but was unable to leave the shed. The vision before her chained her down: dozens of people sitting on their bunks, chewing in silence.

As she stared at this sorry sight, a German soldier appeared at the doorway, screamed *"Achtung!"* and called her name. She was startled. He gestured for her to follow him and led her three-hundred meters, to a square shed gleaming white. He knocked three times, and an order from inside instructed him to come in. Silvana followed him. Behind a long black desk set with a bottle of whiskey and three glasses were two German officers and the man in civilian clothing—Herr Breitner, as it turned out. The officer to his left addressed her in heavily accented English, telling her that Herr Breitner requested that she and her family be released from Bergen-Belsen and be sent to work in his sewing workshop in Italy. At the end of the war, he said, he would return them to their home in Africa. After he finished speaking, he removed his beret, crushed it between his fingers, and fixed his eyes on her. When she didn't speak, he continued, leaning back, saying that he didn't know what Herr Breitner saw in her, but that thanks to his great financial contribution to the German war effort and his acts of bravery during World War I, they decided to grant his request.

Her heart fluttered inside her. She watched Herr Breitner silently. His face was kind as he said she mustn't miss this invaluable opportunity. Her mind was filled with the faces of the people who were taken with them from Libya to Bergen-Belsen. She saw them on the many stages of their way of suffering: in the warehouse in the Tripoli Port, on the ship on the way to Italy, on the snowy path to Civitella del Tronto, in Fossoli di Carpi, and on the train to Bergen-Belsen. Rebecca's face always appeared among them, as if she wereinseparable from the Libyan exiles.

Silvana thanked Herr Breitner wholeheartedly for what he was willing to do for her, but said she would be staying in Bergen-Belsen with her kin. None of the three Germans tried to change her mind. She left the shed determinedly, but the event rattled her nerves all night long: *what a fool I am*, she kept thinking. I shouldn't have done that, *I should have saved us, that's what anyone would have done. My father is beating his fists against his grave.* For a moment she even considered getting out of bed and running to the edge of the camp to tell the Germans she'dchanged her mind, that they would go with Herr Breitner to Italy, but by the end of the night these thoughts subsided. All she could see was the shed, the sight of the people around her. She was happy she didn't turn her back on the children curled into their mother's souls, souls that had long ago abandoned their bodies and now seemed to wrap around them, exposed to all.

She didn't tell Rebecca about Herr Breitner when they met the next day. She knew Rebecca would be mad at her for refusing the offer and bring her doubts back to life. Her urge to tell her friend what had happened was partially satisfied by other stories, including the story of her meeting with the Hebrew soldier. Rebecca showed interest, saying she had no doubt Silvana would see him again after the war, but Silvana thought she might have detected a hint of irony in her words. She couldn't bear it, not because she wondered whether he was alive or dead, and not because she couldn't be sure she would ever meet him again. She helped Rebecca up from the ground and continued speaking about this, until Rebecca said decisively, "You will see him again, I know it."

When she returned to the shed she felt as if she were carried on the wings of this statement. This thought was what allowed her to float above the news of the death of the old lady whose husband passed away as they climbed to Civitella del Tronto, and also to skip over the despair that moved from her mother's face to her sister's face and back again. It allowed her to order the two of them to hold on without waiting for a response. wasnt the camps libecati

At the end of October 1944 the Libyan prisoners realized that the harsh cold they'd felt this far was but a preface to true winter. Bergen-Belsen was covered with snow that concealed the camp's purpose perfectly, and the chill and snow only worsened their suffering. The real torture came from the S.S. From the beginning of November, the treatment of prisoners became much worse. Rumors spread of a cruel commander who would soon replace the current one, about German defeats on different fronts. Some Libyan prisoners thought this was the reason for the Germans' rough treatment of them. One clear example of this attitude took place on a Saturday night, when the shed's dwellers gathered and a pleasant man named Meir blessed the food. Two S.S. soldiers walked into the shed. They looked like the white version of Muhammad and Akram, the candy merchants from the Dark Market in Benghazi—one very tall, the other very short. They ordered the people to walk outside, muttering, "*Schwarze Juden.*"

Silvana pulled her mother by the hand, screaming at her sister, "*Ta'ali,* come on!" From the corner of her eye she noticed that Meir wasn't running with everyone else, but slowly folding the tablecloth that served as his prayer shawl. The short soldier yelled at him, and when Meir didn't respond he shot a barrage of bullets into his head. Meir's younger sister, who'd had a bad hunch, ran back into the shed, lay down by his body, and wailed. The short German soldier screamed at her to get out. When she didn't, another burst of gunfire hit her head, and her body covered her brother's.

Silvana couldn't help but watch. From the moment she saw Meir from the corner of her eye, an inner force made her turn around and look straight at him. She tried to cover her eyes, but her hands refused, unable to prevent the vision from slicing through her gut. She trembled, spat, and threw up. The yelling outside grew louder, turning into screams of horror, but Yona Hachmon rang above them all: "*Weynec, ya rab?* Where are you, God?" The soldiers went outside, leaving the two dead bodies behind. The fact they couldn't understand a word of the prisoners' language frustrated them. The tall soldier muttered a German curse, from which the words "*Arabische Sprache*"[29] could be discerned. A few prisoners kept shouting, and the German ordered them in broken English to speak Yiddish. His friend added an explicit threat, telling them that whoever didn't speak the Jewish language would be sentenced to death.

Eliyahu Hajaj was no longer with them, and so there was not a man among the prisoners who spoke a word of German, let alone Yiddish. They were at a loss. The tall soldier aimed his weapon toward one woman' head, announcing angrily that if none of them said at least one word of Yiddish, she would be shot. Frightened sobs filled the air. Silvana racked her brain to recall the one Yiddish word Rebecca

---

29From German: Arab language.

used once in a while. She couldn't come up with it. The soldier shot the woman. As her blood painted the snow red, Silvana saw it was Mama Regignano, that bashful woman who kept telling everyone during their journey, "*Tuwel amerkum!* Be patient." *yiddish word*

The prisoners froze in their tracks. No one said a word until Silvana cried, "*Gewald!*" Some people looked at her accusingly—she was too late. Others were paralyzed. The tall soldier smiled with satisfaction, and announced in broken English that he was glad, because he thought he might have had it wrong, and that perhaps these people weren't even Jewish. He ordered some boys to carry the bodies of Mama Regignano, Meir, and Meir's sister, and to load them onto a wagon that was submerged in snow halfway up its wheels.

The inner burning in Silvana's soul neutralized her cold. For a moment, she thought of attacking the short soldier who stood beside her. She could snatch his gun—and do what? Die by his hands or his friends'? She didn't do it and was immediately washed with a wave of self-hatred. She loathed herself for yelling "*Gewald*" too late. She saw in her mother's eyes and Toni's that they wanted to hug her but couldn't. Instead, Yona Hachmon walked over and held her close, as if Silvana could fill the hole that had opened in her when God refused to answer her call. Silvana slowly released her grip and sat down on the snow, yearning to disappear.

The soldiers made sure the bodies had been evacuated and began walking back to the center of the camp, leaving the prisoners behind. The sky was clear and bright, the sun illuminating the white expanse, but doing nothing to fight the cold. Silvana knew it was cold, but didn't feel it. The people around them hugged their bodies, as if this would convince the world to cover them. She knew she had to see Rebecca.

Silvana stood up. Her mother and sister got up and hollowly gave her their hands so that she could lead them. She slowly took them to the shed, and the moment they crossed the threshold she deposited them in the shed and turned around. The bright white spread before her again. Beyond the stunningly clear air she saw faint prisoners lying in the snow. For a moment she watched them from the point of view of the Germans soldiers, who saw them as nothing more than a dark spot. To push the thought away, she looked at the fences. They weren't separating her from freedom; there was nothing behind them that made her feel like she belonged. The area outside the camp seemed no less threatening than the camp itself. The open field across it, which saw as an ally, a reflection of Bergen-Belsen, now seemed like nothing more than a continuation of her prison, realizing, as she now did, that she'd led herself astray when she thought she and the white Jews shared the same fate. Now she knew that unlike them, if she ran away there would be no way for her to hide or mobilize in such a foreign space. The knowledge that she had to see Rebecca gave her strength. In those moments, Rebecca was not only a sister from whom she gained power under unbearable conditions, but a homeland in a strange, foreign world. The momentary warmth her friend's image imbued her with returned the feeling to her body.

She returned to the shed, wrapped herself with her woolen blanket, and went out to search for Rebecca. This time she didn't head for the latrine. Something in her heart told her that Rebecca wouldn't be there. She wandered aimlessly in the paralyzing cold. On her way she saw a prisoner that looked suspiciously healthy. When he realized she didn't speak Yiddish or Polish, he addressed her in English, telling her unequivocally that if she came with him behind the sheds and let him kiss her, he'd give her two cigarettes. He added with a smile that he'd heard the gypsies really knew how to make love. She pushed him away with her weak hands and kept going.

A new wave of weakness spread through her. She wanted to sit down, but there was nothing but snow all around her. A few dozen meters away she saw a black object in the midst of white. She hoped it was a large rock. *Imshi l'lkadam, ya Silvana, go on*, she told herself. When she got closer she found a large dog, wounded and bleeding. She leaned over it with her torso. Other than a brief whine, the dog showed no resistance. With the last of her energy she covered both of them with her woolen blanket, absorbed the warmth of his body, and fell asleep.

When she awoke she felt as if she'd slept for centuries. Evening was near, the sky had grayed, still allowing the sun a last bit of grace, allowing fractured rays to filter through the clouds. The cold air hit the back of her neck. She raised her body, looked at the dog, and saw that it was dead. Silvana was filled with shame. She covered it with her woolen blanket and began walking back without it. She was close to becoming nobody. Tino's suicide, her father's death, the murder of the three people earlier that day, her mother and sister's collapse—they all defeated her. She became nothing, a void, a spiritless body advancing aimlessly through the snow. In the distance she saw people gathering outside the shed. She couldn't tell if they were Germans, Libyan Jews, Ashkenazi Jews, or a mixture of all three. Only as she got nearer did she see they were a few German soldiers speaking with Luigi Hachmon while perusing documents. When Luigi saw her he lowered his eyes. This gesture returned her soul to her body, and she was startled. Her heart told her this was bad news. A few seconds later she walked into the shed, where she learned that many people were being transferred to a Wehrmacht British prisoners' camp in Biberach an der Riss in southern Germany.

No one could tell her which unlucky few of them would remain in Bergen-Belsen. She was consumed by Luigi Hachmon's lowered eyes. Her mind now realized what her heart had told her earlier: the news was bad. The three of them—her mother, her sister, and herself—would not be transferred; they would remain in Bergen-Belsen. Though she was certain this was the case, she continued to hope that something would change, that Luigi would come in and tell them they were leaving too. But instead, Hachmon came in with an S.S. soldier, and spent long minutes reading the names of the transferred. When he finished reading without mentioning her family, he looked up from the page and as far away as possible from her mother's bunk.

None of them knew which considerations were taken into account in the decision of who to transfer and who to leave behind. Even without clear knowledge, Silvana blamed Luigi for having played a part in this harmful decision. She didn't allow him to evade her gaze. She walked over and around him, turned around and stood a meter away from him. She looked at him as if through her father's eyes and said, "*Buya dima calna uld hram*. Father always said you were a snake." Hachmon said nothing, looking only at the German soldier, as if asking him to rescue him. The German continued to watch, seeming to enjoy the show. "*Ka kint yidi limna—kint nkitzha*. If you were my right hand, I'd cut you off," Silvana added, using the most contemptuous curse of Benghazi Jews. Then she spit in his face and turned away. People were wailing all around.

Yona approached her, begging her to bless her on her journey, or she wouldn't join the others. Silvana blessed her through tight lips and turned back, avoiding a hug. She went to her family's bunks. Shortly thereafter, everyone on the list packed up their few belongings and left the shed, following Luigi and the German soldiers outside the camp. Only twenty people were left behind. A new layer of depression coated the shed, but within the hour it already felt old as time, their abandonment becoming ancient history.

She resisted the temptation to indulge in the crisis. The cry for help on the faces of her mother and sister left her no other option. But she knew that in order to act she needed first to tell Rebecca what had happened, and to receive her encouragement and warmth. She wrapped herself with two blankets left behind by the transferred and went outside. Even the two blankets couldn't protect her against the cold. She was chilled from head to toe, no limb left untouched. She imagined that the blankets were doing their job and walked to Rebecca's shed. It was almost completely dark, and the only sound came from a distant airplane.

A few dozen meters later, she slipped on the thin ice, becoming tangled up in her blankets, and unable to get up. After the third failed attempt she no longer wanted to. She lay on the ice, bundled and trapped inside her blankets, and watched the sky. Her disbelief in the existence of God was now pure and unadulterated. No questions challenged it, no fear set blocks in its path. It was unconditional, unadulterated lack of faith. "Why?" she screamed at the void that opened up above her.

After a while, she envisioned her mother and Toni's faces. She finally managed to stand up with great effort, and tried to wrap the blankets around her in a way that wouldn't make her trip. She continued to walk toward Rebecca's shed. When she reached a new row of sheds, she thought she recognized Rebecca's. The door was ajar in spite of the cold. She pushed it further and walked inside. A weak light illuminated the space inside. Some bunks were occupied by unidentifiable creatures, while others were taken up by those who still retained their human form. Three healthy looking teenagers sat together on the floor, whispering. Those who were awake looked up at her. She waited for them to say something, but they kept quiet. "Rebecca," she said. "Rebecca Rice." They remained silent, but now their expressions were astonished. Silvana tried to muffle her Arab accent as best she could when she repeated, "Rebecca Rice." Nothing happened. More silence.

As she walked to the center of the shed, a woman addressed her in an unfamiliar language, quickly switching to English. "You are Silvana…" she said. "Rebecca's Libyan friend. I've heard about you. I will take you to her."

The woman wrapped a blanket around her body, took Silvana's hand, and led her out of the shed. Silvana didn't ask a thing, only loosened her hand inside the woman's warm palm and allowed herself to be led. They walked by one shed and into the next. Before she could tell what was going on, Rebecca was running to greet her. She touched her delicately, as if she hadn't seen her in ages, and said emotionally that she'd heard the Arabs had been transferred, and thought she'd never see her again. Silvana wanted to hug her, but couldn't. The moment she met her friend was the moment she realized she couldn't fulfil the thing for which she'd yearned to see her.

It was the first moment in their friendship that Rebecca looked like a stranger. She wondered if it was because of the silence she'd walked into before. It occurred to her that their countries of origin were meddling in their relationship, pushing them apart. For a moment even Rebecca seemed to belong to a completely separate breed of people, people who would never truly accept someone from her culture, and would at most show her affection for the sake of appearances.

This moment quickly passed. Rebecca ignored the distance in Silvana's eyes. She thanked the Dutch woman for bringing her friend to her, and

asked Silvana to follow her without introducing her
to any of the starving people around. They climbed
onto Rebecca's bunk, and Rebecca covered the two
of them with her patched blanket. Now that they
were huddled together, away from the influence of
the outside, Rebecca became the old friend Silvana
had seen in her since the first time they met. As time
ticked by, they became what they'd been since losing
their fathers—true sisters.

Rebecca's body warmed Silvana and she fell
asleep in her lap. At dawn, a bloodcurdling scream
from outside awoke them: "*Raus!*"

The moment Silvana opened her eyes, it was as
if the familiar world had closed its own. Startled,
she looked around her, searching for something safe
and familiar. She didn't see her mother, Toni, or
her Libyan brothers. She didn't hear the Arabic that
filled every corner of her shed. Instead, the air was
tight with Yiddish and Dutch. The foreign language
was cut by Rebecca's words, inviting Silvana to step
firmly as if it were a thin strip of land allowing the
daughter of Israel to cross the Red Sea: "Stand close
to me."

The hunger and cold that hit the people standing
for roll-call did not prevent many of them from
watching Silvana with wonder as she slipped into
their rows. She tried to make herself as small as
possible, hoping she could thus avoid their eyes. She
prayed no one would count them. She knew very

well how S.S. soldiers reacted when someone was missing from roll-call, and she hoped not to find out how they reacted when they had an extra person.

A flushed soldier with one boot a bit taller than the other began counting them. When he passed her she thought she could hear Rebecca's heartbeat. The soldier lingered, watching her, then moved on. He asked his friend a question Silvana couldn't understand. Rebecca took advantage of the other soldier's hesitation and stepped forward, announcing in fluent German, "He counted to thirty, not thirty-one."

When the roll-call was through and everyone headed out to work, Silvana used the guard's distraction to walk around Rebecca's shed and back toward her own, praying that roll-call hadn't been taken there yet. It only now hit her that her mother and sister spent the previous night without her. Questions raced through her mind: *what did they do without me? How did they respond to my absence? Are they afraid for me? Or perhaps they have lost all feeling?* These questions urged her on. She turned to make sure she was far enough from the German soldiers before breaking into a run.

But her legs didn't cooperate for long, and a few dozen meters later she stopped, about to pass out, and collapsed onto the snowy ground. She waited for her breath to slow down a bit, and then kept running. She attributed the footprints in the mud to the people who'd been transferred to Biberach an der Riss. Once more she was enraged for having been left behind, her wrath burning for Luigi Hachmon.

When she peeked into her shed she found it empty except for a family of three that sat in its center, dipping their hands into a large bucket that stood between them. She didn't ask where her mother or Toni were because she was afraid of their answer. One of them said that no one was really watching them anymore, and that a few of them were randomly chosen for work. She ran frantically between their usual work spots. The two first sites were empty. Other than the word "*Haria*"—freedom—painted onto one of the walls, there was no trace of Libyan Jews. She found her mother and Toni in the third site. Toni was sitting on a toilet bowl, her face in her hands, and her mother was sitting on the urine soaked floor. She lay down between them and wailed. They didn't join in, as if barren of all feeling.

"I kept telling her you were with Rebecca," said Toni.

Silvana couldn't take their meekness any longer. She stood up and shouted, "What did you do to me?" They didn't answer, and her frustration grew. She screamed, "I thought they took you away!" She didn't calm down until Toni stood up, punched her, and told her she was the one who left them to be with her white friends. Silvana lay back down next to her mother and sobbed, promising to never leave them again.

And indeed, she hardly left their side in the following weeks. Even on the few occasions they were sent to work in separate locations, she snuck out to see them every couple of hours. Most of their time was spent sitting in the shed with the small group that remained. Her thoughts slowly consumed her, sawing at her insides, not letting go even when she met Rebecca. She fought to survive. Rebecca tried to distract her, but only one of her attempts was successful; this happened when Rebecca joined the Libyan women in Hebrew songs they'd learned from Lavi, the only old Libyan man who remained in the place. They sang without understanding the words:

Ashreynu, ashreynu
Ma tov goralenu
Uma yafa yerushatenu
Ashreynu, ashreynu[30]

Sometimes, on the nights they had any energy left, they accompanied the song with clapping or tapping on the bunks. Toni almost never joined in. Her mother, on the other hand, sang along one night, which lifted Silvana's spirits. Silvana was later

---

[30]From Hebrew: Oh joy, oh joy/What blessed fate/What wonderful inheritance/Oh joy, oh joy.

disappointment when her mother returned to the embrace of grief immediately afterwards.

One night in early January Silvana announced she was going to sleep in Rebecca's shed, because her friend had told her she needed her for the very first time. This night didn't only separate Silvana from her family, it also separated Silvana from herself. As she left them, walking toward Rebecca's shed, her heart wouldn't give her a moment's peace. The whole dark way there she thought she was doing something unforgivable, breaking her promise to never leave them.

Rebecca looked weaker than ever. Silvana could see this even in the dim light of the shed. Her face seemed to have shed its skin. Rebecca hugged her and told her she knew the soldier who would be taking roll-call the next morning, and that she'd already informed him that her friend would be spending the night. Seeing Silvana's concern, she told her not to worry—the man was a German-Dutch prisoner whose family was friends with hers.

Silvana didn't ask Rebecca why she explicitly asked for her to spend the night. Her body answered the question for her in bed. Rebecca burrowed into Silvana's body, asking it to protect her from the noises of the past and future. She laid her head on Silvana's chest and kissed her lips weakly, expecting to be kissed back. Silvana fully fulfilled her role as protector, hugging her, first with one arm and then with two, rubbing her back, neck, and finally her thighs, and giving her the kiss her lips yearned for.

That night, for the first time in a long while, Silvana truly slept. The next morning she ran out for roll-call with everyone else, taking turns pulling Rebecca and being pulled by her. None of the shed's residents looked at her, except for a young, small man whose arms were as long as a monkey's. His eyes told her he knew she didn't belong, and her attempts to ignore him were futile. He didn't take his eyes off her until roll-call was over and everyone went off to work. Silvana did as Rebecca told her, "Go. Now's the time." Even as she walked back to shed 210 she could feel the man's eyes piercing her back.

But this bother soon lost its significance. Her eyes darkened as she reached her shed. She was welcomed by an empty space, but there was something new about it. It was obvious the tenants hadn't been taken to their usual jobs. Most of the blankets were unfolded, the water buckets were upside-down, one shoe was strewn in the middle of the shed, and a note in the doorway was covered with words written hastily in blood. There was no doubt about it: the people left this shed never to return. Just to make sure what she felt was true, she walked over to her mother's bunk, her heart pounding and her palms sweating in spite of the cold. There, in the tiny rectangle between the beams, her mother had hid a tiny box with a silver ring whose value was mostly sentimental. The ring was gone. Silvana knew her mother wouldn't have given it up for anything after carrying it all the way from Benghazi. She was petrified. A little while later some prisoners came in and began cleaning up, completely ignoring her.

She stuttered something. A short prisoner with a kind face explained in weak, clumsy English that he'd heard everyone had been transferred to a British prisoners' camp last night and that the shed was now to be prepared for a new group that would arrive the same day.

She felt her body being taken over by her soul. She was pure spirit. She stepped outside and looked at the abyss of the sky, the place where God dwelled before she stopped believing in him. She yearned for it to fill up for a moment, even if only with a mirage. Rain washed over Bergen-Belsen. This was the first time Silvana realized the true meaning of loneliness. She wanted to run, to stand still, to scream, to say nothing, to disappear, to exist. She wanted very badly to live. Finally she dragged herself through the pouring rain back to Rebecca's shed. There was no person, animal, or vehicle along the enormous carpet of mud; the epitome of emptiness momentarily covering the tangible world.

When she arrived at Rebecca's empty shed she threw herself on her friend's bunk and fell asleep, encased in her smell. She dreamt that her mother and Toni were giving her their hands, calling to her,

"*Ta'ali, ya* Silvana, come." She gave them back her hands, but couldn't hold on. A small yet endless space stretched between them, as if they were the opposing magnetic fields. From the moment she woke up, she felt that she herself was within that space. Her hands hurt and she felt her body shrinking. A dull pressure weighed down on her. This space, so undefined and yet so real, surrounded her from all directions, following her everywhere. It plagued her with constant guilt for having chosen Rebecca over her family.

Hunger began gnawing at her. Her values were falling away. When she saw prisoners returning to the shed, she wanted nothing more but to steal whatever bread they were hiding on their bodies. She schemed to rob them, but quickly realized they didn't have any food, that they were hungry themselves. Even when she saw Rebecca, who'd just returned from a job, her face more thoughtful than usual, she only wondered whether her friend could give her something to eat. Rebecca was hungry too and said weakly that she would soon get them something. Silvana followed her to behind the shed, pausing at the sight of a black plank of wood on the ground.

Rebecca moved it. "Pray to God," she said, digging with her hands through the dirt.

Though Silvana avoided speaking to God, she said confidently, "I am praying."

A filthy rag in the ground contained a rather large piece of bread and two pieces of meat. Rebecca took the bundle apart with trembling hands. She cut the bread into two unequal pieces, quickly placed a piece of meat on each, and gave Silvana the larger of the two. Silvana didn't dwell on the idea of offering the larger piece back to Rebecca, instead wolfing down her food.

Rebecca didn't say how she got the food. She assumed Silvana knew the German-Dutch prisoner from roll-call was the one who came to her aid. Silvana knew that Rebecca understood she wasn't naïve enough to believe that a friendship between the families was the man's motivation, but said nothing. Still hungry, the two faltered back to the shed, but now it was Rebecca's obvious weakness that prevented Silvana from breaking down. They climbed onto Rebecca's bunk. Silvana thought of Toni and her mother. She hoped they weren't thinking about her too much, that they weren't letting her absence fill the place to which they'd been taken. Rebecca fell asleep and Silvana caressed her face. Her fingers hunted a crumb of meat that had clung to her lips and put it in her own mouth. Suddenly someone touched her back. She turned around, startled, and saw the small man with the long arms. He fixed her with a suspicious, threatening look that reflected her foreignness. Then he rubbed her foot, which was poking out of the blanket. She pushed his hand away.

"*Du bist nicht fun undzere*,"[31] he said.

"*Imshi*, get out of here," she barked at him.

Before leaving, he muttered, "I come back."

He delivered on his threat the very next day. After roll-call, Silvana was sent along with ten young men and two other strong looking girls to move large tins a few dozen meters away. The tin she carried was heavy and she dropped it. She wanted to follow suit and collapse to the ground too, but a strange prisoner grabbed her, thus saving her life. A Nazi soldier already had his weapon aimed at her, prepared to shoot her as they shot everyone who was no longer useful. The long armed man, who was among the same group, saw what had happened. At noon, as they were walking to the latrine, he followed her, teasing.

"He kill you," he said, implying that the soldier needed but little excuse to take her out. "He don't like you. You not from us."

The image of the German soldier aiming his weapon at her erased all other images from her mind.

When she crouched down to defecate away from the eyes of the Germans, he crouched down beside her. She said nothing, not even when he put one hand on her breast and the other on his own penis. He kneaded her breast roughly over her tattered clothing, again and again, insatiable, rubbing his

---

[31] From Yiddish: You're not one of our kind.

uncooperative penis. Then he stopped kneading, pulled the rags away from her torso and sucked on her nipple. She wanted to resist, but his threat—that he would snitch to the Germans that she was in their shed—paralyzed her. She closed her eyes and began sobbing, silently cursing the world.

Her body felt filthy in the following days. She was so overcome by this sensation that she could think of nothing else. She wanted with all her might to erase the traces of the man's hand and mouth from her body. She yearned to sanitize their points of contact. Without soap or running water, she searched for other cleaning methods, and, at wits' end, ended up using urine and mud. She sat down in the latrine and peed what little fluids she could manage into her hand. She smeared her urine soaked hand with mud and scrubbed her breasts roughly, again and again, as if wanting them to crumble into dust. They remained hanging off her body like nooses, double monuments of the vile act that had been performed on her.

She avoided touching them. Even on the nights when she sought small comfort by touching her body, she skipped over them. One night she removed Rebecca's hand on its way to her breasts and revealed to her what had happened. Her words imbued Rebecca with newfound power. Her face reddened with rage and she shifted uncomfortably. It was obvious she was going to do something, but

Silvana didn't want to discuss the event further. She only wanted to forget.

The next afternoon, Rebecca approached the man, slapped his face in front of everyone, mentioned her relationship with the German-Dutch prisoner who was in charge of them, and announced that if he ever came near Silvana again he'd be murdered, just like Carl Rott. The threat did the job. The man stayed away from Silvana, and Rebecca grew closer to herself. The power she'd discovered in herself filled her with vitality and a measure of hope.

But not for long. In late January Silvana's and Rebecca's situation visibly deteriorated. The tiny piece of bread they received each day was not enough to sustain their bodies. More and more new prisoners were brought into the camp and it was overflowing with people. But the worst part was the water shortage. They rarely drank clean water, and mostly quenched their thirst through filthy sources— mop buckets or puddles of standing water. They both got ill, and at nights lay closer together to fight their tremors. During the day they dragged themselves through the camp, their bodies burning with fever and their stomachs empty and aching. They took advantage of the loosening order of the camp to spend as much time together as they could. Rebecca thought the disorder was a result of too many new prisoners, while Silvana thought it was first and foremost a meditated act by the Germans.

They once had a real fight about it. They were sitting outside the shed, awaiting orders, watching with burning eyes as a new stream of baffled prisoners walked past. As if possessed, Rebecca kept repeating her opinion on the loosening of order, and Silvana kept shaking her head no. When Silvana finally pointed out that repetition was not enough to make what she was saying true, Rebecca riled. She fixed her eyes, which were glittering with heat, on Silvana and muttered that she didn't understand anything, that she came from an undeveloped country, that Egyptians knew nothing of European logic, that even in a thousand years black people wouldn't be able to understand the white man.

Silvana shivered not from cold or fever. She stood up, pleading with her mind to order her body to punch Rebecca, but her mind refused. Instead she latched on to the question of whether calling her country Egypt rather than Libya had been intentional. She limped into the shed, where she was met with threatening looks. She didn't care. It wasn't the shed's tenants she was being ripped apart from. For the first time since she'd been torn from Libya her feeling of detachment was empty of real or abstract meaning. She wasn't torn from her previous life, her country, or her culture, nor was she torn from her mother and sister's ever reaching arms. The feeling of detachment was so powerful and all-encompassing, and yet Silvana had no idea what she'd been torn away from.

Rebecca walked into the shed, climbed onto the bunk and buried her head in Silvana's stomach. Silvana stroked her friend's burning body. She whispered into her ears, afraid Rebecca would burn alive between her hands, telling her that she would never let her die. She spoke a mixture of English and Arabic. Rebecca nodded, and they fell asleep.

A loud explosion shook the camp in the middle of the night, followed by several weaker ones. Anyone who was able to step outside did. On the way out, Rebecca called to Silvana that people were saying the sheds were about to catch fire, but when they looked outside what seemed to have been burnt was the old order of the camp: prisoners and soldiers mixed together seamlessly, officers were dumbfounded, soldiers kept asking prisoners, *"Was ist hier los?"*[32] A fat German soldier who fell to the ground couldn't get up and asked a prisoner as thin as paper to help him. A rather old soldier screamed at the sky, begging his God not to desert him now. A prisoner held one of her captors, leaning her head on his chest, asking for his protection. The chaos went on for several minutes before the soldiers got a hold of themselves and, with the help of their prisoner liaisons, returned everyone to the sheds with screams and gunfire.

Silvana ran to the shed, one hand holding onto Rebecca's, the other covering her eyes so she

---

[32]From German: What's going on here?

wouldn't see how those who couldn't run were being shot. "*Rabi Yahfadna*, God save us," she screamed at the threshold. In those moments the shed appeared as a realm of freedom, a place to which one escaped from the eternal prison outside. She blocked out everything that was going on and focused entirely on her own survival.

The next day the question of whether or not she would ever see her family again continued to run through her mind and choked throat. She tended to believe the answer was no. She heard a rumor that the Germans were about to retreat and that they would kill as many prisoners as possible before they did.

This rumor was founded on another one, according to which the noise that had shaken the camp the previous night was a bomb that had exploded a few hundred meters away. The common assumption was that American planes had tried to hit the camp, and many prisoner were startled by the idea that after working so hard to survive the hell of the camp they would end up dying by the hands of those trying to liberate them. Silvana heard all this from Rebecca.

Her friend also reported the state of mind of other prisoners. Silvana often wished to be able to forego mediation and hear for herself, but many of the prisoners didn't speak English, and those who did weren't too eager to talk to her. Whenever she tried to start a conversation with another prisoner, her accent made her instantly suspect. With no one to talk to other than Rebecca, she was often forced to talk to herself. She liked the sounds of the Arabic language, rolling its many layers of diction on her tongue, gaining life from its throaty sounds, a life so different from the spirit of death that surrounded her. She covered herself with her words, protecting herself with them, living inside of them.

But the Arabic that was her safe home also raised the hostility of others. Once, for example, she was standing outside of the shed and singing a song that old Jewish ladies in Benghazi sang to their grandchildren. It included the line, "Ya *waldi, ma t'hapesh dima n'habec un'azed, hata ba'ad muti*— my child, have no fear, I'll love you even after I'm dead." For some reason, it was this line that provoked a tall, cross-eyed prisoner. He walked over and pushed her with a force she didn't think anyone in the camp still had, then muttered some dirty words, of which she recognized the word "*Schwarze*," a word which, unfortunately, she was all too familiar with.

This incident and others like it did not prevent her from speaking to herself in Arabic. Nor did the fear that one of the prisoners would report to the Germans that she didn't belong in their shed. After the night when the explosion shook the camp, she stopped fearing that possibility, seeing as how all order in the camp was breaking. It was obvious to everyone that the Germans had no interest in such petty issues. Like the other prisoners, Silvana realized that as far as the

Germans were concerned she no longer belonged to any specific shed or roll-call, but only to her certain, imminent death.

Indeed, the more chaos spread through the camp, the less the Nazis bothered to conceal their intention of killing all prisoners. One day Silvana and Rebecca were sent with a group of female prisoners to clean a warehouse in the southern end of the camp. On their way, they passed by two German soldiers who were having a conversation. They stared at Silvana, and she could tell by their tone that they were joking around. She asked Rebecca what they'd said, and Rebecca said they'd made a comment on how skinny the girls were, but Silvana knew she was lying; they'd only looked at her. She pushed her for the truth, but Rebecca evaded by claiming that if they kept talking the soldiers might shoot them. Only when Silvana threatened to stop walking and begin shouting as loud as she could did Rebecca concede and say that one soldier asked the other what he thought black meat smelled like when it burned, and what color of smoke it produced.

Silvana's mind was a blank. Only in the evening, when they returned to the shed and secretly drank some of the cold water Rebecca had procured through her connections, did she begin thinking again. On the one hand, she yearned to give up what was left of her life, and on the other hand she wanted very badly to keep fighting. She held on to the second option for dear life. Once and again she persuaded herself to hold on until the war was over. Once and again she replayed all possible scenarios that could reunite her with her mother and sister, and perhaps even with the Hebrew soldier.

The next day she took advantage of the relative disarray and walked to shed 185 to search for a prisoner named Johan. She'd heard that he'd taken the opposite route from her family—he came to Bergen-Belsen from Biberach an der Riss.

His appearance was strange. His muscles still hadn't atrophied from malnutrition. His chiseled face resembled that of a regular man. His head was unshaved. Only the deep sorrow in his blue eyes revealed his identity as a prisoner in a concentration camp. Silvana walked over, saying nothing. He didn't react. She spoke to him, and he remained silent. When she finally surprised herself by grabbing his hand he mumbled some words in Dutch. She mumbled back in English.

"What did you say?" he asked.

They began talking. When she learned he hadn't met her mother and sister and hadn't seen a group of Libyan Jews, she asked him about what was going on in Biberach an der Riss. She wanted to know about the living conditions, food distribution, treatment of prisoners, and water, the water. She asked again and again if prisoners there had access to running water.

His answers were hesitant, fractured memories. When she asked about water he kept repeating that all prisoners had access to running water. Still, his answer didn't satisfy her, but kept blending into his other vague answers like a drop in a puddle of standing water. She therefore focused on his appearance, which ignited a force within her, fading and returning to flicker over and over again.

She turned to leave without saying goodbye. On her way back to Rebecca's shed she felt her body heat for the first time in two days. A doughy mass of people wandered before her; marionettes with flailing limbs, buckling knees, their skeletal arms flying in all directions with no coordination, making growing and shrinking elliptical shapes through the air, no direction or purpose, as if their loyal operators feared that if they paused, even for a moment, they would stop moving forever. Silvana wanted to go to the latrine, but was afraid she would run into the prisoner with the monkey arms, and ended up going to the bathroom behind the skeleton of an abandoned motorcycle. She had good reason to be so afraid of running into the man who had so aggressively kneaded her breasts; the day before, the German-Dutch prisoner, Rebecca's benefactor, had been murdered, and she knew there would be nothing hindering the path of the long armed man.

Unfortunately, she ended up running into him near Rebecca's shed. This time he wasn't careful and didn't keep his distance, but rather walked quickly toward her, muttering unintelligible threats. This time she didn't tell Rebecca. She didn't want to burden her with any further worries. She lied when she'd said she didn't think her friend's death would worsen their conditions, explaining that they could use the information he'd given them to get their hands on more clean water. Rebecca looked at her doubtfully, and Silvana promised she'd only have to give up the cigarettes she'd gotten from him.

From the moment she'd moved into Rebecca's shed, she stopped obsessively following the dates. She trusted Rebecca on this matter, due to her relationship with the German-Dutch prisoner. Somehow she knew it was February of 1945. The first days of that month seemed to be taken from another world. The awful cold had ended, the murky, vomity soup given to prisoners was replaced for some reason with proper soup, tasty and reviving, and more and more rumors spread about the nearing victory of the Nazis' enemies, who would soon be coming to liberate them.

At the same time, each day more and more prisoners fell down never to get up again, and random shots were fired everywhere. Rebecca and Silvana were especially careful. They tried never to leave each other's side, and avoided the German soldiers as much as they could. They used the growing crowdedness of the camp to become invisible, trying never to stand out.

One evening in the beginning of the month, when they secretly smoked the last cigarette Rebecca had left from her dead benefactor, Silvana suddenly recalled that the prisoner she'd met from Biberach an der Riss had insinuated that he was also able to procure potable water in Bergen-Belsen. Rebecca said she'd go talk to him. Silvana tried to convince her to let her come along, but Rebecca refused vehemently, and in spite of her exhaustion went to see him alone the very next day.

Silvana awaited her return. As time ticked by, she became more and more anxious that her friend might have collapsed along the way. She couldn't imagine what life in the camp would be like without her. She was afraid of being completely given to the graces of strange prisonersjust as much as she was afraid of the Germans. But the fear of losing Rebecca was much deeper and essential. She couldn't imagine the entire world without her. Rebecca's confident presence had turned the world into something defined within her mind; without her it collapsed into a black hole.

Now she regretted not having been taken to do some menial labor that day. Sitting around aimlessly made waiting much harder. She went in and out of the shed, back and forth, like a desperate passenger on a sinking ship. No one looked at her, no one looked at themselves, everyone behaved as if their life's purpose was to slowly die.

Eventually she fell into an exhausted sleep below the bunk. She only awoke at the sound of Rebecca's voice, speaking the Arabic words she'd learned from Silvana in her strange Dutch accent: "*Kumi, ya mazyanti, ya ruhi, ya nafsi.*"[33]

The Arabic blended into the dream Silvana was having about her childhood, and it took her several minutes to get the images out of her mind and figure out where she was. Even when she did figure it out, she couldn't get a hold of herself. She wanted so badly to return to her dream, even though it had been interrupted by the vision of the terrible beating her father once gave her as punishment for having mentioned Rita's name in public.

Rebecca brought her mouth to Silvana's ear and whispered that she'd gotten them a whole bottle of clean water. Even just those words were enough to make Silvana feel satiated. Rebecca had buried the bottle in the spot where the German-Dutch prisoner used to leave her food. Silvana didn't ask Rebecca how the Dutch man had smuggled the water into the camp or why he'd agreed to give her the full bottle, and Rebecca was in no rush to share the story either, not because she wanted to hide anything from

---

[33]From Jewish-Libyan Arabic: Wake up, my beauty, my soul.

304 | Benghazi-Bergen-Belsen

Silvana, but because the thought of discussing it frightened and exhausted them both.

When evening descended and clouds darkened over the camp, the two left the shed wordlessly and began walking to the hiding place. The area was almost empty, save for few passing silhouettes, but Rebecca still asked Silvana to block her from view as she dug through the dirt. They found the bottle without being noticed. Rebecca held onto it like a blind man feeling the face of a stranger. She said Silvana had better carry it because it would be easier to hide it under her shirt. Silvana nodded and quickly slipped it beneath her wide shirt. Rebecca said they had to find a place to drink in hiding, but Silvana said that if they'd waited this long, they should wait for complete darkness. Rebecca agreed and they returned to the shed.

Inside the shed Silvana saw the faces of all the people who didn't have clean drinking water. She couldn't look at them for longer than a moment. She lowered her eyes as she walked to the back of the shed. Rebecca, on the other hand, spoke to a few of them, and Silvana heard one of the prisoners mumbled the word "wasser," whose meaning she already knew.

The minutes ticked by as Silvana's thirst grew. She waited expectantly for darkness, which was late to come. After a while, she told Rebecca she couldn't wait any longer. Now Rebecca was the one to say it would be much safer if they drank when there was no light outside.

When it was finally dark, they stepped outside. Two prisoners who'd lost most of their minds stood planted in place, not minding the cold, staring at the moon with illuminated glassy eyes. The Germans had recently removed their guard, and even the Capos that had supervised them were gone. Still, Silvana and Rebecca looked around carefully to make sure they were out of sight. Rebecca led them to behind the shed, where she pulled out the bottle. Silvana took the first gentle sip. Rebecca didn't urge her to pass the bottle, only watching her with a look of victory, proud to have gotten them clean water right under the noses of the Germans and their collaborators. When Silvana finally gave her the bottle she'd lost all restraint and downed it in one long, lustful, choking gulp.

The next day, the water had brought a terrible fate upon them. At dawn, her head still buried beneath the torn blanket she'd swaddled herself in, Silvana heard terrified whispers all around. The name Yitzhak Fogel was spoken repeatedly. Everyone looked at the doorway. The dull light of dawn illuminated a very short man, almost a midget, who leaned smugly and possessively against the doorframe, watching the prisoners in silence. They thought he was stretching out the silence as long as he could. Silvana poked her friend in the ribs. Rebecca, who was as still as an object, slowly woke up to add her eyes to the others staring at the doorway. Then she mumbled something in Dutch, of which Silvana could only discern one word—"Capo."

"Rebecca Rice!" the scream shook the shed, cutting through the thickening quiet. "Rebecca Rice!"

Rebecca stepped off the bunk and stood at some distance from Yitzhak Fogel. Silvana folded herself. The Capo walked over, looking straight at them—a hint of a malevolent smile on his lips—stood before Rebecca, and ordered the two of them in Dutch to follow him. They followed wordlessly.

When they arrived at a small, square shed, the Capo stopped. He looked at them for a long time, saying nothing. A minute or two later, a German officer emerged from the shed, and began talking to Yitzhak a few steps away. The Capo turned to Rebecca with a slew of words. Horror twisted her pale face, and pain flashed through it. For a moment, Silvana couldn't recognize her friend. She looked as if she'd aged by years.

The Capo didn't wait for time to resume its course. He ordered them into the shed and closed the door behind them. Rebecca collapsed to the ground. Silvana hovered over her, asking again and again, "What happened, Rebecca? What did he say to you?"

Rebecca couldn't get up. She sobbed ceaselessly. All of Silvana's attempts to get her to talk failed. Silvana pulled on her arm pointlessly. Rebecca kept sobbing, her torso doubled over toward the ground, her legs pulled back, her left hand supporting her body. Silvana pulled Rebecca's face to hers, but this didn't work either. Only after ordering her, while pulling on her hair, to explain what had happened, Rebecca finally muttered, still crumpled on the floor of the shed, that one of them had to die, and that the Capo and officer said they had to choose which one. They had an hour. She wept, her face to the ground, and said those damned men knew they had stolen water and stayed together in her shed. "That bloody Dutchman told them everything," she wailed.

Silvana sat down on the other side of the small room, putting her face in her hands. For a moment or two she saw nothing but darkness. Then she silently said goodbye to her mother and sister, to her dead father, to Rebecca, to the Hebrew soldier, to the broken space of her life, to the desert, to Jeliana Beach, to the Lungomare, to Benghazi, to her memories of everything she once was and everything she'd ever hoped to become. Images of her life blended before her, out of order, a photo album touched by some invisible, amused, and cruel hand that had rid it of any logical order of a life story. Silvana erased the images one by one, shaking herself out of them. One final blurry image from one of her last solitary desert excursions still flickered through her mind: the day when the desert seemed to pounce on itself like a storm, the camels galloping beyond the screen of sand, the darkness that took over the dunes, smudging them until it was pushed away by the rays of sun that sliced through it. Her desert, not far from Benghazi, the Sahara Desert, the place where the wind brought eternity and the single moment together to converge. All at once the will to live ignited within her, burning brightly. She had to stay alive.

Silvana was filled with guilt: *how could you forget all about what Rebecca had done for you? She saved your life!* She fought off the guilt, burying the accusing words alive. She prepared for the battle of a lifetime over her own life, and searched for an enemy. But Rebecca just kept sobbing, saying she wouldn't play this sick game, and that she thought they should tell the Nazi and his Capo to kill whoever they wanted.

At first Silvana took her words at face value, but immediately thereafter she became worried that her friend might be playing a trick on her. If they returned the bullet to the hands of the Nazi, he would be more likely to kill the one he saw as lowlier, meaning, Silvana. The one who wasn't only Jewish, but also black.

Her anxiety had a mind of its own. Silvana told Rebecca this wasn't a good idea, because if they gave the German Nazi and the Jewish Nazi the option to decide which of them to kill, they would both be killed. Therefore, they had no choice but to make the call. Rebecca said nothing. Even when

Silvana shouted that time was running out, her silence persisted. The Capo yelled outside the door, urging them to make a decision. "Rebecca!" Silvana screamed. "Rebecca!"

This time Rebecca answered. One short statement escaped between her yelps: "Tell them to kill me."

Silvana had chills. Pain and relief battled within her, but only for a moment. She then worried that Rebecca might be more familiar than Nazi mentality than she was, and perhaps she knew they'd choose to kill whichever one of them the girls decided should stay alive. She grabbed her head and shook it madly. A loud knocking came at the door, followed by the call, "*Noch fünf minuten.*"[34]

Silvana replayed everything Rebecca said from the moment they walked into the shed. She tried to recognize some sort of regularity that would disclose a secret plan. Rebecca's words were like knives pricking the sides of the merry-go-round that was her mind. Her head felt like it was about to explode.

The door opened. Rebecca jumped to her feet and hurried out. For a moment, Silvana was paralyzed, but then a strange inner force pushed her out after her friend. Before the Capo could even ask what they'd decided, Rebecca said something in Dutch. Within a fraction of a second the German officer, his

---

[34]From German: Five more minutes.

gun already drawn, cocked, and ready, shot Rebecca once, straight into the heart.

Silvana collapsed, mad, crying bitterly, her heart overcome with desire to be saved from this torture, to have the man shoot her too. But the German officer walked away, leaving her with the Capo, who stood around, watching her gaping at the ground and screaming at the top of her lungs, "*Elash?* Why?"

Surprisingly, Rebecca's death improved Silvana's condition. Her suffering was so steady that it was devoid of any ups and downs. Her heart was sealed. She stopped feeling. No one could take pleasure in torturing her ever again. She was an inanimate object.

And yet, in mid-March, her heart cracked: Johan, the Dutch prisoner, mumbled at her one morning that he heard the Wehrmacht was planning on releasing all prisoners from Biberach an der Riss. This news made Silvana feel again, and the feeling was heartbreak. She was happy for her mother and sister, then thought of Rebecca and hated herself. She saw herself as the vilest creature on the face of the earth. She couldn't explain to herself how she'd let her guardian angel die.

One afternoon the chaos in the camp reached a new peak. Everyone mixed together until it seemed like none of the prisoners knew which shed they belonged to. "*Marzo pazzo*," she heard one of them mutter. "Mad march."

Silvana was instantly pushed into the past, to those hot summer days when her father described the weather of each season in Italy, especially the fickle month of March, when no one could foresee what would happen. Beyond the fog that surrounded her soul, she now recalled the way they used to sit around the straw table in the garden, watching her father in wonder, listening intently to his stories. Most of all, she saw her mother's expression. Beneath the restraint that covered it like makeup were hints of sorrow and anger over the fact that her husband never invited her to join him on his trips to Italy. Silvana then noticed the fear in her mother's heart that the rumors of the affair her husband was having with the Fratelli Capone secretary were true. Now she lost herself in longing for her mother. She lay on the bunk, her body writhing with the deep pain that had become a part of her.

The next day, her pain over Rebecca's death defeated all other pain. Her loss glowed like a lone star that no one but her could see. Her absence was apparent everywhere: in the shed, in the dirty water holes, in the latrine, in every clump of dirt, in every move Silvana made. Even at night, when her body was almost completely devoid of feeling, it still had the power to intensely feel Rebecca's absence in the empty space left in their bunk. But more than anything else, Silvana missed her friend's perspective. She no longer had anyone to respond or interpret the situation, no one to encourage her or force her to keep dreamingabout the day of her release.

Another, almost equally painful repercussion was the return of a complete sense of foreignness, or rather, the return of the inability to blur it. In Rebecca's absence she could not forget, even for a moment, that she was significantly different from all the other prisoners—an African desert island in the midst of a European ocean. Even when she wasn't around any Germans or Capos she tried to disappear within herself, getting smaller and smaller, until she became invisible. But the prisoners continued to see her, all as one. Worse still, sometimes they noticed her attempts at disappearing and therefore focused on her even more. Her strange appearance seemed visible from miles away at any time, day or night. Her persistent presence was suspect to them. They questioned the idea that this strange creature could be Jewish like them. She saw her reflection in their eyes: to them she was foreign, unique in the world, a human mutant outside of history, a woman without a home or a homeland, a dark ghost, a black demon in the shape of a human, the Angel of Death walking among them. The more apparent her misery became, the more she frightened and deterred them.

She could bear their looks, but when these were translated into words she became anxious. One day as she was standing in line for a dollop of soup and some bread crumbs—that was the most they got at the time—a woman standing beside her complained that Silvana was getting food at her expense. No one came to her aid. Silvana realized that no one would help her even at the moment she feared most: when the long armed man found out about Rebecca's death.

The moment did come. One night around mid-April, as the sky was covered red, he appeared by her bunk and whispered calmly that he wanted to speak to her. When she asked, panicked, what he wanted to talk about, he said she must have heard they would soon be released, and that he wanted to say goodbye in private and apologize for what he'd done to her in the latrine. He presented her with a rag from which the edge of a loaf of bread peeked out, and said he had a present for her. She stepped outside with him, walking among piles of bodies the Germans no longer had anyone remove, pulled magically by the vision of the bread. They walked for about thirty meters before they reached a long trench. The whole way there it only occurred to her once, briefly, that he might be leading her on. But the sight of the bread had eaten up her fears, not leaving even a crumb.

The long armed man sat on the lip of the trench and pulled out the bread. It was only an edge, not a whole loaf, but even that was enough to make her head spin. Only when three other men appeared to their left did she realize she may have been set up. The men laughed. She turned her back on her atheism and prayed to the Jewish God that these men were German. She knew the Germans were strictly forbidden from physical relations with Jewish women. At most she would be shot and her misery would finally end.

But once more, no god answered her prayers. They were not German soldiers, for whose presence she'd yearned. They were three rather robust Dutch Capos. She hoped they'd be repelled by her wilted, ragged body, but that wasn't the case. One of them, a tall man with an especially shiny bald head, pushed her into the trench. From this point of view, on her back in the trench as he stood above her, he looked enormous. He fixed his eyes on her for what felt like eternity. She now prayed for the sharp stones poking her back to slice through her heart. The tall man jumped into the trench to the sounds of his friends' calls of encouragement: *"Neuk de joodse hoer!"*[35] and tore off her clothes.

She didn't resist. From beyond the fog of her senses she knew that any resistance would only further provoke them. She didn't call for help; who would save her? The S.S.? The prisoners, who could barely stand on their stick legs? Her white Jewish brothers, who treated her like an animal that had cunningly managed to invade their territory? She tried to strangle her consciousness, but the Dutch

---

[35]From Dutch: Fuck that Jewish whore!

men wouldn't let her die. She felt the whole planet leaning over her. The tall man spread her legs forcefully, shoved his penis into her, and gestured for his two friends to join. They didn't hesitate for a moment. One of them, foaming at the mouth, grabbed her head in his left hand, and used his right hand to open her mouth as wide as possible before shoving his partially erect penis into it. She tried to move her mouth and make it harder for him to push his penis in and out, but her mouth refused. It was paralyzed. The third man, the youngest looking of the group, stood over her, masturbating madly, occasionally leaning in and reaching for the place where, light years ago, her breasts once were. Between moans he sporadically muttered something that sounded like a curse.

Their groans mixed together, rising and falling, strenuous and calm, broken and continuous, chords that formed an improvised requiem. After they each, one by one, were satisfied, they stood above her for an eternal moment. Then, by order of their leader, they peed on her. Her mind shut down.

She only regained consciousness after a full day in the trench. She awoke to the worried face of a British soldier. At first she thought she was hallucinating that she was in the arms of the Hebrew soldier. A moment later her mind regained control of her soul for one moment, when she realized he was a British soldier who looked nothing like her Jewish one. He was exceptionally tall, much taller than the players of the Maccabi Benghazi Basketball Team that suddenly came to mind, and wore round sunglasses the likes of which she'd never seen. His hair was even lighter than the tufts of all the German soldiers and officers she'd met. He let her drink slowly from his canteen, and refused the pleas of her open mouth to gulp down as much as possible. She fought him with everything she still had in her, yearning to take hold of the canteen, mumbling "please" over and over again, but he kept his cool and only allowed her to drink a little. When she finished sipping all he would allow, he carried her in his arms over the dead and the dying and outside of the camp. There, inside a British tent, she was laid on a narrow army cot.

For days and nights nothing could break into the fog that surrounded her soul, until she finally emerged anew into the world: on the third day after her rescue, one of the British officers whispered to her that a reporter from the BBC covering the liberation of the camp was about to record some prisoners singing the Jewish anthem. When she heard this, a force broke loose from the lowest cellars of her soul, imbuing her with energy for a few hours. She asked the officer to take her there. He refused at first, seeing howweak she was, but finally conceded.

An hour later, he delivered her to the meeting place. She saw hundreds of prisoners, still wearing their camp uniform, gathered around a rabbi in black attire who reminded her of the ones she'd known in Benghazi. She also saw the British reporter, who held something reminiscent of a recording device she'd once seen an Italian officer carry. The prisoners did not wait for a signal, and, as if according to some invisible cue, opened their mouths and began singing *HaTikvah* with effort. Though she knew the words by heart, she couldn't sing with them. Only when she realized the song was coming to an end did she join in, emphasizing her Arab accent, so they would all know: she too had been there.

Acknowledgements

I'd like to thank the historian Yaakov Hajaj Lilof, who shared his expertise about World War II and his fascinating knowledge regarding the fate of Libyan Jews. Yaakov was always available for any questions, big or small.

I'd like to thank Meir Kachlon, Chairman of the World Organization of Libyan Jews, who opened the Libyan Jewish Museum in Or Yehuda for me whenever I wanted to visit, and taught me some of the Arabic expressions that appear in this book.

Doctor Zvulun Boaron, for his great contribution in all matters regarding the writing of Libyan Arabic.

My mother, Wanda Sucary of the Saban family, who spent days and nights telling me the history of her family in Africa and Bergen-Belsen, sparing no detail, even if it caused her indescribable pain.

Michal Peleg and Ana Kohanim for offering up their terrific Italian.

Assaf Galai and Ran Hacohen, for their help with Yiddish and Dutch, respectively.

I'd like to thank my wife, Yael Weisbord-Sucary, for the patience she showed during the three years I "lived" alone in Libya and Europe of World War II.

Nissim Rubin, for offering his immense knowledge of Arabic and Libyan customs.

Binyamin Dadosh-Doron and everyone I met at Libyan-Jewish conventions, for telling me about their lives during World War II.

67092110R00180

Made in the USA
San Bernardino, CA
19 January 2018